THE CALLED SERIES COLLECTION

VOLUME 1

JOSEPH, NICODEMUS, AND LYDIA

KENNETH A. WINTER

WildernessLessons

JOIN MY READERS' GROUP FOR UPDATES AND FUTURE RELEASES

Please join my Readers' Group so i can send you a free book, as well as updates and information about future releases, etc.

See the back of the book for details on how to sign up.

The Called Series Collection Volume 1

Joseph, Nicodemus, and Lydia

Published by:

Kenneth A. Winter

WildernessLessons, LLC

Richmond, Virginia

United States of America

kenwinter.org

wildernesslessons.com

The Called is an approved trademark of Kenneth A. Winter.

Edited by Sheryl Martin Hash

Cover design by Scott Campbell Design

ISBN 978-1-9568662-7-8 (soft cover)

ISBN 978-1-9568662-8-5 (e-book)

ISBN 978-1-9568662-9-2 (large print)

Library of Congress Control Numbers:

A Carpenter Called Joseph 2021913759

A Teacher Called Nicodemus 2021924987

A Merchant Called Lydia 2022909537

CONTENTS

A CARPENTER CALLED JOSEPH

A TEACHER CALLED NICODEMUS

A MERCHANT CALLED LYDIA

A CARPENTER CALLED JOSEPH

KENNETH A. WINTER

DEDICATION

In memory of my dad,
Bob Winter,
a gifted woodworker and a loving father

who loved his wife, his kids, his grandkids, and his great grandkids well,

but, most importantly, he pointed us all to Jesus,
the One whom he faithfully followed.

∾

The Lord your God cared for you all along the way
… just as a father cares for his child.
(Deuteronomy 1:31)

∾

PREFACE

~

This novella is a fictional work about the life of Joseph, the carpenter. No other man in history has been charged with the tremendous responsibility he was given. He was ordained by the Almighty God to be the earthly father to His one and only Son. That statement alone tells us volumes about the character of Joseph. He wasn't randomly chosen by God. He wasn't chosen simply because he and Mary were engaged to be married. He and Mary were betrothed because God had chosen them both and ordered their steps accordingly ... from before the beginning of time.

Imagine God's criteria for the man who would raise His Son through childhood, adolescence, and early adulthood. Imagine the character and heart the Father would require Jesus's earthly father to possess. We often talk about Proverbs 31 being a gold standard for women. i suggest that Joseph is the Matthew 1 gold standard for men. We only read about a few of his character traits in the chapter. Matthew writes: He was a "just" man. He was a "considerate" man. He was faithful to do what God directed him to do.

But i believe the most important aspect of his character is not specifically mentioned; it's inferred. He was a man after God's own heart! How is it that i can say that with conviction? Simple! Who else do you think the Almighty God would entrust to father His Son?

Through this story we'll explore the heart and character of Joseph as presented in the Gospels of Matthew and Luke. We'll also consider what that may have looked like in their day-to-day lives not recorded in Scripture. The writers of the Gospels were led by the Holy Spirit to write just what the Heavenly Father wanted us to know about Joseph and the earthly family of Jesus. There were many details left unwritten. Those details prompt questions. We will not know the answers to many of those questions until we stand before our Lord. And by then, we may no longer care.

But the purpose of this work is to imagine some of those details and questions. Let me hurriedly point out that not one of those details changes the narrative of the Gospels one jot or tittle. i have taken great care in the writing of this work to guard the sanctity and truth of the Gospel message. i am not attempting to add to those truths. Rather, my goal is to prompt you to consider the truths as recorded in Scripture. My additions are purely for your reading entertainment as you do so.

The story is written in first person with Joseph as the storyteller. Toward the end, his son, James, adds his voice, as he tells a portion of the story as well. My hope is that you draw your chair up close and listen, not just to the story, but to what i believe was in their hearts as they share their very personal reflections about Jesus.

Most of the other characters in the story also come directly from Scripture. You will easily recognize them. However, where the Bible is silent, i have chosen to add background details about many of the people, just like i have Joseph and James, which are either purely fictional or assumptions not confirmed in Scripture. These background details are added to further the telling of the story.

Some of the characters are seen in Scripture – but not necessarily tied to the birth and early life of Jesus. Their inclusion in this work is either conjecture or complete fiction. But i have included them because of the unique perspective they bring to the story.

Lastly, several of the characters are totally fiction. For example, i do not believe Joseph attempted to find a room in Bethlehem at the first century "Holiday Inn." i believe he intended to stay with family. So, a few of the fictional characters are his extended family members whom i have created to receive them. You will not find them in Scripture!

Like my novels and short story collections, you will also encounter fictional twists and turns that are an attempt to fill in the blanks where Scripture is silent regarding certain day-to-day events. Again, my prayer is that nothing in the story detracts from scriptural truth; rather, while remaining true to the biblical story, it tells it in a way that creates an interesting and thought-provoking reading experience.

Throughout the story, some instances of dialogue are direct quotes from Scripture. Whenever i am quoting Scripture, you will find that it has been italicized. The Scripture references are included in the back of this book. Those remaining instances of dialogue not italicized are a part of the fictional stories to help advance the storyline. However, i have endeavored to use Scripture as the basis in forming any added dialogue by a historical character with the intent that it does not detract from the overall message of God's Word.

My prayer is, that as you read this story, you will see Joseph and his entire family through new eyes – and more importantly, that you will be challenged to see Jesus through their eyes.

∽

1

MY FRIENDSHIP WITH ELI

~

I am a carpenter named Joseph. My father, Jacob, was also a carpenter, as was his father, Matthan. As a matter of fact, my ancestors have been carpenters as far back as anyone can remember. Well, maybe not as far back as *anyone* remembers. My ancestor David was actually a shepherd – until he became the King of Israel. And his son Solomon is considered by many to have been the wisest king our people ever had.

Thirteen of my ancestors, who came after Solomon, followed him in ruling over our nation as kings of Judah. Most of them did evil in the eyes of the Lord – so I share my family connection with them with great reluctance. But there is no denying that royal blood courses through my veins.

We are God's chosen people living in the land He promised our patriarch, Abraham, about 2,000 years ago. But though we live in the land God gave us, we have been living here as subjects under foreign rulers for over 500 of those years. Our people have been subjected to the rule of the Babylonians, the Persians, the Greeks, the Seleucids, and now the Romans.

• • •

We have long grown weary under pagan rulers who have little regard for our Lord God Jehovah. We pray for deliverance from our oppression much like our ancestors prayed for their deliverance from Egyptian bondage.

Our God promised, through the prophets, to send His Messiah to deliver us. Each generation for hundreds of years has hoped and believed He would come in their lifetime. But 400 years have passed since the last great prophet, Malachi – and all we have heard from heaven is silence! Our hearts are heavy, and our hope has grown dim, but we live our lives trusting our God for His promise.

Since my ancestor King David grew up in and around the town of Bethlehem, it is considered my family home. Some of my relatives still live there. But over the centuries, much of my family has scattered to other parts of Judea and Galilee.

My great-great-grandfather, Eliud, led his family to settle in the city of Cana. The town was destroyed by the Assyrians many years before, but Eliud and others went there to rebuild it. His carpentry skills were put to great use as the town rose from its ashes.

And the generations of my family that followed him also assisted in that effort. As a matter of fact, my younger brother, Clopas, and I made a steady living there with our carpentry skills for quite a while. But when work began to slow down in Cana, I learned there was more opportunity in nearby Nazareth. Clopas decided to remain in Cana, while my wife, Rebekah, and I moved to Nazareth.

Soon after I arrived in Nazareth, I met a carpenter named Eli. He needed a partner and I needed steady work – so we agreed that Jehovah God had brought us together. Eli and his wife, Abigail, soon became good friends to Rebekah and me.

. . .

I remember the day Abigail gave birth to a baby girl they named Mary. She was the apple of Eli's eye and he doted on her from the day she was born. Eli would occasionally bring her to work with him when she was a little girl. I watched her grow from a tiny infant into a tender young woman.

Mary always had a soft and gentle nature. She honored her parents in all she did and exhibited a great love and reverence for our God. She was a hard worker and had a quick wit.

Abigail died when Mary was nine, and I will never forget the tenderness she showed Eli as he walked through the grief of losing his wife – despite the fact Mary was walking through her own.

Then, not long afterward, my Rebekah died. She had developed a high fever that the rabbi and midwife were unable to cure. Eli and Mary were both a great comfort to me during my time of grief.

Rebekah and I had been married for twenty years before she died. Early in our marriage we came to realize Rebekah could not have children. Though it was a source of great sadness throughout our marriage, we had come to trust that it was the will of God. Still, I always regretted not having a son to mentor.

A few years after Rebekah's death, I started wondering, and praying, if God would give me an opportunity to marry again and give me a son. But I never anticipated how God would answer that prayer!

∽

THE BETROTHAL AND A SENSE OF BETRAYAL

～

*E*li and I watched as Mary continued to mature into a radiant young woman. She caught the attention of all the young men in our town. So, no one was more surprised than I when Eli approached me one evening after we had finished our work.

"Joseph, come, sit a moment," he said. "I have something I wish to discuss with you."

"Of course, my friend," I replied. "I saw you speaking with the rabbi earlier today. Does he have some work he would like us to do? We need a longer term project than those we've been working on as of late."

"Yes, this is most definitely longer term," he responded with a bit of a twinkle in his eye. But it's not a work project I'm considering."

"What is it?" I asked.

. . .

"I'd like you to consider marrying my daughter!" he declared.

I was speechless! Since I am only slightly younger than Eli, I am old enough to be Mary's father. Though such an age difference is not uncommon in marriages of our day, it still was not a match I had considered. However, I admit the possibility was captivating. I told Eli I would pray about his offer.

Over the next several days I made a rather lengthy mental list of all the reasons why I was not the right man for Mary. But I could not think of one single reason why she would be unsuitable for me. As I prayed, I sensed God was leading me to go back to Eli.

"I would be honored and humbled to take your daughter Mary as my wife," I told Eli. "I am grateful for your trust in me that I would care and provide for her. You know I would love her with my whole heart."

"Wonderful!" Eli exclaimed. "I know you will. We will begin making arrangements for your wedding this very day and ..."

I interrupted him, "Not so fast, my friend. Before I can give you my final answer, I must know that this is what Mary wants, as well. I will not enter into a marriage arrangement that she does not desire. So, you need to discuss the matter with her and let me know what she says."

Truth be told, I thought it would be the last time he and I ever spoke of it. I was certain Mary had her heart set on a different match. So, I was shocked when he returned a week later to tell me Mary was also in favor of our betrothal. She was willing to become my wife!

. . .

It was all I could do to keep from shouting with delight – and thanking God for His goodness! Of all men, I was the most envied when three weeks later we announced our betrothal. We set a date for the wedding feast to be held one year later.

Soon after our announcement, Mary unexpectedly traveled to Hebron to visit her cousin for three months. When she returned, she came to Eli and me with startling news.

"Abba … and Joseph," she said as she looked at both of us in the eyes. "I'm pregnant!"

Eli and I stood there in shock and simply looked at each other. But Mary wasn't finished with her news. She assured us she was still a virgin. She told us she had become pregnant by the Holy Spirit.

"An angel by the name of Gabriel appeared to me," Mary explained. "He told me that God has decided to bless me! He said I would become pregnant and have a son. He will be very great, and He will be called the Son of the Most High God. The Lord God will give Him the throne of David. And He will reign over Israel forever. His kingdom will never end.

"I asked the angel how this could be possible, and he told me the Holy Spirit would come upon me, and the power of the Most High God would overshadow me."

She saw the heartbroken expression on my face and Eli's look of despondence.

She continued, "Joseph, I have not broken our vows. This is an act of our Most High God. I do not fully understand what is happening – but I know

I must trust Him. And I need to know that you trust me. Do you believe all I have told you is true?"

My heart was broken! I hadn't really heard much else after she said the word pregnant. She said something about the Holy Spirit coming upon her. But all I could think about was this young woman, whom I thought was without guile, had somehow sullied herself and broken our contract.

I thought about the shame and disgrace to which she and my dear friend, Eli, would be subjected. I thought about the hushed conversations that would occur behind my back.

Without saying a word, Eli got up from his seat and walked out of his home. I didn't know what else to do, so I did the same thing. My heart was full, and at that moment I could not speak.

As I made my way back home, I kept going over what Mary had said. I had gone from having a heart overflowing with joy to having a heart that had been broken into pieces.

But as much as I hurt, my love for her did not diminish in any way. I decided the right thing to do was quietly break our betrothal so as not to disgrace her publicly. Eli could then send her away to stay with a distant relative.

∾

3

CONFIRMED BY AN ANGEL

~

*M*y sleep that night was fitful. In the midst of it, an angel of the Lord appeared to me in a dream. *"Joseph, son of David,"* he said, *"do not be afraid to go ahead with your marriage to Mary. For the child within her has been conceived by the Holy Spirit. And she will have a son, and you are to name Him Jesus, for He will save His people from their sins.*

"All of this has happened to fulfill the Lord's message through His prophet: 'Look! The virgin will conceive a child. She will give birth to a son, and He will be called Immanuel (meaning God is with us).'" [1]

When I awoke the next morning, I ran to Eli's home. Both Eli and Mary wept as I told them what the angel had said.

"Mary," I said, "I trust all you have told me is the truth. I trust you and I trust God. How favored you are above all women! And how favored am I to become your husband and a father to this One who is in your womb!"

. . .

I was delighted to learn that God had led Eli to the same realization. Though we rejoiced in the news, we also knew what people in our town would say. Mary, most of all, would be ridiculed and falsely accused of improper behavior. We trusted God would give her – and all of us – the strength we needed to endure.

Mary came home with me that day to be my wife, but she remained a virgin until after the baby was born.

Nazareth is a small town, so I knew the news about Mary would spread quickly. Eli and I decided the best thing for us to do was go talk to Jacob, our rabbi. Eli, Mary, and I would tell him about all that had happened. The rabbi would know how best to explain it to our neighbors.

When we arrived at the synagogue, Jacob was acting very strangely toward us. He had always been cordial and engaging, but today he was stern and distant. We had already decided Eli would be the first to speak.

"Rabbi, thank you for meeting with us," Eli began. "Certain events have unfolded very quickly for our family, and we have only recently become aware of some very good news."

"What is this good news?" Jacob asked.

"We want you and all of our neighbors to rejoice with us," Eli continued. "So, please allow us to tell you what has occurred. Mary will speak first."

But before Mary could say a word, Jacob interrupted, "Mary, before you speak, I want to remind you all it is my duty as the spiritual leader of this village to know every detail of what has happened so the reputation of this synagogue and our village is in no way tarnished."

• • •

"Of course, Rabbi," Eli interjected.

The rabbi continued, "I have been told that Mary is more than three months pregnant, so events have not unfolded all *that* quickly. I need to determine if anything has occurred that dishonors God or the people of this village. If anything untoward has happened, we will then discuss appropriate action.

"Mary, I have been told you have just returned from a three-month visit with your cousin, Elizabeth, in Hebron. And, as the entire village can see, you are expecting a child. I caution you to be very careful that you speak only the truth to me."

"The day before I departed for Hebron," Mary began, "I was out walking alone in the vineyard when I was approached by one whom I now know to be an angel of the Lord by the name of Gabriel.

"The angel told me, 'You have found favor with God! You will conceive and give birth to a son. The Holy Spirit will come upon you, and the power of the Most High will overshadow you. The baby will be holy, and He will be the Son of God.'"

Mary then went on to tell the rabbi how the angel told her about her cousin becoming pregnant and relayed the story of how this same angel had spoken to Elizabeth's husband, the priest, Zechariah. The angel said the priest's son would be a messenger preparing the way for the baby in her womb.

I confirmed to the rabbi that Mary and I have not consummated our marriage. She is – and will remain – a virgin until after the baby is born. Then I told him how the same angel had come to me in a dream.

. . .

"Oh?" Jacob asked. "And what did this angel of yours say?"

I replied, "The angel told me the child in Mary's womb had been conceived by the Holy Spirit. I was not to be fearful about proceeding with my marriage to Mary. He told me all of this was to fulfill the prophecy of the prophet Isaiah, 'The virgin will conceive a child.'"

Eli spoke up, saying, "God has given me a peace as well that my daughter is to be the mother of the Messiah! This is joyous news! The Messiah for whom we have all waited for centuries will soon arrive! Yes, He is even here with us right now – in the womb of my daughter!"

We all looked at the rabbi with anticipation. We were expecting him to join with us in our celebration. We were earnestly awaiting his thoughts on how we should assemble the entire town to announce this joyous news!

~

4

THE RABBI'S REACTION

~

*A*fter a few moments of silence, Rabbi Jacob responded with a raised voice. "I directed you to tell me the truth and all you have told me are these wild stories! You tell me of an angel coming to you, Mary, in a vineyard, and you, Joseph, in a dream."

"Well, yes, Rabbi," I said. "Isn't it wonderful news?"

Jacob raised his voice even further. "Who are you that an angel of God would come to you? Angels have not walked on this earth for hundreds of years, but you expect me to believe that one has come no less than three times, including the visit to the old priest in the temple!

"If an angel had entered the temple, he would have appeared to the High Priest. If he had come to Nazareth, he would have appeared to me. He would not have come to uneducated people such as yourselves!"

. . .

Eli tried to interrupt, "But, Rabbi …"

"Your story is preposterous!" Jacob continued. "How could a virgin conceive a child? Either you all are completely naïve or have been bewitched by this girl! Or perhaps, Joseph, you decided not to wait for a year as you announced but decided to consummate the marriage sooner. And if so, that is your prerogative if you and Eli have come to that agreement. But don't make up this wild story to cover up your impatience!"

"But, Rabbi, the prophet Isaiah wrote …." I tried to interject.

"Do not attempt to justify your story by tying it to a questionable prophecy from Isaiah," Jacob immediately retorted. "You know our Hasmonean leaders dispute the truth of those prophecies, and they deny the belief that the Messiah will be a descendant of David."

The rabbi continued, practically shouting at us. "You have used statements no one believes to try and justify your lies! How dare you dishonor God and dishonor me by saying these things! This is blasphemy!"

Eli responded first, in a firm but unprovoked manner. "Rabbi," he implored, "we have told you the truth! The Spirit of God will confirm that truth to you if you will but seek Him in prayer – just as we have done!"

But the rabbi quickly replied, "How dare you speak to God's anointed in that way! Joseph has said he and Mary have not consummated this marriage. Either he is lying, or Mary has committed adultery with another man. The idea that the Spirit of God has come upon her is preposterous! But since there are no witnesses to indicate she has committed adultery I can only conclude the two of you have had relations – as is your right – and the baby is a product of that impetuous act!"

. . .

Mary was near tears as she said, "That is not how it happened, Rabbi."

Jacob ignored her and continued, "I will not allow you to tell your outrageous story to the people of this town! If you do, I will denounce it as heresy and call into question whether Mary is an adulteress who deserves to be stoned to death. Otherwise, we will let the people believe you have shamefully broken your commitment to a one-year betrothal period and have consummated your marriage. I will never speak a word of any of this heresy you have told me!"

The rabbi then got up and stormed out the room. As he did, he shook his robes to reflect his disdain for what we had said. As he walked away, I saw the hurt and sadness in Mary's eyes.

Our neighbors responded in much the same way. Most of them kept their distance from us, with the exception of a young neighbor girl named Salome. She was a constant source of encouragement and companionship for Mary in the weeks and months that followed. She was a friend when Mary greatly needed one.

But most everyone else we told about the angel's visits looked at us suspiciously. And others looked at us – particularly Mary – with the same disdain we had received from the rabbi. I hated that for her. God had chosen her to be His vessel. She was to be honored, not despised. But life was never going to be the same. There would always be malicious whispers uttered behind her back.

For centuries our people had waited for the arrival of the promised Messiah. I had always hoped He would come during my lifetime and that I might get a glimpse of Him. But in my wildest dreams I never thought my wife would give birth to Him. I had prayed for a son – and God had chosen me to be the earthly father of *His* Son.

· · ·

All I could think about was how inadequate I was to be His father and Mary's husband. But I knew the same God who could enable a virgin to give birth to His Son would empower a lowly carpenter to be the father and husband He needed me to be. By His grace, I would trust and follow Him!

⁓

5

TELLING MY FAMILY

I knew the next person we needed to tell was my brother Clopas, and I knew we needed to do so sooner than later. A few days after our meeting with Rabbi Jacob we set out for Cana. I prayed this conversation would go much better than the one we had with the rabbi.

Clopas is much younger than I am. Six years ago he married a young woman whose name is also Mary. We apparently share similar tastes in women since our wives have the same name! They now have a five-year-old son, James.

I last saw them three months ago while Mary was in Hebron visiting her cousin Elizabeth. They were delighted when I told them Mary and I were engaged. Though they, like everyone else, were surprised because of our age difference, they were glad to hear joy had once again returned to my heart.

· · ·

The three of them had accompanied Eli and me as we traveled to Jerusalem to celebrate Passover. While we were there, we encountered our cousin Achim, who lives in Bethlehem. I had shared my joyous news with him, as well.

Clopas was surprised when Mary and I now unexpectedly showed up at his home. I explained that we had news to share with him and his family. I was amazed when I looked over at my sister-in-law. She was staring at my Mary with what appeared to be a "knowing" look.

"You look like you are bursting with excitement," Clopas exclaimed. "Tell us your important news, Joseph!"

After we were all seated, I began. "Soon after we announced our betrothal, an angel of the Lord came to Mary and told her Jehovah God had chosen her, and the Spirit of God would come over her and she would conceive a child. The child will be the Son of the Most High God. He is the Messiah – whose coming the prophets foretold."

"I'm not sure I understand what you are telling us," Clopas said.

I attempted to explain, "Isaiah wrote that the Messiah would be born of a virgin – and now God has chosen Mary to be that virgin. Mary told her father and me about the angel's visit after she returned from Hebron last month. By that time, she was three months pregnant."

Mary continued the story, saying, "The angel of the Lord told me my cousin Elizabeth was also expecting a child. My cousin is in her sixties and, to this point in her life, has been barren. Imagine my surprise! I decided I needed to go to Hebron immediately. If Elizabeth was truly pregnant, it would be confirmation that all the angel had told me was true.

· · ·

"I told my father I had learned Elizabeth was pregnant, and I needed to go visit her. But I did not tell him the rest of the story. I needed to see with my own eyes before I told my father and Joseph what the angel had said. And my father was so overjoyed for Elizabeth and her husband, Zechariah, that he never inquired about the messenger.

"As I traveled to Hebron, I kept thinking about how I was going to tell my father ... and Joseph. And now, how was I going to tell Elizabeth? Would she believe me when I told her about an angel appearing to me? And would she believe what he had said?

"When I arrived at their home, I found out that Zechariah was gone. But Elizabeth greeted me. Immediately I could see she was great with child. She had the glow of an expectant mother. I was so happy for her.

"But imagine my astonishment when she cried out to me, 'God has blessed you above all women, and your child is blessed. Why am I so honored, that the mother of my Lord should visit me?'

"I didn't need to worry about what I would say to Elizabeth – she already knew! She went on to say, 'When I heard your greeting, the baby in my womb jumped for joy.'

"Any question I had about what the angel had said to me vanished! I had only been carrying the Son of God in my womb for a matter of days. There was no physical sign that I was pregnant. I had told no one about the angel or what he had said."

"But Elizabeth knew?" Clopas asked.

"She knew!" Mary answered.

. . .

"After I told her about how the angel had visited me, she told me Zechariah had been visited by an angel in the sanctuary of the temple. The angel had told him their son would be called John and he would prepare the way for the One in my womb.

"Three months later, when it was time for me to return home, I continued to ask Jehovah God how He would have me tell my father and Joseph. I knew He would show me and not abandon me."

∽

6

A BROTHER'S ACCEPTANCE

~

*C*lopas looked amazed as he took in everything Mary was saying. So I added, "Clopas, when Mary first told me, I didn't know what to think. But that night Jehovah God confirmed it to me through a dream. An angel told me I should bring Mary into my home as my wife. And I have done so. However, we will not consummate our marriage until after the child is born.

"You are my closest family, so we wanted you to know and understand as soon as possible. We know how shocking this all sounds. We both have experienced that same shock firsthand. So, please, feel free to ask us any questions you have."

I didn't need to wait long to hear exactly what my brother thought. "Joseph, I know you to be an upright man of integrity," Clopas responded. "I know you love God and strive to stand righteous before Him. I know you will not lie about your own actions or anyone else's. Your word and the word of Mary is all we needed to hear to know what you told us was the truth.

. . .

"We join with you in praising Jehovah God for His faithfulness in sending His Messiah, for His mercy in allowing us to now sit here in the baby's presence, and for His grace in the way He is enabling you to walk through this with Him. Mary, you truly are blessed by God above all other women. And Joseph, our God has chosen well to choose you to be the earthly father to His Son."

We all embraced and spent the rest of our time together rejoicing and praising God. Two days later, Mary and I returned home to Nazareth. God had again answered our prayer.

A few months later, we received word the Roman emperor, Caesar Augustus, had decreed that a census be taken throughout our land. We were all to return to our ancestral homes to be registered. Mary and I made preparations for the three-day journey to Bethlehem.

The baby would soon be born. This was not a good time for a trip, but we didn't have a choice. Once again, I admired Mary's bravery – not only for making such a trip during this late stage of pregnancy, but also because of the stares and whispers she would be forced to endure – particularly when we arrived in Bethlehem.

Eli had planned to travel with us since he, too, was of the line of David. But two days before we were to leave, he came down with a fever. The rabbi and midwife had seen this fever before and treated him with an elixir made from herbs and bark.

They assured Mary and me that he would recover, but he did not have the strength to travel to Bethlehem. We would go on without him and one of the midwives would look in on him during our absence.

. . .

I planned for us to stay at the home of my cousin Achim in Bethlehem. He and I had always enjoyed a close relationship, even though we lived far apart. I hoped he would welcome us with open arms.

Shortly before our departure, I received word from Clopas that he and his family would join us on the journey to Bethlehem. We were grateful to have their companionship as we traveled. They would, however, be lodging with his wife's sister when they arrived in the city.

Bethlehem is situated in the midst of rolling green hills, which produce some of the best almonds and olives throughout the province. The soil is fertile because the town sits on top of an enormous aquifer. As a matter of fact, the water from the aquifer is well known to be the best tasting water around. The story goes that some of King David's mighty men risked their lives by crossing through Philistine lines to get him a cup of that very water.

Bethlehem was once one of the fortress towns established by King David's grandson, Rehoboam. It was a defensive military installation designed to safeguard the water source, which also supplied Jerusalem and other surrounding villages. But now under Roman rule, it had become less of a fortress and more of a sleepy village secluded from the fervent pace and activity of Jerusalem.

The hills in and around Bethlehem are ideal for raising sheep. The rich soil and plentiful water provide an abundant food supply. The demand for sacrificial lambs in Jerusalem continues to grow. They are the principal animal sacrifice offered in the temple throughout the year.

And during the feasting days, Jerusalem is filled with pilgrims from all over the land who aren't able to bring their own animals to sacrifice. The pilgrims rely on the lambs and birds available at the temple. That creates great demand – and profit – for the Bethlehem shepherds.

7

A JOURNEY TO BETHLEHEM

∼

*W*e passed by Jerusalem on our way to Bethlehem. Even though this was not one of the feasting days, the city was still bustling with activity. Achim is a carpenter, and since there's not a lot of work for carpenters in Bethlehem, most days he works in Jerusalem. He can work there but still be home most nights, sleeping in his own bed and enjoying his wife's good cooking.

He and his wife, Miriam, have three grown sons who are also carpenters. Each of them is married, and Jehovah God has blessed them all with children – which means Miriam and Achim have been blessed with many grandchildren.

Achim has often reminded me that our ancestor King Solomon once wrote that *"children are a gift from the Lord"* and *"happy is the man whose quiver is full of them."*[2] God continues to enlarge my cousin's quiver!

. . .

Each time I visit Achim, his house is bigger. All his family lives under one roof, so every time a son marries or has children, Achim simply adds another room. Like most of the homes in Bethlehem, his is made of stone with wood timber beams to support the upper floors. The house also abuts a hill, so the stable for the animals is actually a cave Achim enlarged within the hill.

Several years ago, Achim added a third level to his home. The center courtyard is open to allow for cooking, eating, and gathering. That is where they spend most of their time together. The other rooms either surround or overlook the courtyard. Those rooms provide adequate space for sleeping and privacy. When I last saw him, he told me he had added extra rooms to provide space for guests.

Achim and Miriam have graciously invited our extended family to stay with them or with other family members who also live in Bethlehem. As the patriarch of our extended family there in Bethlehem, Achim has made sure space is available for the entire family.

In fact, he sent word that he has reserved a room in his home just for me! I had shared with him earlier the good news about Mary and me. He and Miriam were genuinely pleased. They knew how devastated I was after losing Rebekah.

They had been planning to travel to Nazareth to join in the celebration of our wedding feast the following spring. But now there would be no wedding feast. They didn't yet know Mary would be arriving with me.

Achim appeared in the doorway to greet me before I even had a chance to knock on their door. His arms were outstretched, his eyes twinkled, and his smile extended from one ear to the other.

.   .   .

In his usual gregarious fashion, Achim called out, "Welcome, Joseph! We have been watching for your arrival! We are so happy ..."

Suddenly, he stopped in mid-sentence and pulled away from our embrace, staring over my shoulder at Mary. At that same moment, Miriam arrived at his side. She, too, was wearing a big smile that only broadened when she saw Mary.

"You are radiant, my dear!" Miriam declared. "And you must be weary from your journey. Come in, come in! We won't have you standing there in the doorway!"

But just as Miriam went to embrace Mary and usher us into their home, Achim placed his hand on Miriam's shoulder to stop her. The two of them exchanged disapproving looks. Suddenly there was an awkward silence.

Finally, I said, "Achim and Miriam, this is Mary, my wife."

The two looked at me, then at Mary – followed by a not-so-subtle stare at her obvious "baby bump." The silence became even more awkward.

"I know you must have questions," I continued. "But may we come in so Mary can sit and rest, and we will explain everything that has occurred?"

Miriam nodded her head in agreement and reached out a hand to help Mary across the threshold. But Achim continued to block the doorway and removed Miriam's hand from Mary's shoulder.

〰

8

"THERE IS NO ROOM FOR YOU!"

❧

*T*his time Achim broke the silence saying, "Yes, I do have questions, Joseph, and they must be answered before you can enter my home. When is the child she is carrying due?"

"Any day now," I replied.

I obviously knew what he was about to ask next.

"Joseph, when we last saw you, you said you were engaged to this young woman and the marriage feast was still nine months away. That was only a little more than six months ago. How can she now be expecting a baby any day, and how is it she has become your wife well in advance of your wedding feast?"

. . .

I had hoped to tell them all that had transpired sitting in the comfort of their home. I wanted Mary to be able to sit down and rest. But that was not an option since Achim would not budge from their doorway.

So, I explained how Mary had been visited by an angel who told her the Spirit of God would come upon her, and she would give birth to His Son. Then I told them how the angel had subsequently appeared to me and told me the same thing. As a result, we had gone ahead and formalized our marriage contract right then, and I had brought Mary into my home.

"But she is still a virgin as the prophets foretold," I added. "And we will not consummate our relationship until after the baby is born."

Achim's demeanor showed no signs of softening. He was staring at me with a disgusted look on his face, and I knew his reaction was going to be very different from Clopas's.

"Either she is a liar," he accused, "and you are so lovestruck you have been blinded to her deception. Or you are both liars and have made up this unbelievable story to cover up her adultery.

"If the baby is yours, why have you said you have not yet consummated your marriage? Whoever heard of Jehovah God coming upon any woman to give birth to a baby? Babies are only conceived one way – and it requires a woman and a *man*!"

"Yes, Achim," I said in an attempt to help him understand, "but the message of the angel...."

But he was not going to allow me to interrupt him. He continued, "And whoever heard of angels appearing to anyone? Of course, there are stories in our Scripture about how angels appeared to the patriarchs, but that was a long time ago. That doesn't happen anymore!"

Achim was seething with rage.

He continued, "This is most obviously a violation of God's commandments, and I will not accept it. I cannot allow you into my home because I would be lending credence to this outrageous story and violating everything I believe to be righteous and holy! You are my relative, and until now I have considered you to be my dear friend. But the two of you stand before me as an abomination before God, expecting to enter my home as if everything is all right.

"There is no room for you in my home or in the homes of any of our family members! I will see to it you are not welcome in any home in Beth-lehem! There is no room for you! You have sinned against God, and you have stained our family name."

Then he turned his back to us and shouted, "Go away from my home!"

I saw the hurt in Mary's eyes. I had hoped Achim would realize we were telling the truth, rejoice with us in the news, and embrace us like my brother had. But instead, he unleashed his wrath on us. The baby would be born any day now, and I had no idea where we were to go. I silently began to pray to God.

Almost immediately, Miriam spoke up. "You can spend the night in our stable. It will provide shelter, and the animals will provide warmth from the cool night air. There is straw to provide you with a comfortable resting place, and I will bring you food and water for the night."

.   .   .

As she spoke, Achim turned to silence her, but she gave him a look that left no doubt it was his turn to be silent.

"Thank you for your kindness," Mary said quietly.

The two of us followed Miriam to the stable, and I thanked God for His provision. As the sun began to set, we could hear other distant family members as they arrived and were welcomed into the home. On two occasions, Achim led the animals of his other arriving guests into the stable. But he did not speak a word to us, and other than Miriam, we saw no one else.

Miriam brought us food, water, and blankets. She took great care to make sure Mary was as comfortable as possible given the circumstances. We knew she did not agree with Achim's actions, but to her credit, she never spoke a word against him.

～

9

THE BABY IS BORN

~

$\mathcal{L}$ater that night, Mary went into labor. Neither of us had any experience about what to do, and there were no family members to help her. Miriam was the only one besides Achim who even knew we were here. There was no time to send word to Clopas and his wife or send for a midwife.

Mary was calmer than I was. She told me what to do, and I tried to help her get as comfortable as possible. Beyond that, I prayed to Jehovah God!

I knew God had chosen my wife to bear His Son. I knew she was blessed above all women. But I had never admired her as much as I did at that moment. She showed incredible strength and courage. She may have gotten pregnant without human effort, but I can assure you the birth of Jesus required plenty!

. . .

Mary was in labor for several hours. Even though she was giving birth to God's Son, the painful ordeal of childbirth that resulted from Eve's sin in the Garden of Eden was not lessened for my wife. But Mary endured it all!

Later she told me, "When I heard Jesus cry out for the very first time, all the pain was worth it. As the Son of God, He will always be my God; but as the Son of Man, He will always be my baby boy. I have loved my God as His child for as long as I can remember, but now I will love His Son with a mother's never-ending love."

We knew Jesus was the Son of God, and we knew God had sent Him to this earth. But we didn't completely know why He had come. We didn't know what He would do or what He would endure. But at that moment, as Mary fed Him for the first time, I looked at them both and marveled at this precious gift from God.

Even the animals in the stable seemed to be in awe. Not one of them made a sound. It was as if they realized they were in the presence of their Creator.

We basked in that special moment as we both held Him in our arms for the next hour or so. I added fresh straw to one of the animal feeding troughs, then covered it with one of the clean blankets Miriam had provided for us. Mary had already wrapped Jesus in the swaddling clothes she had brought for that purpose.

As I laid Him in that manger, Mary began to sing the song I had heard her sing many times before:

"With all my heart, I praise the Lord, and I am glad because of God my Savior. He cares for me, His humble servant. From now on, all people will say God has blessed me. God All-Powerful has done great things for me, and His name is holy. He always shows mercy to everyone who worships Him. The Lord made this promise to our ancestors, to Abraham and his family forever!" [3]

. . .

As we looked at Jesus sleeping in the manger, the message of that heart song became even more real to us both. After a while, the stillness of the night was broken. At first, we heard the shuffling sound of feet just outside the stable. It was too late at night for guests to be arriving at Achim's home. We knew it couldn't be Miriam or Achim coming to check on us. Who was it?

Just then, I saw a young boy peer hesitantly into the stable. He was immediately followed by a man who stopped and gently put his hand on the boy's shoulder. Soon I saw several more men standing behind them. I could tell they were shepherds.

The young boy was the first to step inside the stable. He was staring at Jesus lying in the manger and slowly began to approach Him. The others followed, with heads bowed. I knew they had not come to do us any harm.

The shepherd boy stopped and looked at Mary. It was obvious he was seeking permission to come closer to Jesus to get a better view. Mary never hesitated. She smiled and nodded her head for the boy to approach. Then he looked at me, and I did the same. It was as if he and the other shepherds already knew who the baby was.

∼

10

THE SHEPHERDS COME TO WORSHIP

~

One by one, first the boy, then the men began to kneel in front of the manger. The one who appeared to be the boy's father said, "My name is Moshe. This is my son, Shimon. We, together with these other men, are shepherds. Two nights ago, my wife gave birth to my third son. I don't think she and I would have been as welcoming to strangers interrupting this private moment as you two are being to us. Please allow me to explain the reason for our intrusion.

"Tonight we were watching over our flocks in the hills overlooking the town. It has been a clear still night without a cloud in the sky. The sheep were contented, so it was a quiet night in the hills. And as we looked down on the town, it, too, was still.

"Shimon was excitedly telling me how he and his younger brother, Jacob, were going to help me train up their new baby brother to be a good shepherd. When suddenly, our tranquility was interrupted by the appearance of what looked to be a man – but a man unlike any I have ever seen. He was surrounded by a blinding light.

. . .

"While I raised a hand to shield my eyes, I instinctively reached out to pull Shimon close to my side. I squinted at the other shepherds who were near. We all were trying to discern what was happening and what we should do. Did this man mean us harm? Should we run? But we all knew we could not abandon our sheep! Who was this man and what did he want? Instead of feeling threatened, the light seemed to embrace us. Don't misunderstand – we were afraid! But at the same time, we were spellbound.

"'*Don't be afraid!*' the man said. '*I bring you good news of great joy for everyone! The Savior – yes, the Messiah, the Lord – has been born tonight in Beth-lehem, the city of David! And this is how you will recognize Him: you will find a baby lying in a manger, wrapped snugly in strips of cloth!*'[4]

"We were still trying to understand who this being was when, all of a sudden, the sky was filled with a heavenly host. As if in unison, we all fell to our knees in fear and shielded our eyes from the brilliance that radiated above us. At that point, we knew this was a host of angels – the army of heaven – who had come to bring us great news.

"The angelic host began praising God, saying: '*Glory to God in the highest heaven, and peace on earth to all whom God favors!*'"[5]

"As the angels proclaimed their news, time seemed to stop. Even the sheep surrounding us seemed to bow low. No one – and no thing – was capable of moving. We were overwhelmed by the sight and enraptured by the news. I have no idea how long the angelic host remained in our midst.

"Then we did something that shepherds never do! We left our flocks unattended in the field. We didn't hesitate for one moment. We ran into town to this stable just as the angels had directed us.

. . .

"As we approached the stable, we expected to find a large crowd gathered to worship the arrival of the newborn Messiah. We thought the religious leaders would all be gathered to give praise to God – and perhaps even King Herod himself would be here. This is a great night of rejoicing for our entire nation in celebration and worship. Glory to God in the highest!

"But we are dumbfounded that no one is here. Not even Achim, who owns this stable, or his family. At first we thought, surely this isn't the place! And yet, we know it is! Why are we seemingly the only ones who know who this baby is?"

He hadn't really directed that question to us; rather, he was making an observation. Moshe and the others turned their attention back toward Jesus and worshiped Him. Neither Mary nor I knew how to respond. Instead, Mary gave them a tender smile and nodded her head in acknowledgment.

After a while, they quietly stood to their feet and reverently backed out of the stable. The boy was the last to get up. I could see he was staring into Jesus's eyes. He apparently had discovered what Mary and I had seen earlier.

Jesus's eyes are inviting and gentle. They welcome you in and make you feel safe. But they also seem to look into your very soul. Even though newborns are not supposed to be able to focus, Jesus is able to do just that!

After a few moments, Moshe softly called out to his son, "Shimon, it's time to go."

~

11

OUR FAMILY IS SEPARATED

~

*T*he shepherds were not as quiet leaving the stable as they had been arriving. We could hear their excitement as they shared everything they had seen, heard, and experienced. But no one else came to visit us that night except Miriam.

She had evidently heard the shepherds when they arrived. I caught a glimpse of her in the shadows standing just outside the stable but still within earshot of what was being said. When the shepherds left, she returned to the house.

A few hours later, but still well before sunrise, she and Achim came into the stable. They walked directly to the manger. As Miriam looked down at Jesus, I could see her countenance softening. Achim's expression, however, remained unchanged. Miriam turned toward Mary.

She said, "Your baby is beautiful, my dear. What is His name?"

. . .

Mary answered, "His name is Jesus – just as the angel instructed us."

"And how are you feeling?" Miriam continued.

"Jehovah God has been gracious and faithful!" Mary replied. "He gave me the strength I needed and the courage to endure throughout the birth – just as He did in the days leading up to the birth. He has blessed me with a husband who seeks to honor Him as well as honor me. He, too, has been my strength and courage throughout it all.

"Now God has blessed us with this beautiful baby – to love, to care for, and to raise. I am truly blessed above all women! And we thank you for your kindness in providing us with this place for me to give birth to my baby."

"That is why we have come to see you this morning," Miriam responded. "Achim and I can no longer allow you and your baby to remain in this animal stable."

I silently lifted up a prayer. "God, where would You have us go now?"

"We have decided you must move into the room we had prepared for Joseph inside the house," she continued. "It is on the upper floor away from the rest of the family. You will have a comfortable bed and a warm place for your baby. I will provide you with all you need each day.

"It will be a place for you to rest and regain your strength until your forty days of purification are completed. But no one in the house is to know you are there, and you are not to venture out of the room. We all must be agreed on this condition."

. . .

"What will the others think when they hear the cries of a baby coming from the room?" Mary asked.

"We have twelve grandchildren living in our home, a number of whom are crying babies, so no one will be able to distinguish the sounds of one more," Miriam replied. "And the room in which you will be staying is far removed from the others, so that should not be an issue."

But something told me there was something else – and I didn't need to wait long to discover what it was. As I looked at Achim, I could clearly see this was not his idea; but apparently Miriam had prevailed. Achim turned to me and said, "Joseph, there is one condition to this arrangement. You will not be permitted to stay in our home with Mary and the baby. I cannot turn a blind eye to your sinful behavior. You may return on the baby's eighth day for His circumcision and on His fortieth day to retrieve them. Otherwise, you must stay away.

"It is best you leave Bethlehem during this time. There is plenty of work in Jerusalem for a capable carpenter. And I am sure you will be able to find a room in the city where you can stay. The sun will rise soon. We need to move Mary and the baby into the house before the rest of the family awakens. And Joseph, you need to leave now, as well."

I hated to leave Mary and Jesus, but I knew Miriam would take good care of them. Mary looked at me and reluctantly nodded her agreement, but I could see how unhappy she was with this arrangement. The joy we had shared with a group of unknown shepherds over the birth of Jesus was now being overshadowed by the doubts of our own family.

I embraced my wife, saying, "Jehovah God has been faithful in ordering every step that has led us here, and we will trust Him, knowing He will continue to do so."

. . .

Turning to my cousin I said, "Thank you, Achim, for allowing Mary and Jesus to stay in your home, and thank you for the care I know you will provide them."

Achim nodded curtly. Miriam ushered Mary and Jesus into the house, and I set out for Jerusalem.

~

12

MY FIRST WEEK IN JERUSALEM

~

*B*efore I could leave Bethlehem, there were two things I needed to do. First, I went to the synagogue as soon as the doors opened and registered for the census. Then, I sought out Clopas at his sister-in-law's home. I told him what had occurred since we arrived the day before.

I told him Jesus had been born and how a group of angels had announced His birth to shepherds in the hills. I told him how the shepherds had come to worship Jesus. I told him the joys, the wonders, and the awe of everything that had transpired.

"But Achim does not believe any of this is true," I continued. "He does not believe Jesus is the Son of God. He believes that either Mary committed adultery, or she and I violated our betrothal agreement and consummated our marriage before the proper time. He refused us entry into his home, but Miriam prevailed upon him to allow us to spend the night in their stable.

. . .

"Now that Jesus has been born, he has agreed to allow Mary and the baby to stay in the house until her time of purification is complete. However, I am not welcome in their home. I am headed to Jerusalem to find work for the next few weeks until Mary's time is completed."

"Brother, I am so sorry Achim has treated you this way," Clopas replied. "I would see if you could stay here in this home, but I know they have no room."

"That is very kind of you, brother," I responded. "I know Jehovah God has a divine plan in all of this. So we will trust Him that He will use this to further His purpose in all our lives.

"I have come to ask a favor of you. It will be several weeks before Mary and I can return to Nazareth. Would you please stop in Nazareth on your way home to Cana and check on Eli? Tell him Jesus has been born, and we will return as soon as we can."

Without hesitation, Clopas replied, "We most definitely will do so! Is there anything else we can do for Mary and the baby while you are in Jerusalem?"

"No, thank you!" I answered. "Since they are staying in the home secretly, they will not be able to receive you. I am, however, confident Miriam will take good care of them."

I bid my brother farewell and set out for Jerusalem. It quickly became apparent that Achim had been correct about there being plenty of work in the city! Renovations were being made to Herod's palace, and I was hired to help with the work that very afternoon.

•   •   •

Over the years, most of the merchants in the city have added rooms over their shops to accommodate the many pilgrims who come to Jerusalem for the annual feasts. It did not take me long to find a place to stay for the next forty days.

My days were very predictable. Six days per week I arose at the sound of the cock's crow and worked until the evening hours. Then each evening and on the Sabbath day I went to the temple to pray and seek God's face. I prayed for the safety of my wife – and His Son.

I will confess that though I knew Jesus was God's Son, from the moment He emerged from the womb, my heart embraced Him as my own son. He is the Son of Jehovah God who entrusted me to be His earthly father. From the moment He was born, He was both my God ... and my son.

Each night I prayed for the wisdom, understanding, strength, and ability as one who is a sinner to be the father to a son who will know no sin. I prayed I would be faithful to the task to which God had called me. I knew I would never be worthy – and yet, I also knew God had chosen me.

"Heavenly Father," I prayed, "grant me the ability to be the father You would have me be – to Your Son!"

In some respects the days passed slowly. I missed my family. But in other ways, time seemed to fly. Before I knew it, Jesus was eight days old!

13

THE CIRCUMCISION OF JESUS

~

J woke up early in the morning so I could arrive at Achim's home well before the household began their day. Achim and Miriam were expecting me, so Achim met me at the door and quietly led me up to the room where Mary and Jesus were staying. Mary had been anticipating my arrival as well, and we both savored those few moments together.

Mary placed Jesus in my arms, and I quietly followed Achim back outside. The sun was just beginning to reveal itself above the horizon. I would take Jesus to the synagogue and then return with Him by mid-morning in time for His next feeding. The rabbi would not be at the synagogue for at least another hour, so I decided to walk out to the hill country on the eastern side of town.

As I looked at Jesus asleep in my arms, I could not get over how light and fragile He was. It was hard to imagine God would choose to send His Son in the form of a baby. He is the Creator of life, but He had chosen to come in the form of His creation. He is all powerful, but He has chosen to come in the form of a powerless baby.

. . .

I had never held a baby in my arms for this long. I had held my nephew when he was born, and, of course, I had held Jesus soon after He was born. However, in both cases, their mothers were nearby to rescue me if the babies began to cry. For the next few hours, I would be on my own. Truth be told, I was somewhat intimidated – not so much because Jesus was the Son of God – rather because He was a little baby!

As I walked along the hillside, Jesus opened His eyes. He looked up at me with those all-knowing eyes, as if to say, "We've got this! Don't be concerned. Let's just enjoy our time together."

An even deeper love began to swell up in my heart – a deeper love for my God and a deeper love for this little One He had entrusted into our care. I began to think about all the things I would do with Him and teach Him. Then I thought about all He would teach me!

The sun was shining brightly now, and I knew it was time to make my way to the synagogue. Jesus was to be circumcised today in accordance with the covenant God had made with our patriarch, Abraham.

There weren't many people in the streets and only a handful in the synagogue when I arrived; each of them was engaged in prayer. I approached the rabbi and introduced myself.

"Rabbi, my name is Joseph. I am from Nazareth. My wife and I came to Bethlehem to be registered for the census. Soon after we arrived, my wife gave birth. The baby is eight days old today. In accordance with our law, I have brought Him to be circumcised."

"Joseph, my name is Rabbi Levi," he replied. "It is a pleasure to meet you on this joyous occasion. But I am surprised I have not yet seen you here in the synagogue before this if you arrived over eight days ago."

"I have been working in Jerusalem while my wife completes her days of purification here in Bethlehem."

"Where is your wife staying here in town?" he asked.

"The carpenter Achim and his wife, Miriam, have kindly provided her with a room."

"They are kind people," he said, "and it is not surprising they have come to your aid. What is the child's name?"

"His name is Jesus," I said.

The rabbi responded, "That is a noble name. I will be honored to circumcise Jesus."

The rabbi recounted the covenant God had made with Abraham and that through circumcision, Jesus was entering into that covenant. I did not sense a release from the Spirit of God to enlighten him on who Jesus was and how He was a part of that covenant in more ways than one.

Jesus barely whimpered when the knife cut away His skin. I wrapped Him back up in His cloth, and we made our return journey to Achim's stable. Again, I was able to avoid contact with the few people I passed. Miriam was there waiting for us. People were now awake in the house, so I would not be able to take Him back inside to Mary. Miriam would do so. I kissed Jesus on His forehead and released Him to her care.

∽

14

MY REMAINING DAYS IN
JERUSALEM

~

*I*f I thought my first week away from Mary and Jesus was a long time, you can only imagine what the next thirty-two days were like! I was to return to Bethlehem on the fortieth day to get my wife and Jesus. We would then travel to the temple in Jerusalem to present an offering of purification on Mary's behalf and an offering of redemption for Jesus as a first-born son. We would then continue our journey back home to Nazareth.

Truth be told, Mary and I were both concerned about Eli's health. Though I knew Clopas would look in on him and attend to any immediate needs, we would feel much better once we were there and able to provide whatever continuing care he required. But I was also looking forward to being back in Nazareth as a family, living in our own home, and beginning some pattern of normalcy.

I had waited many years to have a son, and though Jesus isn't technically my son, in many ways He is. I looked forward to beginning my new role as His father.

. . .

In the meantime, I continued my routine of working from dawn to dusk six days a week and spending evenings and each Sabbath day at the temple in prayer. Herod's household manager was pleased with my work in the palace, so he had commissioned me to be a part of the team of craftsmen making needed renovations to the great meeting hall. The king was residing at his palace in Caesarea Maritima, so it was a convenient time to get this work done.

I never had reason to visit the palace in Caesarea. But I am told it rivals the handiwork of the great palaces in the world, including Rome itself. Though Caesarea has become the political capital of this region, we all know Jerusalem remains the religious and accepted capital of our land. Herod knows it as well, so periodically he travels to his Jerusalem palace to appease the religious leaders.

Having seen the remarkable improvements he commissioned to be done to the temple, I can imagine the majesty of his palace in Caesarea. The household manager assured us the same would ultimately be true of the Jerusalem palace. No expense would be spared. This king would only be satisfied with the best!

As you know I am a carpenter, but my primary building material is stone, not wood as you might have imagined. Most of the renovations being made to the palace were being done using marble. Though I had not made the journey to Bethlehem to work, a good carpenter is never without his tools.

Our work in the great hall was almost finished – not any too soon, I might add. The household manager announced to us the king would arrive in Jerusalem the next day –our final day of work. We had been working through the night to make sure the work was completed in time. I was ready to be done so I could travel to Bethlehem the following day to get my family!

. . .

The king looked over our work when he arrived and was very complimentary. He gave us permission to continue working throughout the day so we could complete the job – even though he had returned. We were surprised when the household manager entered the hall a few hours later and announced, "A royal entourage from the Parthian empire is making its way through the city in the direction of the palace. Quick! Ready the hall to receive them!"

Herod did not seem pleased by the news whatsoever! He proclaimed loud enough for all of us to hear, "I have not received any message that an envoy is coming. Who has the audacity to show up at my door without my royal permission or invitation? What matters could be so important that protocol would be so blatantly disregarded? I refuse to grant them an audience! Even the Romans extend that simple courtesy to me! I will not condescend to their breach in protocol!"

One of Herod's advisors, a scribe by the name of Annas, spoke up. "Your majesty, you know how important our trade relations are with the Parthian empire. They are also our gateway to the Han Dynasty of China. We can ill-afford to offend them. Perhaps you should at least hear what they have to say."

The silence in the room was deafening. Even the workmen did not make a sound. Finally, Herod reluctantly said, "All right! I will see them!"

~

15

AN UNEXPECTED ARRIVAL

~

The king directed the household manager to have us continue with our work. Though he had decided to receive these visitors, he was not going to treat them as honored guests. They had offended him with their unannounced arrival, and he was not going to be gracious with his reception. However, the household manager did tell us to keep our noise to a minimum as we worked.

The Parthian visitors were very flamboyant. They wore brightly colored clothing unlike anything one would see in Jerusalem, including the king's palace. They entered the hall with a great show of splendor and magnificence as they bowed regally before the king. I had never witnessed anything like it.

After they had dispensed with their initial pleasantries, the one magus, who had introduced himself as Prince Balthazar from Babylon, spoke up. "Your majesty, where is He who has been born King of the Jews? For we saw His star when it rose and have come to worship Him."

•   •   •

His question seized my attention. Was he referring to Jesus? How could he possibly know about His birth? As I looked at the king, I could see he had no idea to whom the prince was referring.

Herod replied, "Oh, the King of the Jews! Of course, that is why you have come! I was just preparing to address another matter before you arrived. I must go and do so, but when I return I will tell you all about the King of the Jews!"

The king then promptly exited the hall followed by his advisors. The door had not fully closed when we heard him shouting, "The King of the Jews! I am the King of the Jews! How dare they suggest that anyone apart from me has been born into those ranks! Antipas, my son, you are one of my heirs. Has news of your birth taken seventeen years to make its way to Babylon? How dare these people suggest one has been born who will displace me and my seed!"

Overhearing the king's rant, the magi looked at one another warily, realizing Herod had no idea what they were talking about. They anxiously awaited Herod's return so they could conclude their visit and continue their quest. However, an hour passed before he came back.

"Thank you for your patience while I addressed another matter of important provincial business," he announced. "Now, as to your question about One who has been born King of the Jews – our prophets foretold of One who will come – the Messiah – who will lead our people to rebel against foreign authority and return our nation to its position of glory.

"Our people have prayed for His arrival for hundreds of years. Perhaps you, yourselves, have read those writings and seek the One whose coming was foretold. When did you first observe the star in the sky?"

• • •

Balthazar replied, "About a year ago, your majesty."

Herod nodded and said, "Yes, that is precisely when I first became aware of it, as well!"

Everyone in the hall knew he was lying. He hadn't seen a star – neither, apparently, had anyone else in his court! But he continued as if he had been earnestly seeking the baby.

He directed one of his scribes to read the prophecy aloud:

"The Christ will be born in Bethlehem of Judea, for so it is written by the prophet: 'And you, O Bethlehem, in the land of Judah, are by no means least among the rulers of Judah; for from you shall come a ruler who will shepherd My people Israel.'"

I had forgotten the prophets said He would be born in Bethlehem! God had known hundreds of years ago that Caesar would require us to travel to Bethlehem for the census. Of course, He did! Jehovah God knows it all!

My thought was interrupted when I heard Herod say, "Bethlehem! You should find the baby in Bethlehem! I had planned to go see Him myself, but I have only just arrived in Jerusalem. I have several affairs I must attend to first, so go and search diligently for the child. When you have found Him, bring me word, so that I, too, may go and worship Him."

The magi seemed pleased with his answer and promised they would return. They departed from the hall with the same pageantry with which they had arrived.

. . .

Herod seemed quite pleased with himself as he turned and addressed his advisors in a softer voice. "If these Parthian magi do, in fact, find that such a child has been born, they will return and tell me about it – and I will do what needs to be done. And if, more likely, they do not find a child, then I will be seen as magnanimous in my response to them and the Parthians foolish in their expedition. It truly is a win-win for me!"

16

THE STAR LED THEM TO ACHIM'S HOME

~

I could have told the magi and the king exactly where they would find the child! But I remained silent. What would they think if a lowly carpenter announced he knew where the Messiah had been born? And what's more, that the baby's mother was this carpenter's wife?

But I was also concerned about what Herod meant when he said he would do "what needs to be done." A chill ran down by spine. I knew I needed to get to Bethlehem to protect Mary and Jesus!

I had planned to head their way early the next morning, but now I knew I couldn't wait. Our work in the hall was nearly complete, so the household manager graciously allowed me to leave when I told him I needed to go attend to urgent family matters. He again expressed how pleased he was with my work and assured me I would be welcome to work in the palace any time.

. . .

I quickly left Jerusalem, stopping only long enough to settle the bill for my lodging. Then, I made my way in earnest to Bethlehem. When I arrived outside Achim's home, I saw a host of camels, donkeys, and servants gathered outside. Obviously, the star had led them right to Achim's door. I did not see the magi, so I surmised they were already inside the house with Mary and Jesus. I knew if I went to the doorway, I would only create a scene with Achim. I decided to watch from a distance and only attempt entry if a problem arose.

Soon I saw a child emerge from the home. It appeared to be Sarah – Achim and Miriam's granddaughter. She was beckoning some of the servants to follow her. The servants appeared to be carrying heavy boxes and chests into the home. They all remained out of my sight for quite some time.

Eventually, I saw Balthazar, together with the other magi and servants, exit the home. I watched as they mounted their animals and left. I remained hidden in the bushes – I didn't expect they would recognize me from the palace, but I didn't want to take any chances. Balthazar was speaking to his servant as they rode past me.

I heard him say, "Tonight, we have knelt before a special child. He is not just any king, but the King of all kings. The star has led us to Him. Though we must leave Him now, we must keep Him in our hearts wherever we go!"

I then heard him call out to his fellow magi, saying, "Let us camp in the hills outside Bethlehem for the night since it is late. We can return to Jerusalem in the morning and report what we have seen to King Herod."

Once again, I felt a chill run down my spine. I was afraid how Herod would respond once they brought him their report.

. . .

I turned my attention back to Achim's house. Everything was calm, and I could not see anyone stirring. I did not want to disturb the household – or Mary and Jesus – after all the excitement from the visit of the magi. I had a good vantage point right where I was, so I decided to just rest there. I would approach the house just before first light.

My sleep, however, was interrupted by an angel. He was the same one who had told me to go ahead with my marriage to Mary. He was again speaking to me through a dream. He said, *"Get up and flee to Egypt with the Child and His mother. Stay there until I tell you to return, because Herod is going to try to kill the Child."*[6]

There was no question in my mind God had again directed me through this angel. I knew what I must do. The sun would be coming up soon. It was time for me to arise and get Mary and Jesus.

As I walked toward the house, Achim met me at the door.

∾

17

SURPRISED BY MY COUSIN

~

*T*o my surprise, Achim reached out and embraced me without saying a word. He lay his head on my shoulder, and I soon realized he was sobbing. His breathing was labored as he attempted to speak. Between sobs, he said, "I am … so sorry, … Joseph. I am sorry I did not believe you and Mary when you arrived at my home. I have always known you to walk righteously before God. And yet, … I allowed the evil one to fill me with doubts. I have thought and spoken wicked things about you when you two were simply being faithful servants to our God.

"I refused you entry into my home! I have kept you away from your wife and the Son God has entrusted to you. I refused entry to … the child of the Living God! I turned my back on you – and Him! God has shown me just how wrong I was! Joseph, please … forgive me!"

I had no idea what God had done to bring him to this point, but a heavy burden had just been lifted from my heart. I, too, began to sob as I said, "I forgive you, Achim! I know what it is like to doubt the ones you love and to question the honesty of those closest to you! Mary and I also had our doubts – and questioned God – along the way. But even with your doubts, you opened your home and provided a place for Mary and Jesus to stay. I forgive you, and I thank you for caring for them these past forty days."

Achim led me to the upper room where his entire family had gathered. Those who could fit in the small space were inside the room. The rest spilled out into the hallway. Everyone was either weeping tears of joy or celebrating with words of adoration. Apparently, they had only just learned about Jesus.

In their midst, I saw my wife. She was smiling with that sweet, tender expression I had grown to cherish. I hadn't seen that smile since our brief time together right after Jesus was born. I missed that smile. I missed her. I missed Jesus.

Our eyes met and lingered for a few moments, then Mary turned her glance toward a young girl who was carefully holding Jesus. It was Sarah – the young girl I had seen last night as she led the servants into the house. Something told me she had known about Jesus long before the rest of the family.

We enjoyed this special time with our family for a short time, but I knew we needed to leave soon and travel to Egypt. I was afraid the magi were headed to Herod's palace with their report, and we would not have much time. But first we must present our offerings at the temple in Jerusalem in accordance with the laws of Moses.

"Joseph, look at the gifts a royal expedition of magi presented to Jesus!" Mary exclaimed. "They traveled from afar to see Him!"

"Yes, I saw them last night," I replied smiling, "and was in awe that Jehovah God had led them to find the King of kings! God in His infinite wisdom enabled shepherds and wise men to seek out His Son. But those whose hearts were hardened, like the religious leaders and kings, He blinded."

Achim graciously provided us with a donkey to carry the gifts the magi had given Jesus. He and his sons helped me secure the gifts, while Mary prepared herself and Jesus for the journey. Since Achim and his sons had work to do in Jerusalem, they would accompany us to the temple.

Miriam and the rest of the family bade us farewell. "We will look forward to seeing you this spring in Jerusalem for the celebration of Passover!" she said, before adding, "and what a celebration it will be!"

I smiled back and waved farewell but doubted we would be in Jerusalem in the spring.

On our way out of Bethlehem, we spotted the magi and their entourage off in the distance. They, too, had recently set out on their journey. But I was surprised to see they weren't traveling north on the road to Jerusalem. They were traveling east toward the Arabian wilderness. They would never make it to Herod's palace going in that direction. I wondered *what* had caused them to change their minds ... or, rather, *Who* had caused them to do so?

When we arrived at the temple, I saw a man staring at us. He looked familiar, but I could not immediately place him. Then it came to me – it was Rabbi Levi from Bethlehem. He was the priest who had circumcised Jesus. He was looking at all of us with great curiosity. He saw me and smiled before bowing his head in a greeting.

I began to wonder if Levi was the one religious leader God had enabled to see the arrival of His Son! Then he turned and went on his way. We bid farewell to Achim and his sons before making our way into the temple.

18

AT THE TEMPLE IN JERUSALEM

〜

*A*s Mary, Jesus, and I made our way through the outer courtyard of the temple, I purchased a pair of turtledoves from one of the temple merchants. We would present the turtledoves to a priest inside the temple to be placed on the altar as a purification sacrifice.

According to our laws, a woman is considered ceremonially unclean for forty days following the birth of a son or eighty days following the birth of a daughter. At the end of that time, a sacrifice is made as an atonement that she might be made ceremonially clean.

Our laws also require that if a woman's first child is a boy, he must be dedicated to the Lord. The law dates back to the night the angel of death visited all the households in Egypt, killing every firstborn son unless an animal sacrifice had been offered and the sacrifice's blood smeared on the door posts. According to the law, the firstborn son is redeemed by the giving of five shekels.

. . .

As we prepared to present our offering of redemption, I realized that this first-born Son did not need to be redeemed! God had sent this Son to redeem *us!* I wanted to shout the words throughout the temple, but God spoke to my heart telling me it was not my news to share. He would reveal His Son in His way and in His time.

We presented the turtledoves and the five shekels to the priest as required. As we turned to leave, we were approached by an elderly man who was being helped by a young boy. I instinctively raised my hand to protect my wife and child. Mary, however, reached up and lowered my hand. It was as if she knew why the man was approaching.

Tears of joy began to stream down his cheeks as he turned to Mary saying, "My name is Simeon, and this is my great-grandson, Ashriel. Almost 100 years ago, Jehovah God gave me a promise that I would see the Messiah with my own eyes before I die. I have come to this temple every day since then looking for the child. And today that promise has been fulfilled!"

He then reached to take Jesus from Mary's arms. I was surprised when she handed Him over willingly! As Simeon held Jesus, he turned his head and looked heavenward.

In a strong voice he proclaimed, *"Lord, now You are letting Your servant depart in peace, according to Your word; for my eyes have seen Your salvation that You have prepared in the presence of all peoples, a light for revelation to the Gentiles, and for glory to Your people Israel."*[7]

After a few moments, he returned Jesus to Mary's arms and spoke a word of blessing over her and me. Before he finished, an older woman came and stood in our midst. She, too, asked Mary if she could hold Jesus. Mary again graciously agreed.

. . .

As she held Jesus, she told us her name was Anna. She spoke words of praise and blessing over Jesus. I was a little startled when Mary began to tell her the story of how the angel had come to her and what he had said. She told her about the shepherds and the magi.

For some reason, I, too, felt compelled to tell her about the vision God had given me to take my family to Egypt. I told her we were departing that very hour, as God had instructed. I added, "I do not know where we will go in Egypt, but we will walk by faith. Jehovah God has ordered our every step in the birth of His Son – and He will continue to do so!"

She abruptly asked us to wait there a minute, saying she had something she wanted to give us. When she returned, she placed a wrapped package in Mary's hands. "This is my most prized possession," she explained. "Wrap Him in this tunic, which has no seams, and use it to keep Him warm. Then one day when He becomes a Man, give it to Him and tell Him about this day."

Mary smiled at her and promised she would. As we left the temple, Mary and I marveled at how God had again enabled two very unlikely people to welcome His Son. But we also knew this would not be the last time we would marvel at – and about – Jesus.

∽

19

OUR FAMILY ARRIVES IN ALEXANDRIA

❧

I had no idea where we were to go in Egypt, but I knew the Lord would show us. We set out from Jerusalem and made our way to Ashkelon on the coast of the Mediterranean Sea. From there we traveled south and west along the coast through the Sinai Peninsula.

When we reached the eastern extreme of Egypt's Nile Delta, I realized the marshes would make our travel too difficult, so we turned inland and traveled along the southern boundary of the delta until we arrived back on the coast in the city of Alexandria.

A month had passed since we left Jerusalem, and I wanted to make sure Mary and Jesus had a comfortable place to rest that night with a roof over their heads.

I had once been told that Alexandria was the largest city in the world, rivaled only by Rome. Now that we were standing in the middle of it, I easily believed that to be the case. It is a provincial capital of the Roman

empire, situated on the trade route along the south side of the Mediterranean Sea, which connects Europe with the eastern empires by land
and sea.

I had also heard there was a large Jewish community living in the city. As a
matter of fact, I was told that Alexandria had become the largest urban
Jewish community in the world, even surpassing Jerusalem. I decided the
community shouldn't be too hard to find!

As we stood on the docks overlooking the sea, we were surrounded by
ships of every size and nationality. Even though Mary was carrying the
Son of God in her arms, we still felt very small and provincial in the midst
of this vast city. We didn't know what we were to do next. So we did the
only thing we knew to do. We called out to God!

"Jehovah God," I prayed, "You have directed every step we have taken in
our lives. Even when we didn't know You were leading us, You have gone
before us. At each turn in our journey, You have shown us where You
would have us go. Please bring us someone to show us where You would
have us go from here."

When Mary and I raised our bowed heads there was a young boy standing
right in front of us. He smiled at us and said, "You look like you need
some help! My name is Khati. How can I help you?"

I was grateful he was speaking in Aramaic!

"My name is Joseph," I replied. "This is my wife, Mary, and our son, Jesus.
We are new to your city and looking for a place we can find some food and
a place to rest."

. . .

"I have a little brother," Khati said, pointing at Jesus. "And he is about the same age as your baby. I can see you are Jews. Where are you from?"

"We have traveled here from Jerusalem," I answered, "but we live in the town of Nazareth."

"Someday I would like to visit Jerusalem," he responded. "I have heard many fine things about it. My family and I live in the delta quarter of our city, where many Jews live. The people there often talk about the grand temple where they say your God lives."

"Well, I wouldn't say God lives in the temple," I told him. "He lives in the hearts of His people. But the temple is a grand place for us to worship Him. We were in the temple just before we left the city! We are so very thankful for your offer to help us."

Khati smiled broadly. "My parents taught me to help others in need whenever I can. My father is a merchant, and his shop is not too far from here. I'm sure he can help you. Follow me and I will take you to him."

As we walked the few blocks to his father's shop, Khati pointed out every shop and person of interest along the way. Not only did he seem to know a lot about his city, but many of the people we passed also seemed to know him!

When we arrived at his family's shop, he introduced us to his father, Alim. He greeted us warmly, saying, "Welcome to my humble shop. You look weary from your travels. Please sit down and tell me how I can help you."

∾

20

THE FATHER'S PROVISION FOR OUR FAMILY

❦

I told Alim I was looking to buy some food for my family. Then, as we continued to talk, I explained I was a carpenter looking for work and a place where we could stay. I never expected Alim's response.

"Up until last week, my cousin and his family lived in the one-room home that is adjacent to my home. At the beginning of the week, he unexpectedly announced he needed to move to another part of the city. So, for the past week, I have been looking for a new tenant. I can usually find a tenant quickly – but not this time. Perhaps it was intended for your family. I also need a good carpenter to make repairs in one of my business establishments."

As Alim went on to explain the stonework he needed done, I told him I could easily handle the job. We agreed on an exchange. Mary, Jesus, and I would move into the home he had available for the next two weeks in exchange for me completing the work he needed done.

• • •

It took me only a week to complete the work, which apparently was much quicker than he expected. "Joseph, you are a skilled carpenter," Alim said. "Your work is far better than that of anyone else I have ever employed. And you finish the work in half the time. I will tell my friends about you, and soon you will be in great demand – and I will have a long-term tenant!"

Alim's wife, Nena, helped Mary become acclimated with the big city life of Alexandria, and the two women became fast friends. Alim's younger son was only a few months older than Jesus, so our families were quickly drawn together.

As time passed, Alim and I became good friends, as well. One day, I confided in him that we had left Judea in order to protect Jesus. I told him I had learned of a plot by Herod to massacre all the male children under two years of age born in the area where Jesus had been born. He never asked me how I learned of the plot.

I explained that we had not set out for Alexandria. We knew we were to come to Egypt, but we trusted God to direct us to the specific place He intended.

"The first patriarch of our Jewish people, Abraham," I continued, "came to Egypt over 1,900 years ago to seek refuge, just like Mary and I have done. Then Abraham's grandson, Jacob, came to Egypt over 1,700 years ago seeking refuge for his family from a famine. Our God has used Egypt in an important way in the continuing story of our people – and now even in Jesus's story."

"I am proud our people have played such an important role in your story," Alim replied. "But I also know about the years our pharaohs subjected your people to slavery. I know any kindness I extend to you and your family will never make up for the pain our pharaohs caused your people. But, perhaps it will be a small way for me to personally make amends."

. . .

Alim always avoided speaking with me about his religious beliefs. The people of Alexandria pride themselves on their acceptance and tolerance of differing beliefs. He and Nena believed in the gods of their ancestors – the gods of the sun and the moon, and the earth and the sea. He knew that we, on the other hand, believe in the one true God who uniquely chose the Jews to be His people. Apparently, Alim's idea of tolerance and acceptance was that we would not speak of our beliefs.

However, one day all that changed. Mary told Nena about Jesus – who He is and how He came to be. She told her how she had been a virgin when she conceived. She explained how an angel had told her the Spirit of God would come upon her, and she would bear the Son of the Most High God.

In Alim and Nena's religious beliefs, stories about one of their gods impregnating a woman were not that unusual, but they had never actually spoken to a woman who had said she had been impregnated by God.

Mary even explained how the angel had spoken to Zechariah and Elizabeth, and also to me. She told Nena about the shepherds who had received an announcement from angels. And she told her about the Parthian magi who had followed a star to find Jesus.

Then she explained how an angel had told us to come to Egypt to protect Jesus. She shared with Nena how she and I believed God had directed Khati to us that very first day.

But it was the news we all received the following week that really got Alim and Nena thinking about everything Mary had said.

21

"WE BELIEVE!"

~

*A*lim and I were talking in his shop when Khati came rushing in. He interrupted, exclaiming, "Merchants from Jerusalem just arrived at the docks today. I overheard them talking about how the Herodian king dispatched soldiers to massacre all the male children under two years of age in and around a town called Bethlehem! I cannot believe a king would do such a thing to the children of his own people! Joseph, can this be true?"

I couldn't help but grieve over the great loss experienced by those families. God had protected His Son, but those families had paid a severe price. After a moment, I responded, "Yes, Khati, I fear that it is true."

Alim spoke up. "It is just as you said it would be, Joseph. Your God has protected your son!"

It was a few weeks before Alim approached me on the subject again, saying, "Joseph, I know you to be a man who fears your God and walks uprightly before Him. Nena and I have heard how your God has spoken to you and directed you – and how Jesus is His Son. I know you are not a devious man, and I know you believe all you have told us.

"But how is it your God would choose a young virgin from a small town, engaged to a poor carpenter, to give birth to His Son? Why wouldn't He choose a king and queen in a spectacular city like Alexandria or Jerusalem? Why would He allow His Son to be born in an animal stable and swaddled in a feeding trough instead of a majestic palace? Why would He allow kings to attempt to harm His child when they should be worshiping Him?

"Why would His angels announce the birth to a group of shepherds instead of making the announcement to people of honor and position? Why would He lead Him to be raised in a single-room hovel on the back-streets of Alexandria?"

These were questions I had wrestled with myself. And God had given me the answer. So I was grateful to now convey that answer to Alim. "Because that is what He said He would do. He said His Son would be born of a virgin. He said His Son would be born in Bethlehem. He said He would be worshiped by shepherds and foreign kings would bring tributes to Him. He said a king would slaughter children in an attempt to kill Him. He said He would direct the child to Egypt. He said He would raise a King from the line of our King David. And He said so much more!

"He said His Son would grow up in humble surroundings. And He said He will grow up to become a Man of sorrows, despised, rejected, and acquainted with the deepest grief on our behalf. He will carry our weaknesses and endure our punishment – not for His sins, but for ours."

Alim asked, "How can this be?"

. . .

"Many years ago," I continued, "Jehovah God provided a ram in a thicket to our patriarch, Abraham, to be offered as a sacrifice instead of his son Isaac. By faith, Abraham believed God would provide the sacrifice. He believed God would provide His own sacrifice on His mountain. I believe one day Jesus will be that sacrifice – the Lord will lay on Him the sins of us all. That is what I believe, and that is why I believe.

"Alim, I don't know why God chose me to be the earthly father to His Son. I have never done anything to deserve it. But I know He did choose me, and I will strive to be faithful to Him with every breath I take.

"And I don't know why He chose you to help us, but I know He did. You, too, are a part of God's plan. Each of us has a part. God is at work in and through all our lives that we might come to believe in Him and His Son. So, the question is no longer – why do I believe? The question now is – do you believe?

"When I didn't know, I asked God to show me. Are you willing – with an open heart and mind – to ask Him to show you?"

Alim remained silent. I knew he was pondering everything I had just said. I decided to give him time to consider my question, so after a few minutes I walked away.

The next morning, Alim and Nena came to our door. As I greeted him, he said, "Last night I told Nena what you said to me. When I was done, I told her, 'I believe.' And she looked at me and said, 'So do I.' Then to our surprise, Khati – who had been listening in the other room – appeared and declared, 'And so do I!' We have come to tell you we believe in your God, Jehovah, and we believe in His Son! Teach us so we can know more about Him."

. . .

From that day on, we were more than just friends – we were family! We taught them from the Scriptures and pointed them to the prophecies about Jesus.

Several weeks later, the angel again returned to me in a dream, saying, *"Get up and take the Child and His mother back to the land of Israel. Those who were trying to kill Him are dead."*[8]

I knew we could not delay. I completed my work and packed for our journey to Nazareth. Though we were glad to be returning home, we were sad to say farewell to Alim, Nena, and their family. We would miss them greatly! But we knew we would see them again one day.

∼

22

OUR JOURNEY HOME TO NAZARETH

❧

*J*ust before we left Alexandria, Mary announced she was expecting a child. I was barely able to contain my joy! This child would be flesh of my flesh. Though I knew I would never love him or her any more than I love Jesus, I rejoiced in Jehovah God's goodness in giving us this son or daughter.

Mary told me she was certain the baby was a boy. But she had no word from an angel or promise from God. This was coming simply from her own intuition. We would see how accurate that was!

Once again, I was traveling with a pregnant wife! But this time, we knew it would be several months before the baby was born. Our journey home to Nazareth would take about a month.

Jesus was now six months past His second birthday. He seemed to be enjoying the journey. He had long ago begun to walk – and it didn't take long before He was running. Now as we traveled, He was exploring every tree, every flower, and every animal we encountered along the way. He seemed to be delighting in His Heavenly Father's creation!

As I watched Him, I knew He would always be at least one step ahead of us! And yet, though He had a playful nature and a constant twinkle in His eye, He was never disobedient.

Unlike anyone else who had ever lived, Jesus was born without a sin nature. He is the Son of God, who knows no sin. That was obvious from the very beginning. He never cried for His own way. He never had a temper tantrum. He never spoke a word of disrespect or acted in any way that was disobedient.

He was also often quiet and reflective. I don't think anything ever missed His notice, and He always thoughtfully considered everything He saw and heard. From the moment He was a baby, He had the ability to look at you with those dark brown eyes as if He were looking deep into your soul. I firmly believe that even as an infant, He knew my deepest thoughts and saw me for who I truly was.

He was – and would always be – a delight to Mary and me. We marveled, simply by looking at Him. But now with another baby on the way, we began to wonder what it would be like for Him to have a younger brother or sister. How would He see Himself as He relates to them? How would they see Him?

While we were traveling home, Mary and I began to discuss what we would tell His younger brother or sister about Jesus when the child was old enough to understand.

During the conversation, Mary said, "It will be hard for His brothers or sisters to grow up with the knowledge their older brother is the Son of God. If God grants us the ability to have many more children, I want them to be close as brothers and sisters. I don't want the other children to be intimidated by Jesus or resent Him in any way. I want them to love Him as their brother – and in the proper time, as their God."

We began to pray then that the Heavenly Father would grant us wisdom in what to say and when to say it. It would be a while before we were faced with the question, but we would need wisdom when the time came.

That journey was a very special time for me. Mary, Jesus, and I were together every moment. I wasn't away working. I was able to enjoy my wife and "our" son. Our delight was always mixed with wonder – and I knew I would never have a time quite like this with the two of them again.

When the angel of the Lord redirected us to Egypt after Jesus was born, I sent word to Clopas to let him know where we were headed and that we would be delayed returning to Nazareth. At the time, I couldn't tell him when we would be able to return from Egypt, because I had no idea.

I also had no way to send Clopas a message while we were in Alexandria, and he had no way to reach us. So, we prayed all was well with Eli, as well as Clopas and his family. Mary and I talked about the possibilities of what we would be returning to when we arrived home. We prayed that Eli had regained his full strength and hadn't missed us too much – particularly his grandson, whom he had yet to meet.

As we got close to home, Mary said, "And now we have news for him of another grandchild! I am certain he will be overjoyed at the news. We will have to enlarge the house!"

"Oh yes!" I replied. "Happy is the man whose quiver is full of children!"

❧

23

UNEXPECTED SURPRISES IN NAZARETH

~

*A*s we entered Nazareth, it looked much the same as it had when we left over two years earlier. Well, almost the same. To my surprise, the first person I saw standing outside Eli's home was Clopas! What was he doing here? We saw each other at the same time. I heard him call out for his wife, Mary, and their son, James, as we all began to scurry toward one another.

"Brother, it is so good to see you! We have missed you!" I exclaimed as we embraced.

"It is wonderful to see you all as well, brother!" Clopas replied. "And who is this good-looking young man? Surely this isn't Jesus! He isn't a baby anymore!"

Both Marys quickly joined us, and we all savored our joyful reunion. They had last seen my Mary the afternoon before Jesus was born, and I had last seen Clopas one day later. Much had happened since then. And yes, Jesus had grown, but so had their son James. He had just turned nine years old.

We all had so many questions, and there was much news we needed to catch up on. "This is an unexpected blessing," I exclaimed. "We never expected to see you here in Nazareth. What brings you here?"

Clopas paused and looked at his wife before answering. Out of the corner of my eye, I saw my Mary anxiously looking for her father. But she remained there by my side so she could hear Clopas's news.

"Brother, when I last saw you," Clopas began, "you asked us to travel back home through Nazareth so we could check on Eli. I promised you we would. As we began our journey home, Mary and I talked about the way the two of you were being treated by Achim and his family and by your neighbors. We decided we needed to move here to Nazareth to help you and encourage you. There was really nothing to keep us in Cana any longer. We knew it was what God would have us do.

"When we arrived in Nazareth, Eli was disheartened you two would be delayed in your return, but he rejoiced in the news of Jesus's birth. Jesus, Your grandfather was absolutely delighted to hear about you! He also seemed genuinely pleased about our decision to move to Nazareth. We quickly realized we were not moving here solely to encourage you when you returned, we would also be encouraging Eli in your absence.

"I traveled to Cana while Mary and James remained here in Nazareth. I settled our affairs, gathered our few belongings, and brought them back here. While we waited for you to return, we stayed in your home.

"Two months later, we received your message that an angel of the Lord had directed you to go to Egypt. You had asked that we continue to care for Eli, but you obviously did not know of our decision to permanently move here. We marveled at the goodness of God as He ordered all our steps!"

Then Clopas hesitated for a moment before continuing. "Mary, I am sorry to tell you your father never fully recovered from his fever. As time went on, his health continued to decline, and within a few months he died. On the day before he took his last breath, he told me how grateful he was to God for all of His many blessings. He told me God had given him a wife whom he had loved with all his heart."

Mary began to weep. I held her in my arms while Clopas continued. "He told me, 'God has given me a special daughter whom He has honored above all other women. She is my pride and treasure, shining brighter than all others. He has given me a son-in-law who is not only a good son but also a good friend and a righteous man. And most of all, God has allowed me to be the grandfather to His Son – the Messiah – whom I will not meet now, but I will meet one day in heaven!'

"Eli died peacefully with those praises on his lips. He loved you all. And he died knowing he will see you again on the day of resurrection.

"Before he died, he asked me to move my family into his home, to watch over your home, and to keep the family carpentry trade going until your return. I promised him I would do so."

Though Eli's death had taken place over a year before our return, for us it had just occurred. We immediately entered a time of mourning.

～

24

OUR FAMILY GROWS

~

*T*hose initial days back in Nazareth were difficult. Mary and I both so wished we could have been by Eli's side during his illness and throughout his last days. We grieved his death – but we also grieved that we hadn't been there with him. We knew God had ordered our steps, but it was still hard.

It was gripping to watch Jesus's response through all of this. He had never known His grandfather – at least on this side of heaven – but He saw the pain Eli's death caused Mary and me. He wept with us. One day He told us, "Death was never part of the Father's plan. He, too, grieves the pain and sadness that it causes. But one day soon, death will be defeated. And one day, there will be no more pain and suffering!"

He spoke those words with an authority that surpasses that of anyone I have ever known – and, at the time, Jesus was less than three years of age! Throughout those days, He reminded Mary that Eli was now in a much better place where there are no tears. His words spoke peace and comfort to His mother's heart.

. . .

As the weeks passed, the grief began to lessen. We began to settle back into life in Nazareth. Clopas and I decided to partner in the carpentry trade. It was just like our younger days when we worked together in Cana. He had done a good job of maintaining the trade in my absence, and it felt right to be working together again.

We also noticed our neighbors had become more accepting of us. Perhaps it was because people were drawn to Jesus. Everyone stopped to look at and talk to this charismatic little boy. People admired how mature He was for His age but also how He brightened every heart wherever He went.

We would still on occasion see a neighbor whispering behind our backs, but the open persecution we had experienced before Jesus was born seemed to have passed. Mary and I also decided it had something to do with our grief over Eli's death. The town had truly tried to minister to our sorrow – even Rabbi Jacob.

One day while Clopas and I were working on a job, James came running to tell me Mary was in labor. I needed to get home right away. When I arrived, my sister-in-law and the town midwife were both with Mary. Though I tried to convince them I was experienced in helping Mary give birth, neither one of them would hear a word of it. They both told me to wait outside with the other men!

Clopas, James, and I all nervously waited. Jesus, on the other hand, assured us everything would be fine. He reminded me that the pain of childbirth wasn't a part of the Father's original plan, either. It never ceased to amaze me to hear a three-year-old say things like that! It wasn't long before I heard the startled cry of a newborn baby and the announcement from my sister-in-law, "You have a son!"

. . .

Jesus and I entered the room to see the newest addition to our family. There weren't any animals in the room looking on, and the baby's bed had never been used as a feeding trough. Otherwise, Mary seemed as contented holding him in her arms as she had been when she first held Jesus. It was a reminder that all life is a precious gift from God!

Clopas and James soon joined us. Clopas asked, "What name will you give him?"

Mary looked at our nephew and replied, "James, if it is OK with you, we are going to call your new cousin James as well! The name means 'one who follows' and it is our prayer he will follow God every day of his life. So, the two of you will share that important name!"

My nephew looked quite pleased with the answer. Jesus looked at His baby brother and smiled. He had always been a Son, but He had never been a brother. He was going to enjoy this! I saw Him looking into James's eyes. He was looking into his very soul – and I knew He could see James and all he would ever become.

It was a precious night for our family. A family of three had now become four, and something told me we weren't finished.

∾

25

OUR FAMILY GROWS EVEN MORE

❧

*A*s the years passed, our family did continue to grow. Two years after James was born, God gave us another son. We named him Joseph. He would be my namesake and a continuing reminder of God's faithfulness.

One year later, God blessed us with Jude, which means "praise." He was to be a constant reminder to us of the great praise that is due to our God and His faithfulness. I had once prayed earnestly for a son, and now God was granting my heart's desire – exceeding, abundantly beyond my greatest hope. One year after that came Simon. Jesus now had four younger brothers – and I had five sons!

Jesus was seven years old when Simon was born. He was already a great help to Mary and me. He was a natural craftsman. I began to teach Him how to use my tools when He was four years old. Very soon, He was fashioning woodcarvings that surpassed the work of many seasoned carpenters.

· · ·

As a matter of fact, when He was six years old, He carved a set of animals for James, together with a small wooden ark. I was amazed by the intricate detail, even on animals Jesus had never seen – at least on this side of heaven.

But then I remembered: He knew exactly what each of those animals looked like. He had been with His Heavenly Father when they were created. His handiwork and craftsmanship were already on display in them and through them.

When Jesus gave James the set of animals and the ark, He repeatedly told James the story of Noah and the flood until James knew the story by heart. He taught James the meaning of a rainbow and the fact that Jehovah God keeps every promise!

When James was a little older, Jesus made dolls for him representing David and Goliath. They became two of his most prized possessions as he repeated the story Jesus taught him about how our ancestor, King David, defeated the Philistine giant. He reminded James that God would give him the strength and ability to accomplish everything He set before him.

After Simon was born, Mary told me to stop praying for sons and to start praying for daughters! Those prayers were answered with the birth of little Mary two years later and Salome one year after that. We chose the name Salome in honor of the young girl who had been a friend to Mary when she was pregnant with Jesus. She had continued to be her friend as the years passed.

We were now a family of nine! Each time our family grew, so did our humble home. We added a little space here and there. The five boys slept in one slightly enlarged room. The girls had a much smaller room. And Mary and I had a small room for ourselves.

• • •

Jesus was a good big brother to them all, and they all looked up to Him. But He and James, as the two oldest, enjoyed a special bond.

Because of their unique relationship, I have asked James to help me tell parts of the rest of my story.

"Jesus helped our parents teach each of us children to be a servant to the others," James said, "and to always think of others in a selfless and loving way. But He didn't just say it in words; He lived it out and modeled it in all He did. I wanted to be just like Him!

"But, no matter how hard I tried, I wasn't able to be just like Him. Jesus never disobeyed our parents. He never did anything to any of us children out of spite or envy. He never got angry or wanted His own way. And when I say never, I mean never!

"It was as if He couldn't sin! I think I started to notice it when I was five. I realized my parents never needed to punish Him for doing something wrong. And it wasn't just that He didn't do anything wrong – He didn't seem to *want* to do anything wrong!

"Our parents taught us we were to care for all of our brothers and sisters – but we were particularly to care for the sibling immediately younger than ourselves. Jesus was to watch out for me, I was to watch out for Joseph, Joseph for Jude, and so on. We were to teach our younger sibling what we had learned. And we were to stick with it until the younger sibling had grasped the skill or the teaching.

"Jesus never got frustrated with me, but I got frustrated with Joseph all the time! Jesus never raised His voice to me, but I would sometimes become so impatient with Joseph I would raise my voice and say things in a mean way. Why couldn't I be more like Jesus?"

26

A TRIP TO JERUSALEM

~

*M*ary and I had not yet told the other children Jesus was the Son of God. We had not felt God leading us to do so. But James, unlike the rest of his siblings, was starting to question why Jesus was so different in His attitudes and actions.

Soon after James turned nine, he and Jesus began to compete with each other athletically. Whenever they were not helping me with my carpentry work or doing their studies, they were often playing together with a ball they had fashioned out of an animal skin stuffed with husks.

"Jesus and I enjoyed kicking the ball back and forth to each other," James recalls, "and we created a game in which we assigned scores for the farthest or most difficult kicks. As we grew older, so did the complexity of our game.

"Jesus was always stronger than I was. We tested our strength by lifting stones. We used heavy round stones of varying weights and challenged each other whether we could lift them to our knees, our waists, our shoulders, or above our heads. Though Jesus always outlifted me, I learned early on I was faster than He was. We were often seen running throughout the Galilean hills.

"I wasn't very old when I learned Jesus's greatest passion was reading and studying the Scriptures. Early in the morning and after the end of the workday, Jesus could often be found at the synagogue reading the Scriptures, listening to teachings, and discussing truths with the rabbis. He instilled within me, as well as all our brothers, a thirst for the Scriptures. This was particularly true of our younger brother, Jude."

When Jesus was twelve, Mary, the children, and I traveled to Jerusalem for the celebration of Passover. Clopas and his family, together with our family, and a number of other families from our town, all traveled together. Those periodic trips to Jerusalem to observe our various religious feasts became a much-anticipated break from everyone's daily routine. The trips were a great opportunity for good fellowship and fun.

The men and women each traveled in separate groups. The younger children and older girls all traveled with the women. Jesus was now old enough to travel with the older boys in their group. It was possible to go for days without seeing an older son because he was off with the others.

The day after we arrived in Jerusalem, our family went to the temple to offer our sacrifice to the Lord. As we continued to pray, Mary and our daughters went to the court of women, and the boys and I went to the men's court.

"After a while, I saw Jesus walk over to the area where the rabbis were teaching," James remembers. "He sat down and joined them. I soon walked over to sit with Him. Before long, He was participating in the conversation – asking questions, giving answers, and quoting Scriptures. I couldn't imagine myself speaking up like that, at my age or His. And apparently some of the men were questioning His right to speak. But soon His knowledge of the Scriptures silenced even His most outspoken critics. My brother always amazed me!

"We remained in Jerusalem for a few more days – and each day Jesus slipped off to the temple to engage in conversation. My father allowed me to join Him twice more. Each time, I noticed that more people were coming just to see the young boy who was speaking with an authority that challenged – or even overshadowed – that of the religious leaders."

The next day, we departed for home. That evening Mary began to ask if anyone knew where Jesus was. He had walked with the older boys on our way to Jerusalem, so we believed He was doing so on our return trip, as well. But soon we discovered that none of the older boys had seen Him.

This was unusual for Jesus. He had never done anything close to disobeying Mary or me! We couldn't imagine what had happened to Him. Mary and I were worried and decided to return to Jerusalem to find Him. Clopas volunteered to join us in our search.

I told the rest of the family to continue the journey home under the charge of my sister-in-law. I instructed James to help his aunt watch out for the rest of his brothers and sisters. I could tell he was proud to be given the responsibility of being the "older" brother!

For three days we searched for Jesus all over the city. But on the fourth, we decided to go to the temple. There we found Jesus sitting among the rabbis discussing the Scriptures. When we saw Him, His back was to us. But we saw the look of astonishment on the faces of those sitting around Him. He spoke in a way that amazed them – and not just because He was so young!

~

27

THE FATHER'S BUSINESS

~

*M*ary, Clopas, and I watched for a short while before Mary spoke up. *"Why have You done this to us? Your father and I have been frantic searching for You everywhere."* [9]

Jesus stood up and looked at her with compassion. He saw the concern on all our faces. But what He said next would forever alter the way we saw Him. He answered, *"Why did you need to search? You should have known that I would be in My Father's house."* [10]

He had not spoken those words disrespectfully. He would never do anything to dishonor His mother or His father – including His earthly father. But He knew He always needed to honor His Heavenly Father and in so doing, He would truly be honoring us all. He needed us to understand that truth.

We all thought about what He said as we made our way home to Nazareth. It was obvious there would still be times we needed to adjust our plans to align with those of the Father. Mary and I had done so in the days leading up to and following His birth, and we would need to continue to do so as He grew through adolescence into adulthood.

We realized the time had come to tell the other children about their brother. Though the younger children would not fully understand everything, we knew it would be best if they all heard the news at the same time. We began by telling them Jesus had stayed in Jerusalem after we left to be in His Father's house and about His Father's business. You can imagine their quizzical expressions.

So, we told them Jesus's story from the beginning while He sat beside us, listening intently but never once trying to interject. He knew His siblings needed to know who He was – but He was still their older brother and did not want that relationship to change. Joseph and Jude received the news with some of the same questions James had. As expected, the others were too young to really grasp what we were telling them.

I have asked James to share how the children responded to the news.

"Our father and mother told us the story of how Jesus had come to be born," James recalls. "They explained that though my father was Jesus's earthly father, Jesus is in fact the Son of God. For all my life, I had known Him as my big brother. Now I was being told He was God's Son.

"A lot of things made more sense after that revelation. His teaching and understanding of Scriptures for one, and His sinless behavior for another. But it also caused me to look at Him much differently – and somehow, I knew our relationship would never be quite the same.

"I am ashamed to admit I secretly became jealous of Jesus. How could I ever measure up to a brother who is the Son of God? I was certain I would always be seen as inferior in the eyes of my mother and father. No angels had announced my birth! And no wise men from distant lands brought gifts to herald my arrival!

"As jealousy began to take root in my heart, so did anger and bitterness. If Jesus was the Son of God, why did we live in such humble surroundings? Why didn't we live in a palace, lavished with the riches of this world? Why does our father have to work so hard to earn a living to provide for us?

"It wasn't Jesus who changed that day, it was me. He never once – before or after – lorded over me as my older brother, let alone as the Son of God. I knew He loved me. He was always humble and gracious. He always treated me with compassion and concern. He always looked out for my best. None of that ever changed."

As the weeks and months passed, the children still had occasional questions, but for the most part life continued on as normal. We still worked hard together. The boys still played hard together. We had many good times together as a family.

Jesus taught his younger brothers how to swim, how to carve like craftsmen, and how to play ball. He made dolls for his sisters and was ever their protective big brother. He taught them all how to honor their parents, how to study the Scriptures, and how to treat one another with love and respect.

Mary and I were always careful not to say, "Why can't you be more like Jesus?" But we knew the children – particularly the older boys – still placed that pressure on themselves.

Mary and I viewed all of the children as gifts from God. But even we had to confess to each other that though we loved all of the children equally … we couldn't help but *marvel* at Jesus.

28

A FALL THROUGH THE ROOF

~

*N*azareth was continuing to grow, so there was no shortage of work for Clopas, our sons, and me. Jesus, now twenty years old, had achieved the distinction of being a master carpenter. In many ways, He had exceeded His uncle and me a long time ago. Many of those wanting to hire us to do carpentry work were now asking for Him specifically.

Few people in our community remembered the story of Jesus's miraculous birth. Rabbi Jacob had long ago died. Many of our neighbors had died or moved away. A handful of people still whispered behind our backs – but their whispers were about the illegitimacy of His conception, not His deity. The town viewed Him as the oldest of my five sons.

Friends and neighbors often commented about how proud Mary and I must be of the man Jesus had become. Each time they did, I saw James grimace a little, but his reaction had more to do with his state of mind than it did with the comments. On the job, however, all my sons took their lead from Jesus, because they knew He was now the master carpenter.

. . .

A few days ago, we were making repairs to the roof of the synagogue. Parts of the roof had begun to deteriorate and leak. It was a fairly routine job. I had performed roof repairs most of my life. But that day I stepped onto a section of the roof I thought was sound – only to discover it was not. Down I fell through the roof.

I landed on the floor two stories below after first hitting a bench. I heard and felt the bones in both of my legs snap just before I struck my head on the floor. I don't remember much after that.

"But I sure do," James recalls. "Jesus called out to Jude, who was already on the ground, to run and get the midwife and find the rabbi. The two of them were the most experienced in our town in providing medical care. Jesus and I quickly climbed down the ladder to tend to our father. We could see his legs were folded beneath him in an unnatural way. Jesus called out to our brother Joseph to go get our mother.

"Jesus looked at our father and assessed his injuries. He cautioned me not to move his legs until the midwife or rabbi had arrived. He tore His shirt, handed me a portion, and told me to use it to apply pressure to the gash in our father's leg, which was bleeding profusely. He did the same to the wound on father's head. As we knelt there beside our father, I knew Jesus was praying.

"It seemed like an eternity before the midwife arrived, followed immediately by the rabbi, and then our mother. Mother took over the task of applying pressure to the wound on father's head. The midwife and rabbi tended to the gash in his leg before carefully straightening both legs. We were all grateful that father was unconscious – otherwise, the pain would have been unbearable.

. . .

"While they treated the wound on our father's head, the rabbi told Jesus to craft a stretcher we could use to transport him back home. He and I quickly fabricated a stretcher from materials available there in the synagogue.

"While we were assembling the stretcher, I looked over at my mother, who was now kneeling beside our father and assisting the rabbi and midwife however she could. Concern was written all over her face. But I noticed something else. She kept looking at Jesus – with expectation."

"'Jesus, please heal him!'" my mother pleaded.

"I thought, 'Of course! Jesus is the Son of God!' Though we have never seen Him perform any miracles, as the Son of God He has the power to do so. Why didn't I think of that? All Jesus needs to do is say the word and our father will be healed! But, why hasn't He thought of that on His own? Why hasn't He already done it? Why did our mother even have to ask Him?

"I looked over at Jesus and nodded my head in agreement, as if to say, 'Yes, Jesus, go ahead and do Your thing. Heal our father!'

"Even amid the jealousy I often felt toward Jesus," James continues, "there was never any doubt in my mind He loved our father with all His heart. I knew He would always do whatever He could to help our father. And as the Son of God, I knew He had the ability to do whatever was needed – even the miraculous!

"At that moment, I became completely overcome with emotion and said, 'Jesus, please go ahead and heal our father!'"

∿

29

"IT'S NOT THE FATHER'S TIME."

～

*J*ames continues, "The rabbi and midwife looked at both my mother and me curiously. It was obvious they were surprised we were asking Jesus to heal our father. They knew He was an experienced carpenter, but those skills wouldn't help Him now. My father needed medical care, and they were the ones with that ability.

"They assured my mother and me they were doing all that was humanly possible. But they looked even more puzzled when Jesus said, 'It is not yet the Father's time. Very truly I tell you, the Son can do nothing by Himself. He can do only what He sees His Father doing, because whatever the Father does, the Son also does.'

"Jesus didn't say He *couldn't* heal our father; He said He *wouldn't* heal our father –because it wasn't the right time! How could it not be the right time? That didn't make any sense! If He's the Son of God, He can do anything He wants to do! I could feel myself getting angrier and angrier.

• • •

"I looked at my mother. Though there was a deep sadness in her eyes, she responded to Jesus's words with a slow nod as if she understood. I turned back toward Jesus. Though I could see it pained Him to not help our father, His expression gave me no consolation. I began to seethe.

"But at that moment, father began to groan. He was starting to wake up. The rabbi and midwife had successfully stopped his bleeding, but now they had turned their attention to setting his broken bones. They asked Jesus and me to gently place the stretcher underneath his body. We all worked together to get it under him while moving his body ever so slightly.

"Jesus then cut lengths of wood to be used as splints. Mother tore pieces of her cloak to be used as ties for the splints. I helped wrap the ties around each leg to hold the splints in place after the rabbi and midwife set the bones.

"Once the splints were in place, Jesus and I carefully picked up the stretcher and began to carry him home. By now, my brother Joseph had alerted our remaining siblings and they accompanied us."

While Jesus and James were carrying me home on the stretcher, I became fully awake. Every part of my body hurt, and every now and again the slightest movement would cause a sharp jab of pain. The trip seemed to last forever, but we eventually made it home. Slowly, they set my stretcher down on the bed.

The rabbi told them to leave the stretcher underneath me. There was no need to move it just yet. I apologized to them all for doing something so stupid as falling through a roof!

· · ·

I could see they were all worried, so I decided to lighten the mood of the moment when I grinned at them all and said, "Let this serve as a reminder to all of you men to always be careful where you step on a roof!"

The midwife told me I would be confined to my bed for several weeks to allow the bones in my legs to heal, and it would be many months before I would be able to return to my work. In the meantime, Jesus, my other sons, Clopas, and his sons would take care of the business; Mary and my daughters would nurse me back to health. I was mindful of how much worse things could have been and how much Jehovah God has blessed me with my family.

Over the years, Mary and I had learned that the best opportunity for the two of us to talk was after the rest of the family was asleep. Tonight was no exception. I could tell something was bothering her as she went about making sure I was as comfortable as possible.

"I asked Jesus to heal you today," she said quietly.

"How did He respond?" I replied.

"He told me it wasn't yet the Father's time."

I could see His answer was bothering her, so I asked, "What did you think when He said that?"

She looked down before replying. "I felt betrayed – by my son and by my Heavenly Father. I know Jesus can heal you. I know the Creator and Giver of Life is able to mend your body. For over twenty years God has asked us to adjust our lives in order to give birth to His Son and raise Him from infancy. I've never asked anything in return until today. But still, His answer was 'no!'"

. . .

Mary had never expressed a word of doubt about Jesus from the day of the angel's announcement until now. She had always been my pillar of faith. Now it was my opportunity to be hers. "Mary," I said, "His answer wasn't 'no.' His answer was 'not yet.' In human terms, Jesus has always been a faithful son to us, and in every way, God has always been faithful to us – and He always will be. His ways are not our ways. His thoughts are not our thoughts.

"The Father set His plan in motion long ago for His Son to come to this earth. His purpose is so much bigger than my few broken bones. It is not for Him to adjust His plan based upon what is happening in our lives; it is for us to adjust our lives to Him!"

～

30

"UNTIL THAT DAY!"

~

*J*ames picks back up telling the story.

"Early the next morning, my mother discovered my father was burning up with fever. We called for the midwife and the rabbi. When they arrived, they told us an infection had set in. They prepared a poultice of roots and herbs to treat the infection. My mother and sisters continued to place cold compresses on his brow and arms to bring down the fever. Several hours passed, but nothing seemed to be helping.

"All of us were gathered there with him. Uncle Clopas and his family were there, as well. The last to arrive in the room was Jesus. It was only then I learned He had spent the night in the garden outside of the village. I knew He often went there to pray. Apparently, He had been up all night praying for our father.

. . .

"The rabbi told us it wouldn't be long now. The infection had spread throughout my father's body. It was all we could do to hold back our tears. I found myself staring at Jesus. Everything within me was demanding to know why He wouldn't heal our father! It was at that moment I saw father open his eyes."

As I looked up at James and the others, I knew God was giving me one last moment with my family. I turned my head and looked at little Salome. I spoke a word of blessing over her. Then I continued to do the same over each one of my children from the youngest to the oldest, concluding with James.

Then I said these words: "Jehovah God has blessed me with a wife who loves Him with all her heart – and loves me with that same heart. For many years I cried out to Him for sons and daughters – and He graciously blessed me with each of you. Clopas, you have stood by my side all your life, and you have never wavered in your trust and support. Each one of you has been an expression of the Father's love for me.

"Jesus, Jehovah God has permitted me to be Your father, as well, and has ordered all our steps for You to be Mary's and my son here on earth – and for all these gathered around this bed to be Your family. I do not know what the Heavenly Father has in store for You while You remain on this earth, but as Your mother's oldest son, I ask you to care for her and all Your family when I am gone.

"And family, I charge you to honor Him and respect Him as your older brother. Jehovah God has given you a great privilege – to know His Son as brother and as Messiah. God will reveal who He is when the time is right. Jesus will follow the Father's timing, and you must trust Him to do so. Some of you have asked why Jesus has not healed me. I say to you simply because it hasn't been the Father's time.

. . .

"Trust the Father and trust His Son – even more than you have trusted me. For I am simply a fallible man like each of you, but Jesus and the Father are infallible. They deserve your trust because they are worthy of your trust."

I'll leave it to James to tell you what happened next.

James recalls, "Jesus looked at our father then turned to look at the rest of us. He told us the time was quickly drawing near for our father to step from this life into paradise. He reminded us that in paradise there is no pain, there is no suffering, and there are no tears. He told us it is a place beyond anything we can imagine that the Heavenly Father has prepared for those who love Him and are looking ahead by faith to the redemption of their sins.

"He told us that if we had seen it – like He has – we would never want to stand in our father's way of entering into it. And He said one day very soon, He will lead our father and the host of others who are gathered in paradise into the presence of the Heavenly Father – according to the Father's timing.

"Then Jesus reached down, wrapped His arms around our father, kissed him on the cheek, and said, 'Father, until that day.'

"With his last breath, our father smiled and looked directly into Jesus's eyes as he said … 'Until that day!'"

∼

SCRIPTURE BIBLIOGRAPHY

∽

Much of the storyline of this book is taken from the Gospels according to Matthew and Luke. Certain fictional events or depictions of those events have been added.

Some of the dialogue in this story are direct quotations from Scripture. Here are the specific references for those quotations:

[1] Matthew 2:20-23

[2] Psalm 127:3, 5

[3] Luke 1:46-49, 54-55 (CEV)

[4] Luke 2:10-12

[5] Luke 2:14 (NIV)

[6] Matthew 2:13

[7] Luke 2:29-32 (ESV)

[8] Matthew 2:20

[9] Luke 2:48

[10] Luke 2:49

～

LISTING OF CHARACTERS
(ALPHABETICAL ORDER)

~

Many of the characters in this book are real people pulled directly from the pages of Scripture — most notably Jesus! i have not changed any details about a number of those individuals —again, most notably Jesus — except the addition of their interactions with the fictional characters or events. They are noted below as "UN" (unchanged).

In other instances, fictional details have been added to real people to provide backgrounds about their lives where Scripture is silent. The intent is that you understand these were real people, whose lives were full of all of the many details that fill our own lives. They are noted as "FB" (fictional background).

In some instances, we are never told the names of certain individuals in the Bible. In those instances, where i have given them a name as well as a fictional background, they are noted as "FN" (fictional name).

Lastly, a number of the characters are purely fictional, added to convey the fictional elements of these stories . They are noted as "FC" (fictional character).

~

Abigail – wife of Eli, mother of Mary (FC)
Achim – cousin of Joseph, living in Bethlehem (FC)
Alim – an Egyptian merchant (FC)
Anna – the prophetess in the temple (FB)
Annas – a scribe and advisor to Herod who later became high priest (FB)
Ashriel – great grandson of Simeon (FC)
Balthazar – the Babylonian scholar and prince (FC)
Caesar Augustus – Emperor of Rome (UN)
Clopas – brother of Joseph (FB)
Eli – father of Mary (FB)
Eliezer – son of Achim (FC)
Elizabeth – cousin of Mary, wife of Zechariah, mother of the baptizer (UN)
Gabriel – angel of the Lord (UN)
Herod the Great – the tetrarch (FB)
Jacob – rabbi in Nazareth (FC)
James – son of Joseph and Mary, half-brother of Jesus (FB)
James (the less) – son of Clopas and his wife, Mary (FB)
Jesus – the Son of God (UN)
Joseph – son of Jacob, husband of Mary, earthly father of Jesus (FB)
Joseph – son of Joseph and Mary, half-brother of Jesus (FB)
Jude – son of Joseph and Mary, half-brother of Jesus (FB)
Khati – son of Alim (FC)
Levi – a rabbi in Bethlehem (FC)
Mary – mother of the incarnate Jesus (FB)
Mary – wife of Clopas (FB)
Mary – daughter of Joseph and Mary, half-sister of Jesus (FN)
Miriam – wife of Achim (FC)
Moshe – a shepherd in Bethlehem (FC)
Nena – wife of Alim, mother of Khati (FC)
Rebekah – first wife of Joseph (FC)
Salome – young neighbor girl who befriended Mary (FC)
Salome – daughter of Joseph and Mary, half-sister of Jesus (FN)
Sarah – granddaughter of Achim and Miriam (FC)
Shimon – son of Moshe, shepherd boy (FC)
Simeon – the prophet in the temple (FB)
Simon – son of Joseph and Mary, half-brother of Jesus (FB)

Unnamed household manager of Herod's palace (FB)
Unnamed midwife who treated Joseph (FC)
Unnamed rabbi who treated Joseph (FC)
Zechariah – priest, husband of Elizabeth, father of John the Baptizer (UN)

∾

A TEACHER CALLED NICODEMUS

KENNETH A. WINTER

DEDICATION

Do nothing from selfish ambition or conceit, but in humility count others more significant than yourselves. Let each of you look not only to his own interests, but also to the interests of others. Have this mind among yourselves, which is yours in Christ Jesus.
Philippians 2:3-5 (ESV)

In memory of my friend, Albert "Pete" Peterson,
a giant of a man, spiritually and physically,
who humbly served the Lord as Billy Sunday's advance man
and always made this little boy feel like he was the most important person in the room.

PREFACE

~

This fictional novella is part of a series titled, *The Called*, which is about ordinary people whom God called to use in extraordinary ways. We tend to elevate the people we read about in Scripture and place them on a pedestal far beyond our reach. We often think, "Of course God used them. They had extraordinary strength or extraordinary faith. But God could never use an ordinary person like me."

That is a lie the evil one desires us to believe. He loves for us to think we can't possibly be used by God because we are too ordinary. But the reality is God has used the ordinary to accomplish the extraordinary throughout history – and He has empowered them to do so through His Holy Spirit.

This story is about the life of one of those ordinary people – Nicodemus, the teacher. Though Nicodemus was a learned teacher, and a member of the elite ruling body called the Sanhedrin, he appears to have been a very humble man. The first time we see him in Scripture, he is coming to Jesus as an honest seeker. Most of the other religious leaders who came to Jesus with questions did so with an arrogant determination to catch Him in a trap. Nicodemus, however, appears to have had no agenda except to sincerely understand who Jesus was and the truth He was teaching.

Their conversation includes one of the best known verses in the Bible – John 3:16 – which is the very essence of the Gospel message: *For this is how God loved the world: He gave His one and only Son, so that everyone who believes in Him will not perish but have eternal life.*[1]

Nicodemus is only mentioned in the Gospel of John. Bear in mind that John only recorded events in his Gospel account that he personally witnessed. That would indicate he was in the room that night when Jesus and Nicodemus spoke. It is also reasonable to assume that John and Nicodemus previously knew one another. Given his position, Nicodemus was taking a chance coming in secret to speak with Jesus. He would have needed a trusted intermediary to set up the meeting.

John also mentions Nicodemus on two other occasions. The second time we see him is when he questions the motives of the religious leaders.[2] That is where we learn Nicodemus was a Galilean. I have chosen Capernaum as his hometown and created a back story about why he grew up in that village. The Bible does not tell us where he was from in Galilee. Placing him in Capernaum created interesting story possibilities regarding his interaction with others who lived in that small fishing village.

The third time we see Nicodemus is when he assists Joseph of Arimathea in the burial of Jesus's body. Again, John's reference suggests he and Nicodemus had more than just a passing knowledge of one another.

It is reasonable to conclude that Nicodemus became a follower of Jesus, though Scripture does not tell us definitively. By assisting in the burial of Jesus's body, both Joseph and Nicodemus put their positions on the Sanhedrin in jeopardy. They would have found themselves alienated and ostracized by the other leaders who had participated in the plot to crucify Jesus. Church tradition also supports the belief that both men became followers of Jesus.

Over the years, i have become intrigued by this humble man who was willing to take great risk to seek out and then stand for the truth. An adage attributed to Alexander Hamilton says, "if you don't stand for something, you will fall for anything." Nicodemus appears to have been one of those men who stood boldly for truth. We, as twenty-first century followers of Jesus, would do well to follow his example.

Obviously, i have taken liberties in developing a "back story" about Nicodemus. i do so in an effort for us to see him as a real person – a son with a family history, more than likely a loving husband and father, and a man who became recognized by others as a leader.

So, i hope you will sit back and enjoy this walk through Nicodemus's life. Many of the characters in the story come directly from Scripture, though their connection with Nicodemus is on multiple occasions either conjecture or completely fictional. You will easily recognize those characters. In some instances, i have chosen to add background details about them that are also either fictional or conjectures not confirmed in Scripture. i have also added fictional characters to round out the narrative. In the back of the book is a listing of characters to help you work through what is historical fact and what is fiction.

Throughout the story, some instances of dialogue are direct quotes from Scripture. When quoting Scripture, you will find i have italicized it. The Scripture references are included in a bibliography in the back of the book. Dialogue not italicized is part of the fictional story that helps advance the narrative.

In conclusion, my prayer is you will see Nicodemus through new eyes as you read this ... and be challenged to live out your walk with Jesus with the same boldness and courage he displayed. And most importantly, i pray you will be challenged to be an "ordinary" follower with the willingness and faith to be used by God in extraordinary ways ... for His glory!

1

MY GREAT-GREAT-GREAT
GRANDFATHER NAHUM

∽

The two friends stood their ground in the midst of overwhelming odds. They had already seen many of their own number fall that day. Now it was late afternoon as they watched the enemy continue to advance. One of the men, Nahum, called out to the other, "Judas, I will stand with you and fight on this field as long as Jehovah God continues to give me strength!"

"Nahum, there is no one else I would rather have fighting here by my side!" Judas replied. Suddenly he shouted, "Watch out there, behind you!"

Nahum turned, and his blade met the enemy just in the nick of time – as it had many times before. "Judas, only a handful of us remain, and the enemy continues to push forward. Most of our men have either fled or lie dead here on the battlefield."

"Nahum, we will trust Jehovah God to grant us victory! He will not forsake us! But if my life is required as a part of the price for that victory, I will gladly lay it down here and now!"

"Judas!" Nahum shouted. But at that moment, Nahum saw his friend fall to his death. An enemy blade had pierced his heart … and moments later Nahum fell to that same fate.

In many respects, my story begins with those two friends who fought side by side that day. My name is Nicodemus, and Nahum was my great-great-great grandfather. He was a priest who fought bravely alongside Judas Maccabeus in what ultimately became a successful revolt against the Seleucid Empire.

Our nation had been under the control of pagan conquerors for over 500 years – far longer than we had endured the slavery of Egypt. Our people were taken captive by the Assyrians about 700 years ago, followed in succession by the Babylonians, the Persians, and the Greeks. At the time Nahum died, our people were under the rule of the Seleucid Greeks. If those years taught our people anything, it was that none of our captors had any regard for the God of Abraham, Isaac, and Jacob.

Throughout the 500 years of captivity, we had seen our worship continually restricted and our temple repeatedly desecrated. The Seleucids were no exception. It was their blasphemous desecration of our temple in Jerusalem that prompted a priest named Mattathias, along with his five sons, to lead our people in revolt against the Seleucids.

One year into that revolt, Mattathias died from injuries he received in battle. Just before he died, he designated his third son, Judas, to replace him as leader. Everyone, including his brothers, agreed that Judas was best suited for the role, having witnessed his valor in battle and his decisive military skills.

Though the Seleucid army was far superior to the small Judean force in number and in training, Judas's decision to employ guerilla warfare tactics gave the Jews a slight advantage. My ancestor Nahum quickly rose in the Judean ranks due to his bravery and fighting skills. He soon became one of Judas's most trusted commanders.

One day, Judas directed Nahum to lead 3,000 men to attack the Seleucid outposts scattered throughout Galilee and to free the Jews living in those settlements. Jehovah God granted him favor, and they achieved great victory. From there, they advanced on the forces in Gilead and the settlements east of the Jordan River. Fighting continued for six years, during which time both sides suffered defeats and casualties. But still, our people continued to trust that God would ultimately bring them victory.

Seven years into the fighting, the Seleucid King Demetrius determined to put down the Maccabean revolt once and for all. He dispatched 20,000 of his infantry and 2,000 of his cavalry to lay siege to Jerusalem. Judas and Nahum brought their forces together on that battlefield. They were overwhelmingly outnumbered, and many of their men deserted. But those two leaders, together with just under 1,000 soldiers, stood firm until they were brought to death by the swords of their enemy.

Their bravery became an inspiration to the Jews. Judas's brothers assumed command and, after several more years of fighting, defeated the Seleucids. Judea was finally freed from foreign rule – at least for a period of eighty years, until the Roman general Pompey laid siege to Jerusalem.

Those eighty years of freedom between the rules of the Seleucids and the Romans are known in our history as the Hasmonean dynasty. Judas's younger brother, Simon, became the first Hasmonean leader and high priest. Upon his death, he was followed by a succession of his descendants.

The Hasmoneans chose to honor the memory of my great-great-great-grandfather and reward his bravery by bestowing tributes upon his descendants. Those tributes greatly impacted each subsequent generation of our family ... including me.

∾

2

A VILLAGE ESTABLISHED IN HIS HONOR

❧

*F*ollowing the defeat of the Seleucids, the Hasmonean kings realized towns and villages needed be established throughout the wilderness lands north of Jerusalem if the Jewish nation was going to maintain its independence. King John Hyrcanus I appointed my great-great-grandfather Adir to lead the effort by establishing a new fishing settlement on the northern shore of the Sea of Galilee.

The king chose Adir because the settlement was to be named in honor of his father, Nahum, known for his military achievements in the region of Galilee. It was to be called Capernaum, meaning "Nahum's village."

The Hasmoneans also bestowed a financial tribute to Adir in honor of Nahum. A portion was designated to fund the settlement of the village, and the remainder was a gift to our family. Up until then, my ancestors had never enjoyed great wealth, but all that changed that day.

Adir, together with his family – his wife, Devorah, and their young son, Menahem – along with one hundred men, women, children, and their flocks, set out from Jerusalem to establish the new settlement.

After they had been traveling awhile, Devorah asked, "Husband, how long will it take us to arrive at this new place along the sea?"

"The king tells me it will require eight days considering the large number of animals and materials we are bringing with us," Adir replied. "So, it will be nine days before we arrive, counting the Sabbath day we will observe along the way."

"You and I have never lived outside of Jerusalem. What will we do when we arrive at this place in the wilderness?" Devorah asked, not for the first time.

"First, we will thank Jehovah God for our safe arrival and His great blessing and provision for our family," Adir answered. "And then we will jump into the sea and wash the dust from our travels off of our bodies!"

"But we don't know how to swim!" Devorah exclaimed. "We've never lived near a sea!"

"Then the second thing we will do, wife, is learn how to swim!" Adir responded with a grin.

Jehovah God had equipped this group of settlers with all the skills needed to establish the village. Once they arrived, several men, who were carpenters, quickly went to work constructing shelters for them to live in.

A handful of others were boat builders and fishermen. They began building the settlement's first two boats so the fishermen could get to work plying their trade. Fish would not only be a staple of their diets but also a primary source of the village's income.

Still others began cultivating portions of land that were best suited for growing crops. The land was fertile, and by the time the harvest season arrived, the settlers enjoyed a bountiful gathering of grain. Soon the plentiful olive crops followed. Gratefully, the oil and grain mills were finished just in time to receive the harvest.

Adir and the other men decided not to build a defensive wall around the settlement. Since the Lord had situated the village on the shores of the sea, they did not want to be partitioned off from its beauty or its natural breezes.

In addition to overseeing the development of the settlement, Adir made sure the synagogue was built and established in the center of everything. The village was thriving as the settlers marked the first anniversary in their new community, and more families had begun to arrive. The village now boasted a population of 200, including the small fighting force the Hasmonean king had sent with them for protection.

Adir gathered the people in and around the synagogue to commemorate that first anniversary with a time of praise and thanksgiving to Jehovah God. Sacrifices were offered to God, and the joy of the people could be heard from far away as Adir opened the Scriptures and read:

"Shout with joy to the Lord, O earth! Worship the Lord with gladness. Come before Him singing with joy. Acknowledge that the Lord is God! He made us, and we are His. We are His people, the sheep of His pasture.

"Enter His gates with thanksgiving; go into His courts with praise. Give thanks to Him and bless His name. For the Lord is good. His unfailing love continues forever, and His faithfulness continues to each generation."[1]

Then Adir went about the task of ensuring the continued welfare of his own family and the generations that would follow.

～

3

A MERCHANT NAMED SHEBNA

~

*S*oon after the Hasmoneans began to rule, our priests and teachers began to divide into two factions. The first was the Pharisees, who believed Jehovah God gave an oral law, or Talmud, in addition to the written law, the Torah. The oral law was given by God as a way to apply the written law. Another distinction was their belief that an afterlife exists. God punishes the wicked and rewards the righteous in the world to come.

The second faction was the Sadducees, consisting primarily of people of wealth or priestly position. They rejected the oral law and traditions, and insisted on a literal interpretation of the Torah. They also flatly denied the existence of an afterlife. Over the years, their beliefs were influenced by Greek philosophy and were considered liberal by the Pharisees.

My great-great-grandfather Adir was one of the first Pharisees, and each generation of my family since him has followed that same line of thought – including me. But while our religious beliefs aligned with the Pharisees, our status as wealthy merchants aligned more with the Sadducees. That turn of events mostly took place through Adir's grandson, Asher, who subsequently became my grandfather. Please allow me to explain.

Many Jews chose to remain in Babylon even after Persian King Artaxerxes granted permission for them to return to our homeland. And when the Seleucids seized power in the region, these Jews saw no advantage to leaving their adopted homes to return to a region under a more severe pagan control. But, when our people achieved their independence from the Seleucids through the revolt, many of the Jews in Babylon began to reconsider their options.

Three of those were brothers: Hillel, Shebna, and Camydus. You have probably heard of the oldest brother, Rabbi Hillel. He became a revered sage, scholar, and leader of our people. His youngest brother, Camydus, was also a respected leader. As a matter of fact, both had already achieved significant status before they left Babylon to migrate to Jerusalem.

The lesser known of the three brothers was Shebna. He was an astute merchant who had already begun to build his wealth in Babylon. Having a more adventurous spirit than his brothers, he decided to migrate to the emerging frontier of our people – specifically the village of Capernaum. When he arrived, he immediately sought out my grandfather, Asher, who by then had assumed the role as leader of our village from his father, Menahem.

My grandfather greeted Shebna by extending a hand of friendship, just as he did to all new families coming to Capernaum. "Shebna," he said, "welcome to our village! I am so grateful that Jehovah God has led you to settle here. Please let me know how I can assist you as you get your family settled."

"Asher, even though I have only just arrived, I have already learned you are the man who can be of greatest help to me as I establish here," Shebna warmly replied. "I am told you are a man of vision and great initiative. I, too, am such a man, and I know the Lord God has led me here to help further the prosperity of this village – and our two families."

"Then it would appear that we have much to discuss!" my grandfather responded.

The two men quickly became trusted friends and ardent business partners. When Rome subsequently conquered our land and placed Herod the Great as ethnarch (governor) over our people, they saw it as a major business opportunity.

Though our Hasmonean kings had led us to keep strict observance of God's laws, they had done little to further the economic health of our region. Herod, on the other hand, was committed to allowing us to worship God without pagan influence as well as bring about economic expansion. Shebna and Asher took full advantage of those fiscal plans.

Since Capernaum was located on the sea, they invested in building our harbor into a thriving seaport for trade with other parts of Galilee and Judea. Herod and the Romans obliged by constructing a major trade route called the Via Maris. It connected Damascus with Alexandria in Egypt and passed through Capernaum, as well as Herod's new city of Caesarea Maritima along the Mediterranean Sea. This meant many travelers, caravans, and traders began to pass through our village.

Shebna and Asher thrived in this new environment. Their mills produced most of the olive oil being exported from our village, and they built a warehouse on the shore where fish could be salted and dried for export. Soon they were the sole exporter of the fish caught daily by our local fishermen. Everything the two men touched seemed to turn into gold.

My grandfather was able to take the financial legacy given to Adir and passed down to him through his father, Menahem, and multiply it into much greater wealth. Shebna soon joined Asher as the other leading elder of our village; their two families occupied the largest homes in our settlement. One of those homes became my birthplace and has since passed from one generation to the next.

4

GROWING UP AS A SON OF MEANS
IN A POSITION OF PRIVILEGE

~

My grandfather and Shebna's deep friendship and profitable business partnership lasted for the remainder of their lives. As a matter of fact, the two men planned for their sons, Yaakov and Ishmael, respectively, to follow in their footsteps and continue the partnership. The problem was that Yaakov had a different idea. At age fifteen, he approached my grandfather, Asher.

"Father," he said, "Jehovah God has not given me the passion for business He has given to you. I believe He has called me to become a rabbi – to teach His people the truths and ways of God. I fear that to do anything else would be disobedient to God. I do not want to disappoint you, but I also do not want to disobey God."

Though my grandfather was disappointed, he received the news with grace and compassion. "Yaakov, my son, I have only ever wanted the best for you. And doing what Jehovah God has placed before you to do – no matter what it is – will always be the best! If God is leading you to become a rabbi, then we must send you to Jerusalem to study the Scriptures under Shebna's brother, Rabbi Hillel."

Yaakov studied under the rabbi for five years. When his time was completed, he returned to Capernaum to serve as a rabbi in the local synagogue. Soon afterward, he became interested in a young woman he had known since they were children but who had blossomed during his absence. Her name was Nissa, and she was Shebna's daughter. To the delight of their parents, Yaakov and Nissa seemed to be drawn to each other – so the families wasted no time in arranging their marriage.

Soon afterward my grandfather declared, "Friends and family, though the next generation of Shebna's and my families will not be bound in a business partnership, our children will be bound through a marriage partnership that will carry forward to our future generations. And that is an even greater delight to us both! Instead of anticipating the financial profits our children could produce, we will look forward to the many grandchildren they will produce instead – and that is a much greater blessing!"

Shebna's son, Ishmael, showed a great talent for commerce and was put in charge of his father's business ventures. Asher and Shebna were both pleased with how the Lord had ordered their steps for the continued success of their future generations.

After several years, God blessed Yaakov and Nissa with a son, Nicodemus. And that is where my personal story begins. I enjoyed an idyllic life growing up in Capernaum along the Sea of Galilee. My family was well respected on both sides of my ancestral tree, and I was a son of means and privilege. My father was the respected rabbi of our village. And while I was still a young boy, he was selected by the men of the village to take a seat as a member of our local Sanhedrin.

Each city and town throughout the provinces of Judea, Galilee and Samaria selects up to twenty-three men to serve as judges to settle local disputes, make administrative decisions related to the village and oversee religious affairs requiring interpretation beyond the purview of the local rabbi. Affairs that cannot be settled by these local Sanhedrin are referred to the Great Sanhedrin in Jerusalem.

My father made sure I grew up knowing the teachings of the Torah from as far back as I can remember. He taught me to have not only a knowledge of God's Word but also a love for the God of the Word. He taught me to hide God's Word in my heart.

He often reminded me, "God spoke these words, saying, *'I am the Lord your God ..., you shall have no other gods before Me. I will show My favor to those who love Me and keep My commandments.'*"[1]

By the time I was fifteen, I knew God was leading me to follow in my father's footsteps to serve Him as a rabbi. I had been traveling to Jerusalem with my father to observe the annual feasts since I was twelve years old. Each time, as we approached the temple, I did so with great reverence and awe. But this time when I set off with my father for Jerusalem, it was harder because I knew I would be remaining there for several years to complete my studies.

We arrived just prior to the start of Sukkot, a celebration often referred to as the Feast of the Tabernacles. It is a time of joyful remembrance of God's deliverance, protection, provision, and faithfulness to our people – remembering the forty years He led us through the wilderness.

My father spotted Rabbi Hillel at the temple, and we walked over to him. "Teacher," my father began, "please allow me to introduce my son, Nicodemus. He has come to sit at your feet and learn from you, just as I did at his age. Nicodemus, this is your mother's uncle, Rabbi Hillel. There is no finer teacher in all of Israel. Listen to his every word and hold his teaching in your heart."

5

A SECOND-CLASS JEW IN JERUSALEM

~

R abbi Hillel frequently took his students to the temple where we would sit in one of the outer courtyards as he asked us questions. He was always patient with us, even though we often gave him incorrect answers. One morning he asked, "Who was the prophet Isaiah quoting when he wrote, *'The Spirit of the Sovereign Lord is upon Me, because the Lord has appointed Me to bring good news to the poor. He has sent Me to comfort the brokenhearted and to announce that captives will be released, prisoners will be freed, and the blind will see'*?"[1]

"He was writing of the Messiah who will come from the royal line of David," I responded.

Annas, one of my fellow students, quickly spoke up. "Teacher, you know our Hasmonean leaders questioned the accuracy of Isaiah's prophecy that the Messiah will be a descendant of David. The next thing Nicodemus will want us to believe is that the Messiah will also be a Galilean!"

Several of the talmidim (disciples) chuckled, but Rabbi Hillel looked at them disapprovingly. "The Hasmonean leaders discredited the prophecies of Isaiah in order to usurp the legitimate royal line of King David and legitimize their own ascension into the role," he said. "That is what motivated them to also seize the lawful priestly role of the Zadokites. Annas, you would do well to rightly interpret the Scriptures instead of blindly following in the footsteps of the Hasmoneans."

Several of the other talmidim now chuckled at Annas's expense. Rabbi Hillel also cast a disapproving glance their way before he continued. "And Annas, there is nothing to prevent the Messiah from being a Galilean. Be careful you do not use your own racial prejudices to shape your interpretation of Scripture. You may very well find yourself on the wrong side of the argument."

Hillel looked over at me after making that last statement. He was aware Annas and some of the other young men from Judea looked down on me, as well as the others who were from the province of Galilee. The rabbi knew some of that prejudice had been passed down to Annas from his grandfather, Camydus, who also happened to be the scholar's younger brother. The two brothers had often debated that subject.

Rabbi Hillel's own grandson, Gamaliel, was also in our group of talmidim. He and I usually agreed on most things, whereas I *disagreed* with Annas on most everything. Gamaliel was a Pharisee like me, and not surprisingly, Annas was a Sadducee. Though not all Sadducees shared Annas's prejudice toward Galileans, it didn't take me long to discover that many did.

As time passed, I discovered more of that prejudice in Jerusalem than I expected. Some of the looks and comments directed at me made me wish I could return to Capernaum. But I was grateful for the teaching of the rabbi; I was growing exponentially in my understanding of Scripture.

Instead of being called a student, those of us under his teaching were called a talmid. There is an important distinction between the two terms. A student seeks knowledge from the teacher to earn a grade, whereas a talmid wants to be truly like the teacher. Most of us wanted to follow in Rabbi Hillel's footsteps, though I questioned whether that was true of Annas and a few others.

It was obvious Annas was an ambitious young man. I heard him bragging on more than one occasion that he would become the youngest high priest in our history – and I had little doubt that would be the case.

Since we spent a lot of our time at the temple, we would often meet many of our religious leaders. The high priest at the time was a Sadducee named Simon ben Boethus. He had been in that position for thirteen years when I first arrived in Jerusalem. He seemed to enjoy the favor of the Romans, as well as Rome's appointed governor, King Herod.

As a matter of fact, Simon ben Boethus's daughter, Marianne, was Herod's current wife – his third. No one was certain whether it was Simon's influence through Marianne, or Herod's own sense of grandeur, but the ethnarch was having the temple renovated to rival or eclipse its appearance at the time of King Solomon. There was no denying the impressiveness of the work and the attention to detail.

One of the additions being made was the Hall of Hewn Stones, constructed as a meeting place for the Great Sanhedrin. It was built into the north wall of the temple with half of the hall extending into the sanctuary and the other half extending outside. With doorways in both directions, it symbolized the authority the Great Sanhedrin had over all aspects of our lives – both religious and civil. It truly was a corridor of power.

Though my father was a member of our local Sanhedrin in Capernaum, those members did not command the same respect and power as the members of this Great Sanhedrin. I equated the local group as being servants and this group as being rulers – even though I knew that wasn't the case across the board.

I suspected that many of the teachers and religious leaders in Jerusalem held their positions because of the power they sought and not a desire to worship or serve God. I was grateful that Rabbi Hillel was an exception. But I was still thankful to the Lord when my time finally arrived to return to Capernaum.

6

THE LEADING RABBI OF CAPERNAUM

~

"Welcome home, my son!" my father called out, even before I arrived at the door.

"It is so good to be home, father!" I said as we embraced. "I have missed the smells and sounds of the sea."

My father looked at me and smiled. "When you greet your mother, I hope you will also tell her that you missed the taste of her good cooking and the comforts of her company!"

"Of course, father, that goes without saying," I said matter-of-factly.

"Perhaps, but make sure you say it!"

I could tell by the twinkle in his eye that he was teasing, but I also knew I would be wise to heed his advice. I honestly had not realized how much I missed him and my mother until that moment. I would not be in any hurry to leave them or my beloved Capernaum any time soon.

As we sat down to catch up, I remarked to my father how much the village had grown during my absence. "The number of fishing boats appears to have doubled, and I saw there were many more children playing along the shore."

"Yes," he responded, "Jehovah God is leading more people to our village. We are pushing out one of the walls of the synagogue to accommodate more people. The footprint of the village is expanding, and your Uncle Ishmael tells me the family business is prospering. God has been very good to the people of Capernaum."

The conversation then turned to my time in Jerusalem. I told my father how Rabbi Hillel's teachings had expanded my thinking and deepened my understanding of the Scriptures. I also told him about the religious leaders I had met, as well as some of my fellow students, who were focused only on the worldly desires of position and power.

"Father, I pray God will turn the hearts of many of our leaders back to Him," I said, "and we will truly become a people who seek Him with our whole hearts, souls, and minds."

"Well, always remember, my son," he wisely replied, "it must also be true of us. Make sure you stay rightly oriented before our Lord, seeking to love Him and honor Him with your whole being. Ask Him to keep you from becoming distracted by the words and actions of those around you – no matter how godly they may want you to believe they are!"

Just then my mother entered the room. She had been away tending to a sick neighbor, and she looked tired. I remembered my father's advice and told her how much I had missed her – which was true because I truly had!

Over the next few days, I savored the time with my parents, family, and friends as they stopped by to welcome me home. We laughed together and shared wonderful memories, and I entertained them with stories about the great city of Jerusalem.

As the days passed, I noticed my mother becoming weak and frail. By the end of the week she had developed a high fever. Apparently, she had contracted our sick neighbor's illness. The village midwife prepared an herbal remedy, but it did not help. One week later – several days after our neighbor died – my mother died, as well.

My father was inconsolable. Gratefully, Uncle Ishmael made all the burial arrangements so I could tend to my father. But he refused to eat. Nothing I said eased his anguish. After two days, I realized his sorrow was masking his physical pain and fever. The midwife began to treat him for the same illness my mother had battled. But her efforts again proved to be in vain. My father died – exactly one week after my mother.

The joy I felt the day I returned home now seemed like a distant memory. In less than a month I had lost both my parents; I was overcome with grief. Though I was grateful God had given me a few weeks with them before they died, I had always thought we would have many more years together. People in our village joined me in mourning. They had lost their beloved rabbi and his devoted wife.

Gratefully, the illness did not spread through our village; it was limited to my parents and our neighbor. But my parents' deaths left a huge hole in the hearts of our entire community.

Someone needed to step into my father's shoes and minister to our friends and neighbors. Someone needed to speak God's truth to hearts that were hurting. That responsibility fell to me. I soon became the leading rabbi of Capernaum. It was not a position I sought; it was a position that sought me.

∿

7

GOD GIVES ME A FAMILY

~

*W*hile I was ministering to the people of our village, my Uncle Ishmael and his family took on the responsibility of ministering to me. Though our families had always been close, my parents' deaths brought us even closer. Ishmael became more than a business partner, friend, and uncle – he became a surrogate father, and his family embraced me as one of their own.

Ishmael's daughters – Salome, three years my elder, and Tali, five years my junior – had been like sisters to me growing up. In fact, Tali was the little sister who far too often we ignored! But since I'd been home, I saw Tali in a whole new light.

Her tenderness and her beauty had blossomed while I was away. I didn't quite know what to do with these new feelings. I regretted all those years I had cast her aside as an annoying little girl, but I had far too many responsibilities now to give her any attention.

I wasn't the only man with feelings for one of Uncle Ishmael's daughters. A young fisherman from Bethsaida named Zebedee was spending a great deal of time in Capernaum – particularly in the presence of Salome. He said it was because he was selling the fish he and his partner Jonah caught each day to Uncle Ishmael at the fish packing warehouse. But obviously his interests in Capernaum extended well beyond his fishing trade!

It wasn't long before Salome and Uncle Ishmael both confided in me that a marriage agreement was being considered. Of course, Uncle Ishmael seemed more hesitant than Salome; after all, she was his eldest daughter, and no one would ever measure up in his eyes to be worthy of her. But even I could see Zebedee was an honorable man who strived to be right-eous before God. He was a hard worker and would be a good provider. He obviously had deep feelings for Salome and she for him. Eventually my uncle agreed to their marriage.

As the rabbi of the village, I was privileged to conduct their marriage cere-mony. Though Salome moved away to Bethsaida, the happy couple visited Capernaum often. It was a delight to see how their relationship continued to grow – and to rejoice with them one year later when God blessed them with a son, James.

Life in the village continued to thrive, and more people were added to our number each week. More people also meant more opportunities for ministry. My work continued to increase. I was engaged in ministry from dawn to dusk with little time for anything else.

However, I occasionally took solitary walks along the Sea of Galilee to clear my head. These were times when I could speak with Jehovah God without any distractions or interruptions. It was during one of these walks that God spoke to me through another's voice.

"Good afternoon, Rabbi!" I heard a voice call out.

I had not realized anyone was walking behind me, so her voice startled me. I knew even before I turned around it was Tali. She saw my obvious surprise.

"Good afternoon, Tali," I replied. "Please forgive me for not realizing you were there. I am afraid you caught me deep in thought."

She looked at me with a playful smile. "You apparently have been deep in thought for many weeks now because you haven't said two words to me in as many months. Even when you come to our home for dinner you seem preoccupied when you are near me. Have I done something to offend you?"

"No, not at all!" I said hastily as I struggled to find the right words. I was more tongue-tied around her than I had been in front of Rabbi Hillel! "I must apologize for my behavior. Each day I spend all my time and energy ministering to the people of our village. Regrettably, I often have little of either left to share with those who are closest to me. Please forgive my lack of attention!"

"Do you think of me as one of those closest to you?" she asked with a shy smile.

Her question took me off guard. For months I had denied my feelings for Tali and had foolishly barricaded them behind a wall of silence toward her. Her question was causing that wall to crack, and I blushed at the thought of how I truly felt about her.

Hesitantly, I answered. "Yes, I do, Tali. I am so sorry I have not acted in a way that showed you how I feel toward you. When we were young, I always treated you like a little child undeserving of my attention. But now that we are older, it is I who has behaved like a little child not expressing my feelings toward you."

"So, you have feelings toward me?" she said coyly.

We stood in silence as her mouth slowly formed a tender smile. I could feel my face turning bright red. For the first, and perhaps the last time in my life, I was at a loss for words. So, I just continued my walk along the shore in silence – but now with Tali walking by my side.

8

GOD CONTINUES TO BLESS OUR FAMILY

~

Six months later, Tali became my wife. Ishmael, who was not only my uncle but now my father-in-law, too, was overjoyed to bless our union. He shared with me awhile later that God had assured him Tali and I would have a son who would one day take over the family business enterprise. I told Ishmael we would see if God blessed us with a son, and if so, how He would lead the boy in the future. Each time Ishmael would reply, "Yes, we will see!"

Words cannot express the joy God brought into my life through Tali. I had told the story of creation many times, but it was only after she and I were married that I fully understood what the Lord God meant when He said, *"It is not good for the man to be alone. I will make a helper as his complement."*[1]

We had been married for one year when our daughter Leah was born. Ishmael was somewhat disappointed the baby was not a boy. But he quickly got over it! Leah not only took after her mother in appearance but also in temperament. She quickly had her father – and her grandfather – wrapped around her little finger!

A year after that we welcomed our son, Reuben. Ishmael wasted no time in again reminding me of God's promise.

"It is a little too soon to make that decision, Ishmael," I told him. "We will see how the Lord God directs Reuben's steps when he is old enough to make that decision on his own."

To which Ishmael smiled and again replied, "Yes, we will see!"

Two years later our daughter Rebekah was born. Tali and I could not contain our joy over the many ways God was blessing our family. Friends and neighbors often told us God was blessing us because of our righteousness before Him. And as a rabbi who was still young, I often acknowledged their statements in a way that affirmed that belief.

But that all changed when Rebekah was fourteen months old. We awoke one morning to discover Rebekah had died in her sleep. There was no physician living in our village; local midwives always treated any illnesses or injuries. But they could not explain what had caused Rebekah's death.

I began to question what Tali and I had possibly done to deserve this punishment from God. If our blessings were the result of our works of righteousness, it only stood to reason that Rebekah's death was caused by our unrighteousness! Though they did not say it to us directly, it was obvious some of our friends and neighbors thought the same thing.

In the midst of our grief the Lord God began to lovingly correct me in my misunderstanding of His ways. He led me to the writings in the books of poetry, beginning with Ecclesiastes. He reminded me our lives contain a mixture of joy and sorrow, pleasure and pain, life and death. Each is a part of the season of life. He inspired me to teach these truths to our neighbors when we next gathered at the synagogue.

I told them, "The Lord has reminded me through His servant Job who lost everything: *'The Lord gave me everything I had, and the Lord has taken it away. Still I will praise the name of the Lord.'*[2]

"There will be seasons that are difficult for us to understand. We will not comprehend why God has permitted it. I am only beginning to grasp this with the death of my little daughter.

"The painful parts of our lives are the result of the sin that entered into this world through Adam and Eve. But our God is not a vindictive God. He does not send death and calamity to punish us. As the psalmist King David wrote when he was walking through grief, *'Even when I walk through the dark valley of death, I will not be afraid, for the Lord is close beside me. His rod and His staff comfort me.'*[3]

"As a matter of fact, He has promised us through his prophet Isaiah that He is sending One who will swallow up death forever and wipe away all our tears. In the meantime, we must trust Him as He is fulfilling His purpose in His timeframe. Perhaps ours will be the generation that welcomes the arrival of the Messiah. Perhaps ours will be the generation who sees death defeated.

"Until then, Tali and I will continue to bow before Him and say, 'We praise the name of the Lord,' and we will thank Him for the fourteen months He gave us with Rebekah and for the blessing of Leah and Reuben."

The Lord God did not choose to give us any additional children. He did permit us to help nurture many children who were a part of our village – some of whom became as close to us as our own Leah, Reuben, and Rebekah.

9

TWO PROMISING STUDENTS

～

$\mathcal{O}$ ne of those children was a boy whose family had been intertwined with mine for many years. When my grandfathers, Asher and Shebna, began their business partnership, they needed a carpenter to oversee the construction of their warehouses and mills, as well as their homes. They hired a craftsman named Uziel.

When my Uncle Ishmael took over the business, he employed Uziel's grandson, Betzalel, to build whatever was needed for our family's business enterprises. Betzalel was a gifted craftsman who would have made a handsome living in Jerusalem. But, like his father and grandfather before him, he chose to remain in Capernaum and enjoy the idyllic life along the sea.

Betzalel's eldest son was a young man named Jairus. He was four years old when I returned to Capernaum from Jerusalem. I discovered he had an insatiable hunger to learn. Growing up, he demonstrated he could recall the Scriptures better than those who were twice his age. And on more than one occasion he posed a question to this rabbi that caused me to dig deep for the answer.

"Rabbi, why did Jehovah God accept Abel's offering but reject Cain's offering?" he asked one day. "Were they not both the fruits of their labor – Cain's as the gift of a farmer and Abel's as the gift of a shepherd?"

"We now know what God requires," I replied, "but back then Cain and Abel did not have benefit of the law. How were they to know what would be acceptable to God? Was God saying the fruits of the shepherd were better than the fruits of the farmer? Then what did that mean for the carpenters or the fishermen?"

My fellow talmidim and I had once had that same conversation with Rabbi Hillel, but we had been twice Jairus's age when the thought crossed our minds!

"Some would tell you," I continued, "that God rejected Cain's offering because there had been no shedding of blood, which was required for the angel of death to pass over the homes of the Jews that night in Egypt. But there is nothing in Scripture to indicate God had established that requirement those many years before.

"Others would say Cain brought an offering of inferior fruits and vegetables. But again, there is nothing in Scripture to tell us that.

"The simple truth is God knew what was in Cain's heart. It wasn't the condition of his gift; it was the condition of his heart. And Cain's immediate reaction of anger toward God revealed what was clearly already there!

"We would do well to remember that truth ourselves. It is not the size of the gift we bring to God; rather, it is the condition of our heart. God is not impressed with what we give but how we give it. There are many whose hearts are as hard as stone who are walking into the temple in Jerusalem today presenting gifts that appear to be grand. But God is no more accepting of those meaningless offerings than He was of Cain's."

There was an even younger boy among the students that day listening to our conversation. He was my nephew John – the youngest son of my sister-in-law, Salome. Though they did not live in Capernaum, John always came to the synagogue whenever his family was in the village.

Jairus and John became my best students, and their lives reflected this important truth: "First and foremost, we are to love God because He first loved us. Yes, He gave us the law, but He gave it to us because He loves us. We do not obey the law to earn His love; we obey His law because He loves us, and we love Him. Be careful you do not do what others have done. Do not turn the law from the blessing God intended it to be and turn it into a burden. Do not lose your joy under the weight of the law man has corrupted. Seek the Lord God with all of your hearts, souls, and minds!"

Eventually I knew I had taught these young men as much as I could. I recommended to their families that the boys be sent to the School of Hillel in Jerusalem for more training. By the time Jairus made the journey, his father knew his son would not follow in his footsteps as a carpenter. God was leading him to become a rabbi.

Since John was younger than Jairus, a few more years passed before he left for Jerusalem. In fact, by the time he arrived, Hillel's grandson Gamaliel was the teacher. But John did not stay there long. He was not studying to become a rabbi, though he understood God's Word better than most talmidim. He planned to continue assisting his father, Zebedee, on their family's fishing boats. But something told me God was going to use this fisherman in a different way – a way that would have great impact for generations to come.

10

SERVING IN OUR LOCAL SANHEDRIN

~

*W*e were beginning to hear rumors that our village's growth and prosperity were attracting Rome's attention – though we had rarely seen a Roman official or soldier. Nonetheless, Galilee remained under the authority of Herod Antipas, who had taken over as governor when his father, Herod the Great, died. It seemed Rome would not interfere with us as long as we continued to send them our taxes through our new tax collector, Matthew.

When Antipas became ruler, he began the development of a new Galilean capital, Tiberias, on the western shore of the Sea of Galilee. It was located about a day's journey south of Capernaum over land or half a day by sea. All the new construction and expansion ushered prosperity into the entire region, including Capernaum.

I had now been serving as a member of our local Sanhedrin for almost twenty-five years. I took my father's place on the council soon after he died. During that time our village had more than tripled in size. Though the growth had brought greater wealth, it had also brought greater conflict – most of which Antipas and Rome left for our local Sanhedrin to resolve.

When our citizens had a dispute they could not settle on their own, they would bring it before our Sanhedrin. Most often, the disputes had to do with finances. Sometimes they involved accusations between two parties over whether a Jewish law had been violated. On rare occasions, accusations involving criminal acts were brought before us. Gratefully, the latter were very rare.

On those extremely rare instances when we could not resolve a dispute, we would refer the matter to the Great Sanhedrin in Jerusalem. That body is comprised of seventy-one members from throughout the region. Serving on that council is a full-time responsibility.

Since all of us on the local council also had other duties, we would meet only when necessary. When I first began to serve, we convened once each month; now we were meeting once a week at the end of a workday. It made for a very long day.

While many of the disagreements brought before us were rather mundane, one particular one stands out. It was a complaint made by a husband about his new wife.

The husband stood before our council and declared, "After having slept with my wife on our wedding night, I found that she had slept with another man. I discovered she was not a virgin when we married. She must be stoned to death for the disgrace she has caused me."

Then the woman's father stood and said, "I gave my daughter to this man to be his wife, and now he has decided he no longer wants to be married to her. He is accusing her of shameful things – claiming she was not a virgin when he married her – simply to end their marriage contract."

Speaking on behalf of the council, I turned to the father and said, "Do you have any proof of her virginity at the time of their marriage?"

"Yes, I do," the father replied. "Here is the proof for all to see! This is the cloth from their wedding bed on the night their marriage was consummated!"

As we stared at the cloth, we quickly came to a decision. I turned to the husband to issue our verdict. "We find you guilty of making a false accusation against your wife and before this council. You have falsely accused a virgin of Israel. You will pay the woman's father the sum of one hundred pieces of silver. The woman will remain your wife and you may never divorce her. Do not ever let us hear you have done anything in retaliation against her, or it is you who will be taken to the edge of the village to be stoned to death!"[1]

Whether disputes were the result of false allegations like this one, or simply misunderstandings like most of them, our duty was to bring about resolution, judgment, or reparation for everyone.

One day I received a message from Jerusalem. A member of the Great Sanhedrin from the province of Galilee had died. I had been selected to take his seat on the council. Though the message came in the form of a request, it was not one I could decline. I truly had no interest in leaving my home and going back to Jerusalem, but apparently Jehovah God had other plans for me.

I was grateful I had continued to mentor Jairus after he returned home from his studies in Jerusalem. He had developed into a wise and godly leader. I did not hesitate to name him as my replacement as chief rabbi of the village. I could not have possibly thought any more highly of him.

After all ... I had permitted him to marry my daughter, Leah, a few years earlier ... and now he was the father of my granddaughter, Ilana!

11

CHOSEN TO SERVE IN THE GREAT SANHEDRIN

❧

*I*t was with sadness that Tali and I left our family behind in Capernaum and moved to Jerusalem. Our son, Reuben had become a very capable businessman under his grandfather's tutelage and was progressing nicely in his ability to manage the day-to-day affairs of the family's enterprise. Ishmael and I both knew the future of the business would be in good hands under his leadership.

The one we regretted leaving most of all was our precious little grand-daughter. We would miss watching Ilana as she grew. And we knew we would dearly miss the people of our village. They had become such a part of our lives over the years. But I knew Jehovah God in His sovereignty had placed this position in the Great Sanhedrin before me. I was not drawn by the power or prestige of the position; rather, I was going to serve and honor my Lord God by serving His people.

We traveled by cart with enough possessions to establish a small house-hold in Jerusalem. It took us a little more than four days to make the journey. We were glad when we finally entered the city walls through the Fish Gate on the northern wall.

Though I had lived in the city as a student, and Tali and I had been here on multiple occasions to commemorate our annual feasts, it felt different that day. We had a sense of foreboding that somehow our lives would never be the same. Some may have said it was because of the responsibility I was about to assume on the high council, but Tali and I both sensed it was more than that – we just didn't know what.

We made our way to the Hall of Hewn Stones. Tali went to the Women's Court in the temple while I entered the hall. Soon afterward I heard a familiar voice say, "Does anyone else smell the pungent odor of fresh fish? Either some delivery person has mistaken our chamber for the kitchen, or our newest member from Galilee has just arrived to take his seat among us! Ah, yes, I see it is the latter. Join me in welcoming Nicodemus of Capernaum into our midst!"

I knew before I spotted him it was my fellow talmid Annas. Twenty-eight years had passed since we had sat at the feet of Rabbi Hillel, but he had obviously not changed his opinion of people from Galilee. Annas had gone on to become the youngest high priest in our history. He had served in that role for nine years but had since been succeeded by one of his sons and then by his son-in-law Caiaphas, who was the current high priest.

Several other men were standing with him. The smirks on their faces showed they shared Annas's low opinion of Galileans. Their appearance confirmed that they, too, were Sadducees, one of them obviously being the current high priest.

"Thank you for your greeting, Annas," I replied. "I see that you are still as gracious and cordial as ever!"

But before Annas could respond, the current high priest spoke up. "Nicodemus, forgive my father-in-law's poor attempt at humor. We do welcome you into our midst, and we are grateful that you chose to accept the appointment. I know our families share much in common. And though our lives have followed different paths, Jehovah God has brought all of us together at this time and in this place to serve Him. So again, welcome to you, our fellow brother within the Sanhedrin."

Though his comments were much more gracious than his father-in-law's, I knew that as high priest he needed to be more diplomatic and politically savvy. I was fairly confident that underneath his polished façade were the same prejudices and biases of his father-in-law.

Caiaphas introduced me to the other men who were standing with him. Three of the men were Annas's sons – Eleazar, Jonathan, and Theophilus. Two others were also former high priests – Ishmael and Simon. It was obvious, even at this first meeting, that these men wielded great power within the Sanhedrin.

We were interrupted by another familiar voice who approached me from behind saying, "Hello, old friend! It is so good to see you!"

I was pleased to see Gamaliel as he reached out to embrace me – somewhat to the surprise of the other men. But I knew this fellow Pharisee was being sincere.

"Hello, my friend," I replied. "I have been looking forward to seeing you! I have much for which to thank you, including the way you trained up your talmid, Jairus. He is now the chief rabbi in our village, as well as my son-in-law. Thank you for your investment in him. He has made excellent use of the training you poured into him."

"I cannot take all of the credit," Gamaliel responded. "He came to me with a solid foundation in the Scriptures – and I know that was a result of your training. So, I thank you for sending him to me!"

Gamaliel pointed to the Pharisee who was accompanying him and said, "Nicodemus, allow me to introduce Joseph of Arimathea. I am certain you two will become good friends in the days ahead."

After I spent some time of getting better acquainted, I was directed to the home chosen for Tali and me. It was located in the upper city, not far from where all these other men lived. I excused myself and set out to find Tali so we could make our way to our new home.

12

ADJUSTING TO LIFE IN JERUSALEM

❧

*L*ife in Jerusalem was very different from Capernaum. In Capernaum, everyone knew everyone else; there was little to no pretense. There was very little class consciousness. Though I had been the chief rabbi of the village, a member of the local Sanhedrin, and the living patriarch of one of the founding families – I never felt I was above anyone else.

The people of Capernaum all saw one another as friends and neighbors, though each of us had different responsibilities. But that was not the case in Jerusalem. The people here were very aware of everyone's social class because it was modeled and mandated by the religious leaders.

Most members of the Sanhedrin walked through the streets with an air of superiority, regardless of whether they were Pharisees or Sadducees. They projected to everyone around them that they were the unquestioned experts on the law, both in knowledge and practice. And whenever they spoke, prayed, presented offerings, or did any good deed, it was always done in public with great fanfare and exaggerated largesse.

I had been loved and admired by the people of our village in Capernaum. However, in Jerusalem I was feared and set apart from them. The only "friends" the Sanhedrin had were each other, and those relationships were only valued for the power or prestige derived from them.

While this was true of most members of the high council, there were exceptions. Gamaliel was particularly humble for a man revered as the most respected teacher of the law among those living. His grandfather, Hillel the Elder, would always be the most highly esteemed, but he had been dead now for over fifteen years.

Gamaliel did not teach about the stern and dispassionate God as many of our fellow members did; instead, he taught about a loving God we were to love, honor, and obey. But I quickly noticed that Gamaliel held a unique place of respect among all the members regardless of their position. They showed him great esteem and always paid him deference whenever he spoke.

Joseph of Arimathea was another member who demonstrated humility and love for God in all he did. He was often considered an outsider by other council members, much like I was. They rarely welcomed or embraced our opinions when we spoke up in meetings.

As a result, Tali and I often felt like outcasts in Jerusalem. Neither the other religious leaders nor the citizens befriended us due to the barriers of our station. For the most part, we were extremely lonely during our years living in the city. But still we knew God had led us into this role – for His purpose.

Our favorite times of the year in Jerusalem quickly became the annual festivals – not so much because of the reason for the feasts; but rather, because many of our friends from Capernaum would come to the city. The festivals became brief respites from the loneliness and isolation we otherwise felt.

Those times also provided an opportunity for us to catch up on news from home – and, even more, to enjoy time with our family when they came to celebrate the feasts. One such visit occurred the second fall after we had been in Jerusalem. Our family arrived for the Celebration of Sukkot.

"Papa and Mama," Leah said as they arrived, "I promised to embrace you and give you kisses from Reuben. He had planned to come himself as you know, but Grandfather Ishmael became sick the night before we set out on our journey. Reuben did not feel he could leave him, so he remained in Capernaum and told us to come ahead.

"The two of you may want to join us when we return in a few days so you can see grandfather yourselves. Reuben is sending word to Aunt Salome that she, too, should come and bring James and John with her."

"The illness sounds serious," Tali responded with a worried look on her face. "Should we go sooner?"

"The midwives believe he will still be with us for some time," Jairus answered, "but they also recommend the family come to see him within the next few weeks to say their final goodbyes. I think we will be fine if we remain here for the days of the festival and return when it is over."

"Then we will both return with you at the end of the week," I said.

"Aunt Salome will also need to get word to my cousin John," Leah added. "He has become the disciple of the one called John the baptizer. Apparently, my cousin is convinced this John is the one Isaiah said would come to announce the arrival of the Messiah. The baptizer is preaching and baptizing at the Jordan River. It will take a few days before they can get a message to John to come see grandfather in Capernaum."

"Then we will pray that Jehovah God will order our steps in a way that enables all of us to have time with Ishmael before He takes him home," I replied.

∽

13

AN UNPLANNED TRIP TO CAPERNAUM

~

*T*en days later we arrived in Capernaum. Our joy at returning was overshadowed by our concern for Ishmael. Even though Leah had done her best to describe his condition, Tali and I were still not prepared for his appearance.

Although Ishmael was more than thirty years my senior, he had always had as much or more energy than I did. He never missed a day of work – other than the Sabbath or for a religious festival. I never knew him to spend a day in bed due to illness or injury. But now, he did not have the strength to raise himself in the bed.

The midwife told us she did not expect him to live out the week. She encouraged us all to express our goodbyes now while he could still hear us and respond. Tali and I went into his room together; suddenly, he seemed to have a burst of energy.

Ishmael raised himself and said, "Tali and Nicodemus, come near to me! My heart just leapt! Seeing you both brings me such great joy. It has been too long since these tired eyes have seen you. Come, sit with me, and tell me about your life in Jerusalem!"

Tali knelt beside his bed and took his hands in hers. "Papa, we will tell you, but first tell us how you feel."

"Tali, I am an old man," he said haltingly, "and for the first time in my life I feel like an old man. I have asked Jehovah God to cause the shadow of the sun to go backward on the sun dial, like He did for King Hezekiah, to give me more time, but He has chosen not to do so. I have resigned myself that this body can no longer do what my mind wants it to do. I have come to peace with that – and with God.

"The midwife tells me there is nothing more that can be done, so I have decided to enjoy whatever time I have left with my family around me. And here you are! Now tell me about your life in Jerusalem!"

Tali and I told him about our many new experiences in the city, but we had already decided not to burden him with the prejudices we had encountered from some of his distant relatives. He expressed his pride that I was now one of the most powerful men in the entire region.

Ishmael already knew how I felt about the role, so he smiled faintly as I said, "I am first and foremost a servant of the Almighty God, placed in this role by His divine hand. Any power I have is His, by His grace and for His purpose. I am grateful to serve Him wherever He places me."

After we had visited for a while, we told him to get some rest and we would talk more later. Within moments he was fast asleep, and we made our way out of his bed chamber to the central part of the house. Salome and her sons, James and John, had just arrived.

Salome's older son, James, continued to work as a fisherman with his father. Zebedee had sent his wife and son to see Ishmael, but had stayed behind to tend to their fishing business. As he often reminded us, if he didn't catch any fish, he didn't make any money. What's more, our family would have less fish to process and sell through our warehouse. He seldom failed to tell us he was keeping all of us fed! Salome assured us Zebedee would come see Ishmael as soon as he could.

Her son John had also been one of the fishermen on the boats until he left Bethsaida to seek out John the baptizer. Zebedee had graciously released his son to go because he knew his son had a special calling from God. That's why he had also allowed John to study with me in Capernaum and continue his training in the Scriptures at the feet of Gamaliel in Jerusalem. Though John had been born a fisherman, Zebedee knew his God-given passions lie elsewhere.

In recent days, the Sanhedrin had spent a great deal of time discussing the baptizer. Annas and others were expressing great concern about his growing popularity. After the death of his parents, the baptizer had been raised by his uncle, who was an Essene. Annas knew the Essenes held little regard for the Pharisees and even less for the Sadducees. So Annas and the others were convinced the baptizer's teachings would undermine the authority of the Sanhedrin.

He convinced Caiaphas to send a delegation of priests and scribes to question the baptizer. But, knowing the baptizer was being held in such high regard by the people, Annas also instructed them to be baptized by John so the people would believe his teaching was under the authority of the Sanhedrin. Though I knew I could not agree with another one of Annas's schemes, I also knew I needed to learn more about John the baptizer.

Now was my opportunity! Later in the day, I drew my nephew John aside so we could talk about his time with the baptizer.

14

WHO IS THIS BAPTIZER?

～

"*T*here is no question John is the one God sent to prepare the way for the Messiah," my nephew told me. "The Spirit of God rests mightily upon him. Though he rightly proclaims the truth of God, he is not an eloquent speaker. The people are not being drawn to him by his gift of oratory, they are being drawn by God's Spirit.

"As one of his disciples, I can tell you he is not looking for fortune or fame. His clothing is simple, his diet is modest, and he sleeps in a cave or under the open sky. He seeks no money from anyone. All he seeks is that people repent of their sins and turn their hearts toward Jehovah God and the One who is coming.

"I have grown up around religious leaders. Some, like you, have a servant's heart. But most have become corrupted by the power and wealth of their position. John is not anything like them! He seeks to serve God with all that he is. The religious leaders need not fear that he seeks to take their power; rather, he prays that we might all turn from our sinful ways and return to the only One who has all authority and power."

"What happened when the most recent delegation from the Sanhedrin arrived to question the baptizer?" I asked.

"They asked him if he claimed to be the Messiah!" John responded. "Anyone who has listened to the baptizer for more than five minutes knows that he makes no such claim. It was a foolish question he flatly denied. So then they asked, '*Well then, are you Elijah returned from God?*'[(1)]

"When he told them no, they asked, '*Then who are you? Tell us so we can give an answer to those who sent us. What do you have to say about yourself?*'[(2)]

"The baptizer replied, quoting the prophet Isaiah, '*I am a voice shouting in the wilderness. Prepare a straight pathway for the Lord's coming!*'"[(3)]

"The Pharisees and Sadducees responded, 'Then baptize us so we might be prepared for the Lord's coming.'

"But the baptizer knew what was in their hearts when he exclaimed, '*You brood of snakes! Who warned you to flee God's coming judgment? Prove by the way you live that you have truly turned from your sins and turned to God. I baptize with water those who turn from their sins and turn to God. But Someone is coming soon who is far greater than I am – and He will clean up the threshing floor, storing the grain in His barn and burning the chaff with never-ending fire!*'"[(4)]

"The baptizer made no secret as to who the chaff was. The religious leaders turned in a huff and walked away with haste!"

"They may have walked away for now," I interjected, "but I am certain they will return. They fear him too much to ignore him."

"I understand, uncle," John replied, "but the One they should really fear is the One who is coming soon – the One who will clean up the threshing floor."

I nodded my head in agreement. "Yes, they should! But I fear their hearts will be too hard to receive even Him!"

Just then the midwife entered the room and told us Ishmael had taken his last breath. "Jehovah God has allowed him to die peacefully in his sleep," she said.

I pronounced a traditional word of blessing over his body. "Blessed are You, Oh Lord our God, King of the universe, the Just God. You are the Giver of life. The very breath that we breathe comes from You. We thank You for the time You have given us with Ishmael. Blessed be Your name."

We then prepared his body for burial and carried him in procession to the tomb before the sun set. Tali and I remained in Capernaum for the next seven days for a period of grief and mourning. The people of Capernaum showered our family with love and affection – which made it even harder for us to leave one week later. But we knew it was time for me to return to my duties in Jerusalem.

As we made the journey back, I had a lot of time to think about my conversation with John about the baptizer – and about the One whose coming He said was soon. We had looked forward to His coming for generations. Each generation had prayed He would come in their lifetime. Could now truly be the time?

My thoughts drifted to Annas and Caiaphas and the men who were a part of their inner circle. How would they receive this news? For that matter, how would any of us in the Sanhedrin receive the news? Would we welcome Him with open arms – or would some members plot against Him like they were doing against the baptizer?

And what about me? Would I be a part of the grain or the chaff? Something told me we wouldn't have long to wait and see!

15

REPORTS ABOUT A GALILEAN CARPENTER

~

*W*hen Tali and I arrived back in Jerusalem, the members of the Sanhedrin were in an uproar. As expected, they were up in arms about the baptizer. Most of them were arguing that he needed to be brought to Jerusalem for questioning before the full council. As I walked into the great hall, Annas's son, Eleazar, was already speaking.

"This wild man must learn his radical teaching will not be tolerated by this council," he bellowed. "We cannot have him dividing our people. He disrespected those we sent to question him, which essentially was disrespecting this entire body and the authority granted to us by Jehovah God.

"The people are watching to see what we will do. If we do nothing, people will think he is in the right and we are weak! We must take swift action! Send a contingent of the temple guards to arrest him and bring him before us."

Gamaliel was the first to respond. "Eleazar, if we do that, the people will rebel against us. The people are beginning to flock to him to be baptized. They believe he speaks with the authority of the prophets. If we arrest him, we will look like the evil kings who persecuted the prophets.

"What part of his message do you think we should discredit? Should we tell the people they should not repent? Should we deny the prophecies of a coming Messiah? Or perhaps you believe we should tell them not to be baptized?

"How hypocritical! Do we not, ourselves, tell the people they need to repent and present sacrifices? Do we not also teach about the coming Messiah in our synagogues? Are there not over 700 mikvah pools surrounding this temple where we tell the people to purify themselves in water before walking through these gates?"

Caiaphas raised his hand to preclude anyone else from speaking. When the hall was silent, he said, "Gamaliel again speaks wisdom to us. If we take any action right now, it will only enhance the baptizer's influence over the people. We must find a way to affirm his message of repentance while correcting him for his youthful impetuousness in disrespecting those of us in authority. Let's continue to watch and see what he does while we wait for the right opportunity.

"Besides, we have an even greater concern before us. I have just received news the Roman emperor is sending a new prefect (regional governor) to replace Valerius Gratus. Though I will not personally miss him when he is gone, we have at least been able to come to an understanding with him.

"Do not forget that when he first assumed his office, he demanded a new high priest be placed in office every year. He did so to keep us off balance. And as you recall, his plan worked!"

Annas interrupted. "Until I was able to convince him of the wisdom of continuity of leadership, and he wisely selected you, Caiaphas, to assume the role."

"That is true, Annas," Caiaphas acknowledged. "And since then, thanks to you and the others who stood with you, we have been able to function with some degree of mutual tolerance. But now, with his departure, we have a new prefect who is unfamiliar to us. How will he view us? Will he seek to disband us or strip us of some of our authority over civil affairs?"

"What do we know about him, Caiaphas?" Annas asked.

"Very little," Caiaphas replied. "His name is Pontius Pilate. He is a distinguished cavalry officer and the grandson of an influential leader in the Roman senate. He has caught the eye of Emperor Tiberius and been rewarded with this position. But he knows nothing about us, our history, or our beliefs. He is a pagan like all the rest of them and has the potential to cause more trouble than good."

Annas spoke up again, but this time he was clearly addressing all the members. "That of course is true, Caiaphas. But we still have friends in Rome – alliances that we have built over many years. Tiberius does not want trouble here in Judea. He wants us to pay our taxes, and he wants to maintain the peace. He is content to leave us alone if both of those things continue."

Then he added with a smile, "I doubt Pontius Pilate will want to upset that proverbial apple cart. Let us watch and see. If the need arises for us to convince him to go along with us, I'm sure we will find a way."

Sensing it was time to move on to another topic, Theophilus addressed the high priest. "Caiaphas, I have another matter we need to discuss."

"What is it, Theophilus?" Caiaphas asked.

"I am hearing reports of a Galilean carpenter who is beginning to make a name for Himself up in that region," Theophilus answered. "It is said He is a miracle worker. He apparently amazed a large group at a wedding feast in Cana by turning six washing pots of water into wine. And the guests reported it was the best wine they had ever tasted.

"Then, after He was done teaching from a boat on the sea, He instructed the fishermen to cast their nets in a place that shortly before had yielded no fish. But at His word, they cast their nets and their boats nearly sank from the quantity of fish. Word of these deeds – and others – is beginning to spread, and He is starting to gather a following."

16

A SURPRISE IN THE TEMPLE

~

*A*nnas quickly interjected. "It sounds like He is worthy of watching, Theophilus. Anyone who can provide great quantities of fish and good-tasting wine will always be welcome at my table!"

Annas began to laugh heartily as others quickly joined in. Then he turned to me and said with a smirk, "Nicodemus, what about you? What do you know about your fellow Galilean? Is He a carpenter, a fish monger, or a vintner? Should we afford Him any more attention than we would give to any other Galilean? Perhaps you are the best equipped to investigate this miracle worker and give us a report. After all, you have much in common!"

Caiaphas interrupted before I could respond. "Annas, enough of your sarcastic goading about Galilee. Perhaps I should give Nicodemus the floor to tell us what Galileans think of Judeans. But then again, he is far too much of a gentleman to do that. Let us turn our attention to more important matters!"

As the weeks passed, I continued to hear reports about this carpenter named Jesus of Nazareth. With Passover now approaching, I wondered if I might see Him here in Jerusalem. But with so many pilgrims coming to the city, how could I possibly hope to recognize Him?

The day the Passover celebration began was no different from any other year. People came from all over to bring their offerings to the Lord. Those who traveled from afar usually purchased their offerings of animals or birds from the merchants in the temple. King Solomon had implemented the practice many years ago.

But in recent years, while Annas was high priest, the merchant tables and stalls had been moved into the outer courtyard of the temple instead of the stoa outside the walls as King Solomon had decreed. We were told the move was needed because of increased demand. But truth be told, it had become a lucrative enterprise for the temple treasury – and for those who oversaw it.

The temple priests were instructed to reject any offering that had even the slightest blemish. This meant the pilgrim must forgo presenting an offering or find an acceptable substitute. Since the whole purpose for coming to the temple was to present an offering, the merchants were only too happy to help the pilgrim rectify the dilemma.

The whole process had evolved gradually over time, and no one gave much thought to the significant financial gains being pocketed by some of our leaders. It was meeting a need, so it became an accepted practice.

That is ... until the day Jesus arrived at the temple.

Our council was meeting when we heard shouts and screams coming from the outer courtyard. We hastily went to see what all the commotion was about.

Chaos was everywhere. The moneychangers' tables had been overturned, and the merchants were feverishly gathering their coins from the ground. Portions of the animal stalls were lying in pieces on the ground, and men were hurriedly driving the oxen, cattle, and sheep out through the gate.

Several of the bird cages had careened onto the ground and the doves were taking flight. In the center of it all was one Man. He had a whip made of rope in His hand and He was chasing all the merchants out of the temple. The pilgrims stood there watching in amazement. No one had ever witnessed such a sight – particularly in the temple.

Even amid all the noise, I could hear the Man shouting, *"Get these things out of here! Don't turn My Father's house into a marketplace!"*[1]

Who was this Man? And who had given Him the authority to do what He was doing? He kept referring to the temple as His Father's house. Of course, it is our Father God's house, but He was saying those words in a much more personal way.

And His anger was not uncontrolled emotion. This Man was very much in control. At that moment, I was full of remorse. I realized He was doing something we all should have done – a long time ago. We had desecrated the temple by permitting this merchants' fair to take place in it. We had sinned. And only this Man had the presence of mind and courage to confront it for what it was. Only this Man was willing to stand up on His own and confront the sin.

Though I didn't know who He was, I stood ashamed before Him. I looked up and saw Annas and Caiaphas watching from a corner of the courtyard.

They were obviously seething – but neither said anything. I looked around and saw several of my Sanhedrin brothers who were obviously conflicted over what was happening. But no one dared to move. I saw shame in the eyes of Joseph of Arimathea, who was now standing beside me. "Who is this Man?" I asked him.

"He is Jesus of Nazareth – the carpenter from Galilee!" Joseph replied.

~

17

WHO GAVE HIM THE AUTHORITY?

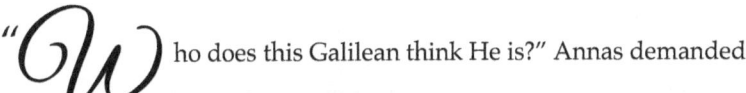

"Who does this Galilean think He is?" Annas demanded.

We were all back in the great hall. The crowd in the temple courtyard had dispersed, but not before Annas and Caiaphas had decided to confront Jesus over His actions.

"What right do You have to do these things?"[1] Annas asked Him.

Jesus had looked at them with a piercing gaze but did not answer. That seemed to enrage Annas even more.

"If God has given You the authority to do this, show us a miraculous sign to prove it!"[2] Annas shouted.

Jesus's demeanor was a sharp contrast to the men who stood before Him. The anger He had displayed a few moments before was much different from what I saw in Annas's eyes. Jesus stood before them calmly and in control. He was not intimidated by these high priests. He responded to them deliberately and firmly. *"All right. Destroy this temple, and in three days I will raise it up."*[(3)]

Even I was startled by His answer.

"What!" Annas shouted. "It took forty-six years to build this temple, and You can do it in three days?"[(4)]

But again, Jesus remained silent. He had given His answer. He obviously saw no need to repeat it or justify it. Instead, He walked on into the temple and left Annas and Caiaphas to stare after Him incredulously.

As I watched this unfold, a prophecy from the Scriptures came to my mind: *"Passion for God's house burns within Me."*[(5)] And I thought – who is this Jesus?

The great hall was abuzz. Many were taking the same position as Annas. This council, led by the high priest, was given the authority under God to direct what could and could not take place inside these walls. Who was this Man to question their authority?

But slowly the conversation began to turn. It was Joseph of Arimathea who was the first to bravely speak up. "But He is right! There was a reason our ancestors kept that activity outside the temple. By bringing it inside, we have turned the courtyard from a place where those entering the temple should be preparing their hearts for prayer and worship into a huckster's market. I, for one, was ashamed that He needed to correct us. In our hearts, we knew it was wrong – or at least we should have – but we did nothing!"

Annas raised his voice to object, but to my surprise his voice was drowned out by a number of voices agreeing with Joseph. Annas watched in amazement as the tide in the room turned against him. Probably for the first time, he sensed he had lost control of the discussion. He did not have the support of the majority.

Seeing what was taking place, Caiaphas intervened. "These are both valid concerns! Annas asks an appropriate question about this Man called Jesus. But Joseph also raises a valid concern. The two matters need not be connected to one another. We will defer further discussion until we have had adequate opportunity to investigate both matters. Until then, the stalls and stables will remain outside in the stoa. As in all things, we will reconsider these matters only after we have had time to pray and fast."

Annas obviously did not like Caiaphas's answer, but he nodded his head in deference to his son-in-law. I was certain there would be much conversation later that night around the family dinner table – but until then we would move on.

As I left later that afternoon, I saw a large crowd surrounding Jesus. Many who were sick were being brought to Him for healing. I personally saw those who had been lame now walking. I saw vision restored to a blind man. And I saw deaf men who could now hear.

Each day throughout the remainder of Passover, the crowds around Jesus increased. He was teaching them from the Scriptures with an authority that surpassed that of great teachers like Gamaliel. I had never witnessed anyone like Him, and I knew I needed to know more about Him. Also, as a member of the Sanhedrin, I needed to be certain this Man was not leading our people astray.

I doubted Caiaphas would select me as one of the members assigned to formally investigate Jesus, but I still felt the need to do so on my own. He was from Galilee, after all. I wasn't sure how I would go about accomplishing this – until I saw my nephew John standing beside Jesus.

18

I WANT TO SEE FOR MYSELF

~

I walked over to John and asked, "How is it that you are here in the temple with Jesus of Nazareth?"

"Greetings, Uncle!" John replied. "You look surprised to see me! I have come to Jerusalem to celebrate Passover with the Master."

"The Master?" I asked. "Why do you call Jesus the Master? When we were last together you were a disciple of the baptizer. Is he here in Jerusalem, as well?"

"No, the baptizer is not here," John answered. "He continues to preach his message of repentance and baptize those who respond in the Jordan River. I am now a disciple of Jesus."

I couldn't contain my surprise as I asked, "How has that come to be?"

"One afternoon several weeks ago," John began, "my friend Andrew and I were standing beside the baptizer when he told us, *'Look! There is the Lamb of God!'*[(1)] He was pointing at Jesus. You can imagine our confusion. So, we asked him what he meant.

"He told us, 'Six weeks ago, this Man came to me and asked me to baptize Him. At first, I didn't know who He was. I should have recognized Him. I actually saw Him a few times when we were both boys. I am told we first met when we were both in our mothers' wombs. You see, our mothers were cousins.' But the baptizer's mother had died long ago, so their families hadn't seen one another since.

"Then he continued, 'When God told me to begin my ministry several years ago, He told me that one day I would see the Holy Spirit descend and rest upon Someone when I baptized Him. God told me He would be the One I was looking for – the very Son of God! That happened when I baptized Jesus that day. And I heard a voice from heaven confirm it by saying, *"You are My Beloved Son, and I am fully pleased with You."'*[(2)]

"As soon as Andrew and I heard the baptizer's words and saw Jesus, we knew He was the One we were to follow. The two of us, together with another one of the baptizer's disciples who was standing with us, immediately turned and followed Jesus.

"We never looked back. From that moment, I have continued to follow Jesus. I was with Him at a wedding feast several weeks ago when He turned water into wine. I was one of the fishermen in a boat when He directed us to cast our nets, only to draw in the largest catch of fish anyone has ever seen!"

These were the stories Theophilus had reported to the Sanhedrin a few weeks ago. And now my nephew was confirming he had been there, and these things were true!

John continued. "Since then, I have witnessed Him heal the sick and make the lame to walk, the deaf to hear, and the blind to see! And what's more, He speaks the words of heaven with an authority I have never heard – and as you know, I have been taught by some tremendous teachers. But Jesus's knowledge and authority exceeds each one, including you, Uncle. Jesus is without a doubt the Son of God!"

I interrupted him saying, "John, that is quite a declaration to make! If it is true, all our people have cause to rejoice! But we must know it is true – without any reservation!"

"Uncle, He is in the temple each day teaching the people," John offered. "Come join them, listen to Him, and know for yourself. Everyone is welcome at His feet when they come as honest seekers. Come, let me introduce you."

"I can't come to Him right now," I answered, "or any other time here in the temple. After what He did a few days ago – when He drove out the merchants – many of my Sanhedrin brothers do not trust Him. If I were to be seen in public speaking with Him, those same men would no longer trust me. I must speak with Him in private. Are you able to arrange a time and place for us to meet?"

"Yes, I believe I can," John replied. "Do you know the shop of Yitzhak the weaver here in the city?"

"Yes, I do."

"He has a room over his shop," John added. "Come to that room two nights from now after the dinner hour when the city has become quiet."

"Can you assure me no one else will know about our meeting?" I asked.

"Only Jesus and I will know," John answered. "I will be there to introduce you."

For the next two days I thought about little else other than my upcoming meeting with Jesus. I told no one other than Tali about my plan, including my friend Joseph of Arimathea. I needed to know for certain who Jesus was before I could admit to seeking Him out. I knew other members of the Sanhedrin had been sent to question Him – but they were trying to discredit Him. I wanted to speak to Him so I would know for certain if He is the Son of God.

I knew I was risking my position in the Sanhedrin and in the community. I truly believed there were some in the Sanhedrin who would never look on Jesus favorably – even if it was proven beyond question that He is the Son of God. As a matter of fact, they would see Him – and anyone who associates with Him – as an even greater enemy.

19

"YOU MUST BE BORN AGAIN!"

◇

I was very familiar with the shop of Yitzhak the weaver. Tali had purchased all the fabric she used to decorate and furnish our home from Yitzhak. He was a well-known and respected merchant in the city.

He was working at his bench when I arrived. I decided to greet him before quietly making my way up the stairway to meet Jesus.

"Welcome to my shop, Rabbi Nicodemus!" he exclaimed. "What brings you here at such a late hour?"

Not wanting to tell him the real reason for my visit, I replied, "I was walking by and saw the lights in your window. I could see you were busy at work, but I decided to stop and extend my greeting."

"I am so glad you did," Yitzhak responded. "How are your wife and your family?"

"My wife is well and very pleased with the fine fabrics you sold us," I answered. "It has been some time since we have heard from our children, but we know Jehovah God is watching over them. And how are your wife and family?"

I had no idea how his answer would better prepare me for my conversation with Jesus. "We, too, know Jehovah God is watching over us!" Yitzhak told me. "Earlier this week, my son, Uriah, was helping me finish the construction of our upper room. We were setting the final roof tiles when he lost his footing and fell to the street below. I scurried down as fast as I could.

"I felt so helpless as I stared at him lying there lifeless. All I could do was cry out to Jehovah God to help me. Just as I did, a Man knelt beside me. He appeared to be just one of the many pilgrims who had traveled to Jerusalem for Passover.

"The next thing I knew He took my son by the hand and said, 'Young man, I say to you, arise!' Immediately, my son sat up. Uriah looked at me, then he looked at the Stranger. The Stranger returned my son's look and said, 'Young man, behold your father.' Then He looked at me and said, 'Father, behold your son!'

"It was as if my son had never fallen. Just a moment before he had been lying there lifeless on the street! I was bewildered. I looked up at the Man and asked, 'Who are You? And what have You done?'

"'Yitzhak,' He said, 'you cried out to the Father for help. He heard your prayer, and your son has been made whole. All so the Father might be glorified.'"

I couldn't contain my joy over God's miraculous intervention. "Praise be to Jehovah God our Protector!" I exclaimed. "Yitzhak, I praise the Lord with you!! Who was the Man?"

"His name is Jesus of Nazareth!" he replied.

For the previous two days, I had asked Jehovah God to show me clearly through this meeting that Jesus was His Son. And now, Jehovah God had shown me even before I had spoken a word to Jesus.

After a short while, I bid Yitzhak a good night and made my way up the stairway to the upper room without being seen. When I entered, only Jesus and John were present.

After my nephew introduced me to Jesus, I asked, "*Rabbi, we all know that God has sent You to teach us. Your miraculous signs are evidence that God is with You.*"[1]

Jesus wasted no time with shallow compliments. Instead, He moved right to the heart of the matter as He replied, "*I tell you the truth, unless you are born again, you cannot see the Kingdom of God.*"[2]

I didn't understand what He meant, so I asked, "*What do You mean? How can an old man go back into his mother's womb and be born again?*"[3]

Jesus replied, "Nicodemus, *I assure you, no one can enter the Kingdom of God without being born of water and the Spirit. Humans can reproduce only human life, but the Holy Spirit gives birth to spiritual life.*"[4]

I still didn't understand. *"How are these things possible?"*[(5)] I asked.

I felt like I was a talmid sitting at the feet of my Teacher as Jesus answered. *"You are a respected Jewish teacher, and yet you don't understand these things? I tell you what I know and have seen, and yet you won't believe My testimony. But if you don't believe Me when I tell you about earthly things, how can you possibly believe if I tell you about heavenly things? No one has ever gone to heaven and returned. But the Son of Man has come down from heaven. And as Moses lifted up the bronze snake on a pole in the wilderness, so the Son of Man must be lifted up, so that everyone who believes in Him will have eternal life.*[(6)]

"For this is how God loved the world: He gave His one and only Son, so that everyone who believes in Him will not perish but have eternal life. God sent His Son to save the world through Him.[(7)]

"There is no judgment against anyone who believes in Him. But anyone who does not believe in Him has already been judged for not believing in God's one and only Son. And the judgment is based on this fact: God's light came into the world, but people loved the darkness more than the light, for their actions were evil. All who do evil hate the light and refuse to go near it for fear their sins will be exposed. But those who do what is right come to the light so others can see that they are doing what God wants."[(8)]

∾

20

WHAT DO I DO NOW?

∾

a s I made my way home, I pondered what Jesus had said. But His last statement in particular kept echoing in my mind: *"Those who do what is right come to the light so others can see that they are doing what God wants."*[1]

I wanted to do right. That's why I had come to talk to Jesus that night. I wanted to do what God wants me to do. I always have. But I knew something had been missing in my life. Was obeying the law of Moses not enough? And who was able to always obey the law? Try as I might, I knew I couldn't.

Jesus had said only those who believe in God's Son will have eternal life and that God had sent His Son to save the world through Him. Is that what was missing in my life? Must I believe in God's Son? And if so, is Jesus truly God's Son as He says? My nephew, John, believes He is. But do I?

As I asked myself that question over and over again, I began to realize I *did* believe Jesus is the Son of God! And if I were to be completely honest, I had known it when I was standing before Him that night. For that matter, I had known it the day I had seen Him drive the merchants out of the temple.

No longer would I deny that reality, which meant I must also acknowledge that everything Jesus said to me was true! He was the promised One. He was the One God sent to deliver His people from their sins. So, what was I to do now? Do I leave the Sanhedrin to follow Jesus as John has done? Or do I follow Jesus from within the Sanhedrin? Does God want me to be light from within the council?

When I arrived home, I told Tali about my time with Jesus. I conveyed everything He had said and all that I had considered as I walked home. I told her I believed Jesus to be the Son of God.

When I finished, she looked at me and said, "I have been praying God would reveal Himself to you through your time with Jesus. The Spirit of God reminded me earlier tonight of the words written by the prophet Jeremiah: '*If you look for Me wholeheartedly, you will find Me.*'[(2)] Nicodemus, I know you are a man who has sought God wholeheartedly. Tonight, He has enabled you to find Him! Give all praise to Jehovah God – and trust what His Spirit is saying to you."

"I do trust Him," I said, "and I know what Jesus told me is true. Now I need to know what He would have me do with this truth."

Tali took me by the hand and said, "Then we will ask Him to show you and trust Him to do so."

It was late when I went to bed, and my mind continued to replay my time with Jesus. I kept hearing Him say, "*so others can see. ...*" By the time the sun rose, I knew what I must do.

God had placed me in the high council; not by chance, but according to His plan. I was to shine His light in the midst of the great darkness within the Sanhedrin. It would not be well received. But His Spirit reminded me I was not responsible for the results – I was responsible to shine the light.

The Spirit prompted me to speak with Joseph of Arimathea first. He listened intently with an open mind and an open heart. When I finished, he thanked me and told me what I shared was helpful, but he was not ready to believe Jesus is the Son of God.

After that conversation, I realized each of us needs to have a personal encounter with Jesus. We cannot convince others of who Jesus is – that's the work of the Spirit of God. My responsibility was to be light pointing others to Jesus. So that's what I set about doing in the days and weeks that followed.

Joseph came to me several weeks later. He had been asked to accompany Annas and Caiaphas on a journey to Arimathea to question Ashriel, the local rabbi. He was the great-grandson of a priest named Simeon who, in his old age, had supposedly seen a baby he believed to be the promised Messiah. Rabbi Ashriel was said to have been with his great-grandfather that day.

Joseph had agreed to make the journey if Gamaliel and I accompanied them, too. He wanted unbiased witnesses to the conversation. Annas and Caiaphas had agreed, so he was asking me to go along. I did not hesitate for a moment!

Given the number of years that had passed since that event, the baby would now be a man of about thirty years of age. My heart raced as we made the journey to Arimathea.

21

A JOURNEY TO ARIMATHEA

❧

*W*hen we arrived at the home of Ashriel in Arimathea, Caiaphas told us Annas would lead the conversation. Ashriel looked at our group warily until he spotted Joseph. His face lit up as he exclaimed, "Joseph, it is good to see you! We miss seeing you and your family at the synagogue!"

The two men embraced as Joseph replied, "And we miss all of you, as well! We look forward to the day we can rejoin you here in Arimathea."

To the consternation of Annas, Joseph went on to explain why we were there. Ashriel clearly trusted him, so Joseph was able to set his mind at ease. After the two men exchanged updates about their families, Joseph relinquished the conversation to Annas, who asked, "Why did Simeon believe the baby he saw was the Messiah?"

We all listened intently as Ashriel relayed the story. "My great-grandfather never doubted that day would come. Even though it had been almost one hundred years since God had given him the promise he would see the Messiah before he died, his faith was as strong that day as it had been on the day God first spoke to him.

"That morning, when he saw the baby and His parents, he just knew! He told me to help him walk over to the baby. His step grew quicker and steadier, and he told me his heart was pounding in his chest. When we arrived at the family, Papa asked if he could see the baby. I'm sure his actions seemed strange to them, but they kindly turned their young son so Papa could look into His eyes.

"Tears began to stream down his cheeks! I'll never forget his words when he turned to the baby's mother. 'This Child of yours will cause many people in Israel to fall and others to stand. The Child will be like a warning sign. Many people will reject Him, and you, young mother, will suffer as though you had been stabbed by a dagger. But all this will show what is really in the hearts of people.'[1]

"She didn't speak a word but simply nodded at my great-grandpa. I was struck by her tenderness. I could see why Jehovah God had chosen her to be the mother of His Son. When Papa reached to pick up the baby, she willingly handed the tiny bundle to him.

"The baby didn't stir or make a sound as Papa held Him. Rather, the baby seemed to look intently into my great-grandpa's eyes. It was as if the baby knew him. And I became convinced the baby *did* know him.

"As Papa held Him in his arms, he looked toward heaven and said, '*Lord, I am Your servant, and now I can die in peace, because You have kept Your promise to me. With my own eyes I have seen what You have done to save Your people.*'[2]

"Papa returned the baby to His mother's arms and blessed her and the father. We watched as they walked away. Papa turned to me and said,

'These people have no idea they have been in the presence of the Son of God,' as he pointed to those moving about the temple.

"Papa died not long after that. But he did so knowing his lifelong mission was complete."

Annas asked the question that was on all of our minds. "Did they tell you the baby's name or where they were from?"

"No," he replied, "they did not, and we never asked."

As Annas continued to ask questions, I found myself believing Jesus was indeed that baby. I think the other men did, too – or at least thought it was possible – but no one said it out loud. I thought about what Simeon had said to the baby's mother, "He will show what is really in the hearts of people." And I knew that was true!

During the years that followed, Caiaphas and Annas frequently brought up the subject of Jesus before the Sanhedrin. They repeatedly raised false accusations. "He is Beelzebub!" "He is a demon." "He is a false witness." "He is a fraud." Occasionally they would say things that were closer to what they truly believed. "He is leading the people away from us. He is usurping our authority. We are in danger of losing our power."

Both men became obsessed with defeating Jesus. This went far beyond their embarrassment the day He cleansed the temple. These men feared Him, and they knew if they didn't discredit Him soon, it would be too late. But they didn't want to just discredit Him – they wanted to destroy Him.

For months they sent messengers trying to entrap Jesus into saying something they could use against Him. But every time, Jesus responded in a way that revealed their treachery.

As time passed, I began to openly ask the question in council meetings as to whether Jesus might be the Promised One. One day, as I looked around the room at each man, I asked, "Have we allowed our fear of losing our power and positions to blind us from seeing the very One we have waited for so many years? Instead of plotting against Him, should we not be welcoming Him into our midst?"

The silence that followed was deafening!

22

TWO MIRACLES IN CAPERNAUM

~

Soon after Tali and I moved to Jerusalem, Jesus's mother, Mary, had moved to Capernaum. Several of the young men from our village – my nephews, James and John; as well as our former tax collector, Matthew – were now numbered among His disciples. My sister-in-law, Salome, was also traveling with Jesus. As a result, He visited Capernaum often to see His mother and permit His followers to spend time with their families.

Whenever Jairus, Leah, and our granddaughter, Ilana, came to Jerusalem to celebrate the feasts and visit with us, they would captivate us with stories of what Jesus had said or done on His last visit to the village. But we were completely amazed by one particular event Jairus relayed to us. "A few weeks ago, a royal procession arrived in Capernaum. It was King Herod's chamberlain, Chuza, and his wife, Joanna. I soon learned their ten-year-old son, Samuel, was ill with a high fever, and they had come seeking Jesus.

"Mary told them He was expected any day. The last she had heard He and His followers were in Samaria near Sychar. They would be returning by way of Cana. Chuza decided to leave his wife and son in the village and go out alone to meet up with Jesus. I promised to look in on the boy until Chuza returned.

"I was there the next day. It was a little after the noon hour and there was still no sign of Chuza – or more importantly, Jesus. We had all heard about the power Jesus had to heal those who were sick, but I feared the boy would soon die. I believed Jesus was going to be too late to save him. I couldn't imagine the grief these parents would experience. Just then, I heard Samuel gasp as he crossed what I feared was the threshold into death.

"But suddenly, the boy began to stir. He sat up in bed as if nothing was wrong. I quickly realized his fever was gone! I looked around the room to see if Jesus had entered without my knowing – but He was not there. It was about one o'clock in the afternoon.

"It was the next day before we learned from Chuza that Jesus had simply spoken the words there in Cana, '*Go back to your son. He will live!*'[1] He had spoken those words at the exact moment I heard Samuel gasp. Jesus had spoken, and a boy who was miles away had been healed!"

Jairus confessed that he and Leah both believed in Jesus that day. By the grace of Jehovah God, He was permitting our entire family to come to know and believe in His Son.

Several months later, Jairus and his family returned to celebrate the Festival of Lights with us – and the story they told us this time was much closer to home! "Two weeks ago," Jairus began, "Ilana started to run a high fever. It was the same fever we had all witnessed in many others. Most of those people had died – except Samuel, the boy Jesus had healed.

"Jesus had been in the village the day before Ilana got sick, but then He and his disciples had departed by boat and crossed over the sea. Many of His followers had remained in Capernaum, though, so I knew He would be returning soon. I continued to keep watch for Him. I knew He could heal Ilana!

"Before long I began hearing a commotion in the street. I heard people shouting, 'Jesus is back! They are about to arrive on the shore!' I ran as fast as I could and got there just as He was stepping out of the boat. I fell at His feet and pleaded with Him – '*My little daughter is dying. Please come, lay Your hands on her and heal her so she can live.*'[(2)]

"Without saying a word, Jesus reached down, helped me to my feet, and the two of us began to make our way toward the village. Our progress, however, was slowed by the crowd pressing in on Jesus from all sides. As we were making our way, messengers arrived to tell me Ilana had died. '*There's no use troubling the Teacher now.*'[(3)] It was too late!

"But Jesus overheard the messengers, took me by the arm, and said, '*Don't be afraid. Just have faith.*'[(4)] Then He stopped the crowd and told them to remain on the shore.

"When we arrived at our home, Jesus saw the weeping and wailing of the people who had gathered to mourn. As we walked by, Jesus asked, '*Why all this commotion and weeping? The child isn't dead; she's only asleep.*'[(5)]

"The people in my house looked at one another and then started to laugh at Jesus. I knew many in the crowd had not seen Him perform miracles like I had – but they had heard of His miracles!

"As Jesus looked at them, their laughter stopped and turned into an uncomfortable silence. Because of their faithlessness, He told them all to leave my home. Afterward, Jesus walked with Leah and me into the room where Ilana was lying. Then He took her hand in His and said, '*Little girl, get up!*'[(6)]

"Immediately, she sat up! Just like Samuel had! It was as if she had never been sick. Ilana stood and began to walk around!"

I looked over at my precious granddaughter as tears of joy streamed down my cheeks. Tali and I both wrapped our arms around Ilana as we praised God for His goodness and mercy to us. We were overcome with a feeling of indebtedness to the One who had brought our granddaughter back to life! Jesus was already our Savior – but after we heard what He had done, He became our Lord and Master. Some have foolishly said Ilana wasn't really dead, she was only asleep. I, however, would suggest they talk to us – her family – or any of those who mistakenly chose to laugh at Jesus.

∽

23

A LINE IN THE SAND

~

*A*s time passed, Sanhedrin members became even more fearful that Jesus was undermining their authority. More than once, He had refused to submit to their rule. They were afraid the people would do likewise to the point the Sanhedrin would be stripped of their power and their positions would become irrelevant.

But Annas, Caiaphas, and the others no longer openly plotted against Jesus; they knew some of us would not support their plans. Instead of discussing their schemes in front of the entire council, they held hushed conversations in the hallways or at the high priest's private residence.

This past October, Jesus was back in Jerusalem for the observance of the Feast of Tabernacles. As expected, throngs of people flocked to Him as He taught and healed in the courtyard. It was obvious that certain members of the council did not like it!

One morning we were gathered in the hall hearing a petition forwarded to us by the local Sanhedrin in Jericho. It was a civil dispute between two citizens in the city.

During our deliberation, two priests entered the hall followed by four temple guards. Two of the guards were grasping the arms of a disheveled woman. A collective gasp arose from the council. Women were not permitted in the council hall, and this woman was certainly not dressed appropriately for any venue, let alone the temple or the Hall of Hewn Stones.

The two priests quickly approached Caiaphas. I recognized one of them. I had seen him speaking with Caiaphas on several previous occasions.

The priests spoke with Caiaphas and Annas in hushed tones. Soon a smile crossed Annas's lips. I couldn't imagine why he was smiling. Nothing about this situation merited a smile. After a few moments, Caiaphas turned to the guards and ordered them to take the woman into the courtyard where Jesus was teaching.

Caiaphas then instructed several members of the Sanhedrin to accompany the priests into the courtyard. I knew these men were some of his key allies in plotting against Jesus, so I feared what was about to take place. I got up and followed them out so I could witness whatever happened.

The crowd in the courtyard began to stir as soon as they saw the woman. Jesus stopped speaking. All eyes turned toward the woman. I noticed that both priests, as well as those sent by Caiaphas, were each picking up a stone. They were obviously preparing to stone the woman. Suddenly everything became quiet. One of the priests, who had spoken with Caiaphas, addressed Jesus. *"Teacher, this woman was caught in the act of adultery. The law of Moses says to stone her. What do You say?"*[1]

Jesus looked at the woman, who bowed her head in fear and shame. In contrast, her accusers stood scowling at her with looks of contempt. Surrounding them was the crowd – leering at her and craning their necks to see what Jesus was going to say. He was the only One who didn't look at her with condemnation.

After a few moments, He stooped down and began to write in the sand, paying no attention to the woman or those around Him. I was close enough that I could see what He was doing. He was writing a list of names, and beside each name He was writing a sin. By one He wrote "adultery." By another He wrote "blasphemy." By still another He wrote "thievery." And on and on. He listed the name of each man standing behind the woman. But the woman's name appeared nowhere on the list!

I wondered what would happen next. Was He going to accuse them? These were obviously sins these men would want to keep private. Not only would these sins be a great source of embarrassment, but if they were made public, they could cost these men their positions of influence. Perhaps some of them might even be stoned to death themselves.

The priest who had spoken continued to demand an answer. When Jesus looked up, He didn't look at the woman, He looked at the men and said, *"All right, but let the one who has never sinned throw the first stone!"*[2]

No one moved. They just stared at the writing in the sand. The men were restrained by their own guilt. After a few minutes, I heard the stones start falling to the ground. The men made no attempt to explain themselves but simply hurried away as if they had an important appointment.

Jesus stood up, looked at the woman, and asked, *"Woman, where are your accusers? Didn't even one of them condemn you?"*[3]

The woman replied in amazement, *"No, Lord."*[4] To which Jesus responded, *"Neither do I. Go and sin no more."*[5]

The men had fled in fear. But their fear had fled with them. What would happen if Jesus ever revealed what He knew about them? Each of these men was now even more committed to silencing Jesus.

24

THE ENTRY OF THE KING AND A SURPRISING VOTE

⁓

*T*hat brings us to the week that was unlike any other – the Passover celebration. Hordes of pilgrims gathered in Jerusalem; some having traveled for weeks to get there. Many had come for a reason other than Passover – they had come to see Jesus!

Word of His miracles had spread far and wide. Some people had come seeking a miracle for themselves, while others simply wanted to see Him perform a miracle. There was excitement in the air as everyone waited expectantly for His arrival.

It was the first day of the week and I was in the temple. Since Jesus had always entered the city quietly and come straight to the temple to teach, I decided if I was going to see Him, it would be there.

But soon I heard shouts echoing throughout the city. At first, it was cheers and an ever increasing clamor, but soon the shouts became a chant as the crowd yelled in unison, "Hosanna!" There was no doubt the people were heralding the arrival of Jesus!

I walked outside to observe. Surprisingly, the people were moving toward the eastern gate, which historically was used by kings and reserved for royalty. But then I realized how appropriate it was for Jesus to enter in through that gate.

Then I saw Him, riding on the back of a colt. Not only was He entering through the royal gate, but He was also riding in the style of a king. At that moment, the writing of the prophet Zechariah came to mind:

Look, your King is coming to you. He is righteous and victorious, yet He is humble, riding on a donkey – riding on a donkey's colt.[1]

I watched as several men placed their garments over the colt to make riding more comfortable for Jesus. People began to spread their garments on the road ahead of Him. Others laid down palm branches they had cut in nearby fields.

The crowd began to repeatedly shout, *"Praise God for the Son of David! Blessings on the One who comes in the name of the Lord! Praise God in highest heaven!"*[2] Some of the people standing around me were surprised when I added my voice to the refrain.

The cheers grew even louder as more people joined the procession. Soon it seemed the entire city was in an uproar. I noticed some of my fellow Sanhedrin brothers had also come out to see what the commotion was about. When they saw Jesus, they indignantly called out to Him, *"Teacher, rebuke Your followers for saying things like that!"*[3]

Jesus responded, *"If they kept quiet, the stones along the road would burst into cheers!"*[4] The men indignantly retreated back into the hall. I knew they were fearful that the crowd was preparing to crown Jesus as King.

When He arrived at the temple, Jesus dismounted the colt, and the crowd parted so He could enter. As He walked through the Court of the Gentiles, I saw Annas standing off in a corner with Caiaphas. They were watching Jesus's every move. Annas was speaking to the younger man in hushed tones, while Caiaphas nodded his head in agreement. Their smug expressions told me they were plotting something.

I expected Jesus to make His way to the court and begin teaching. But surprisingly, He did not. After spending some time walking around the temple in prayer, He departed – much more quietly than He had arrived. I expected I would see Him again the next day.

That evening Caiaphas sent word to all of us to gather in the great hall, though he did not explain why until after we arrived.

"The number of pilgrims pouring into the city is increasing with each day," he announced. "We have never seen so many people. The priests have advised us we must allow the merchants and the stables back into the outer court so they can accommodate the great need for animals to sacrifice and temple coins to exchange. They are fearful the stoa will be overrun, and the seriousness of the offerings and sacrifices will be interrupted.

"I know we have chosen not to do so for the past few years, but I fear we do not have a choice this year. Because we have been divided over this issue, I have called you together to put it to a vote. What say you?"

Several of us looked at one another in astonishment. How could Caiaphas even consider this proposal? Our members had consistently and overwhelmingly agreed to keep the animals and the merchants out of the courtyard. Why would he place it forward for a vote at such a late hour?

But it was I who was surprised, along with a few of my fellow council members, when the vote was overwhelmingly cast in favor of doing so! I suddenly realized the conviction of many of my Sanhedrin brothers had given way to their fear of Jesus. This vote was obviously for the sole purpose of creating a charge against Him.

25

JESUS CLEANSES THE TEMPLE ... AGAIN

❧

*J*wanted to get word to Jesus about the vote and what was being set up in the temple, but I did not know where He was spending the night. At first, I worried what would happen when He walked into their trap. Then the Spirit of God calmed my heart, reminding me Jesus is the Son of God. He knew what these men were going to do – even before they knew themselves.

I made a point of arriving at the temple just as the sun rose. The stalls and tables were in place. The animals were in their stalls, and the merchants were attending to final details. Annas and Caiaphas were in the far corner of the courtyard making sure everything was in order.

As I walked past one of the stalls, the merchant recognized me as a member of the Sanhedrin. "Rabbi," he asked, "how does everything look to you? We didn't have much time to get this done. But we worked hard all through the night and did the best we could."

"I am sorry you had to work through the night," I replied.

"We are here to serve our leaders," he added, "and the people – and Jehovah God, of course. So, I want to be certain I serve well. That's why I asked if everything looked okay to you. Rabbi, can I ask you a question?"

"Yes, go right ahead."

He began somewhat tentatively. "How do you think Jesus is going to react when He arrives this morning? I was here when He chased us out three years ago. I saw His anger; but more importantly, I understood the reason for His anger. And then, a year ago, He healed my son. My child was lame, but Jesus enabled him to walk. I saw the tenderness of Jesus, and my heart affirmed His teaching to be true.

"Begging your pardon, I don't think Jesus was wrong to clear out the temple. I think what we are now doing is wrong. Please sir, I do not mean any disrespect, but I wondered what you think. How do you think Jesus will react?"

I answered him as honestly as I could. "I believe Jesus will act as Jehovah God would have Him act. I believe Jehovah God is sovereign over all things – even this decision. And I believe He will use it all for His glory. So, I will trust Him, no matter what happens – even when I don't understand. That is my word of counsel to you as well, my friend. Thank you for your service."

As I walked away, the merchant slowly nodded his head as he pondered what I had said.

Neither one of us had long to wait. Jesus arrived at the temple within the hour. As I suspected, He was not surprised by what He saw. The moment

He stepped into the courtyard He shouted, *"It is written: 'My house will be a house of prayer.' But you have made it 'a den of robbers.'"*[1]

He immediately began turning over the tables and chairs, driving the merchants from the temple just as He had three years earlier. But this time the merchants were not surprised. They exited the court quickly and returned to their stalls and tables in the stoa. They knew they had been used as pawns in a game they did not understand.

I kept watching Annas and Caiaphas as this played out. They looked quite smug and victorious. Obviously, Jesus had reacted just as they expected. After the courtyard was cleared, Jesus continued into the temple with people following Him. Jesus received them all, healing them and teaching until He departed at the end of the day.

The next morning, Caiaphas and Annas asked their co-conspirators in the Sanhedrin to join them in the courtyard so they could confront Jesus when He arrived. As a part of the orchestrated plot, they acted shocked and offended by His actions. They voiced their objections to what He had done, saying He had completely undermined their authority. He had never once come to them seeking their approval for His actions.

As far as they were concerned, they had never delegated Him any authority, and He had ignored their official positions for far too long. They were now unified and emboldened by the fear they would lose their power over the people. Caiaphas spoke on their behalf: *"By what authority are You doing all these things? Who gave You the right to do them?"*[2]

But Jesus knew what was in their hearts. He wisely asked them, *"Did John's authority to baptize come from heaven, or was it merely human?"*[3]

Two years earlier, the baptizer had been arrested and beheaded by Herod Antipas. These same leaders had avoided having to confront him for what they viewed as his disrespect of their authority. I had often wondered what part they had played in his death. But Jesus was now forcing them to take a public stand regarding John.

They knew whatever answer they gave Jesus, the crowd would turn on them and they would lose their authority, position, and prestige. So, they refused to answer His question by pleading ignorance. That prompted Jesus to respond, *"Then I won't tell you by what authority I do these things."*[4]

The group turned and left in a huff with Caiaphas and Annas leading the way. They sequestered themselves behind closed doors – and away from piercing eyes – so they could discuss the next step in their twisted plot. I was not invited to join them. Neither was Joseph nor the others who had voiced opposition to their plan the night before.

∾

26

A TUMULTUOUS TUESDAY THAT LED
TO A QUIET THURSDAY

~

*N*ine of us had voted against bringing the merchants back into
the temple. We all believed doing so was a desecration of the
temple. Forty other members had once agreed with us, but their fear of
Jesus had caused them to abandon their convictions.

Of the nine who remained, only Joseph and I truly believed Jesus to be the
Son of God. The other seven, which included Gamaliel, had not yet come
to that place. But we were all upset that Caiaphas was now excluding us
from Sanhedrin meetings. The guards refused to let us enter the meeting
hall.

Gamaliel pulled us aside and said, "The high priest has no legal authority
to exclude us. A member can only be excluded if he is unseated. Unseating
a member requires a vote of at least two-thirds of the entire Sanhedrin, and
I know for a fact he is not able to garner that much support. This is an
illegal action that must be confronted."

Gamaliel, a respected teacher, was not one to be trifled with. He sent messages to the influential members notifying them their assembly was illegal because they had excluded the nine of us. Caiaphas soon came out of the hall to see us.

"I apologize for any confusion, my brothers," he said. "I'm not sure why you were told you could not enter the hall. I will find out who was responsible for issuing that erroneous order to the guards. I can assure you they will be dealt with harshly. I had not noticed your absence, so thank you for bringing it to my attention. Please return to the hall with me so we can all proceed with the business at hand."

We knew none of that was true – except for the fact some guard would be punished for simply carrying out an order he had been given. When we took our seats, our fellow members feigned their extreme displeasure over how we had been mistreated. Caiaphas formally extended apologies to us and assured everyone the matter would be investigated and dealt with swiftly.

He then announced there would be no further action taken regarding the merchants or the placement of the stalls. They would remain outside in the stoa for the remainder of the Passover celebration. The council would revisit the matter at some future point.

No mention was made of Jesus or His actions in the temple that day or for the next two days. It was early Friday morning before we learned the members had voted during our absence to delegate twelve men to form a special high council under the leadership of Caiaphas. They had the responsibility and autonomy to take whatever action was necessary to eliminate Jesus as a threat to the Sanhedrin. Even though it was an illegal action since the nine of us were absent, no one ever spoke a word about it.

The next day, I saw this new group gathered in one of our smaller meeting rooms – Caiaphas, Annas, Ishmael ben Phabi, Eleazar, Simon, Jonathan,

Theophilus, and six others. I knew they were discussing Jesus – but that wasn't unusual because that was all this group of men seemed to talk about these days.

I was surprised, however, to see a man I knew to be one of Jesus's disciples enter the room. I could not imagine why Jesus would send him to meet with these men. But He must have, I reasoned, since Jesus was there teaching in the courtyard.

The next day was Thursday, the day before the beginning of Passover. Jesus was conspicuously absent from the temple. The courtyard had been full of people anticipating His arrival, but they eventually drifted away as the day went on. It turned out to be an unusually quiet day, despite the record crowd gathered for Passover.

As I walked home, I couldn't shake the feeling that this was the lull before the storm. I was truly puzzled.

When I arrived home, I told Tali about Jesus's absence from the temple.

"I wonder what kept Him away?" she mused.

"I can't imagine," I responded. "Each day this week I have expected Him to declare to the people that He is the Messiah. They are ready to follow Him. They are just waiting for Him to say the word. I think many thought He might do so today on the eve of Passover. But obviously that wasn't His plan. Perhaps tomorrow will be the day."

～

27

A SURPRISE ARREST

~

I settled into bed early that night. The first part of the week had weighed heavily on me, so I needed the rest. I fell into a deep sleep quickly and began dreaming I was on the shore of the Sea of Galilee. It was a bright day, and the seas were calm. But suddenly, a storm seemed to arise from nowhere. Gale force winds began to blow. The sea surged, and a wave started to crash over me. I heard Tali crying out to me from somewhere down shore.

I awoke with a start, drenched in perspiration. It had been a terrible dream – but gratefully, only a dream. However, I sensed someone standing near the edge of my bed. It was Tali, calling my name. That part hadn't been a dream.

"Nicodemus, get up!" she exclaimed. "You must get up! Joseph of Arimathea is here for you! You must get up and hear what he has to say!"

I opened my eyes and tried to clear the fog from my mind. I could see my wife was extremely upset. Something had happened – and my heart filled with dread.

"Nicodemus, you must hurry!" she said a little louder this time. "Joseph has important news for you."

"What is it, wife?" I asked as I tried to gather my senses.

"Something has happened to Jesus," she cried. "Joseph has come for you."

I was instantly awake. I jumped to my feet, threw on my cloak, and walked to our outer room to meet Joseph. I could see the worry written all over his face. "They have arrested Jesus!" he exclaimed.

"Who has arrested Jesus?" I asked.

"Caiaphas and Annas sent the temple guards together with several priests to arrest Him," he replied. "Jesus was in the Garden of Gethsemane with His disciples and the priests arrested Him. All of His disciples scattered and abandoned Him."

I could not believe what I was hearing. "They arrested Him? For what? And by whose authority?"

"Apparently the Sanhedrin voted on Tuesday while we were kept out of the hall to establish a special council that was given complete authority to do whatever was needed to eliminate Jesus as a threat. They have accused Him of blasphemy against God and sedition against Rome," Joseph explained. "They mean to have Him crucified."

"They mean to do what?" I implored. "That can't be possible! Have they gone mad? The council is illegal. They were chosen and empowered by an illegal vote. This must be stopped!"

Joseph knew we needed to act and not waste time talking. "Nicodemus, get dressed," he said sternly. "They are holding Jesus in the cell beneath Caiaphas's home. We must go now and see if we can talk some sense into them!"

When we arrived at the high priest's home, no one tried to prevent us from entering. Out of the corner of my eye, I noticed my nephew John standing by the window. "What is he doing here?" I wondered.

Before Joseph and I could ask any questions, Caiaphas addressed us. "A few moments ago, in this very room with all of these witnesses gathered, Jesus publicly declared Himself to be the Son of God! Earlier this week, we all heard the crowds refer to Him as King and Jesus made no attempt to correct them. As a matter of fact, He was heard to say, '*I tell you, if these were silent, the very stones would cry out.*'[1]

"By virtue of His declaration before all these witnesses, no further proof is required. A simple majority of the Sanhedrin is all that is needed to convict Him. The forty men who heard His proclamation unanimously voted to convict Him of blasphemy, and we have enough evidence to bring a charge of sedition before Pontius Pilate. We are planning to take Jesus to the praetorium to stand before Pilate even now. The matter is done. It's out of our hands!"

"What do you mean the matter is done and it's out of our hands?" I cried out. "It's very much in your hands! You and the others have set this in motion. Jesus is guilty of nothing, other than being the Promised One sent by God. He *is* the Son of God! I know it's true –and you know it's true."

"I know no such thing!" Caiaphas responded in a calm but stern voice. "And I would advise you to remain silent or this council will charge you with blasphemy!"

A man near the back of the room moved, and I recognized him as the disciple I had previously seen meeting with Caiaphas and the others. "*I have sinned*," he shouted, "*for I have betrayed an innocent man.*"[2]

"*What do we care?*" Annas retorted. "*That's your problem.*"[3] Caiaphas motioned to the temple guards to remove him.

All of a sudden, the man threw pieces of silver on the floor and stormed from the room. It was apparently blood money they had given him for betraying Jesus. Caiaphas directed one of the servants to pick up the coins. Earlier during the week, one of our discussions in the hall had centered around what to do with foreigners who die in Jerusalem.

Seeing the coins on the floor, Caiaphas declared, "*It wouldn't be right to put this money in the temple treasury.*"[15] Use it to buy a field that can be used as a cemetery for the burial of foreigners. Call it the 'Field of Blood.' Now guards, make ready the prisoner. We will leave now to deliver Him to Pilate."

Caiaphas brushed past Joseph and me as he left the room. The two of us stood there, not knowing what we should do. I turned and saw my nephew still standing by the window.

෴

28

"IT IS FINISHED!"

~

*J*ohn turned to us and began to explain. "Earlier this evening, Jesus announced that Judas was going to betray Him, but we didn't completely understand what He meant. We never imagined Jesus would be arrested – nor, in our wildest dreams, did we imagine He would be condemned to death. It all happened so quickly. I am ashamed to tell you we all ran in fear when they came to arrest Jesus. Not one of us stood by His side!"

John was weeping as he gave his account. He was broken over what was happening to Jesus – but also over his own failing. "Is there anything that can be done to stop this?" he asked desperately.

Neither Joseph nor I knew what to do at this point. But I still hoped God the Father would intervene for His Son. "Not once Pilate issues His death decree," I said. "Hopefully, he will see that Jesus has not done anything worthy of crucifixion. Joseph and I will go to the praetorium and see if we can convince Caiaphas to stop this madness!"

"I will go and find Jesus's mother," John replied. "I'm sure the others have already told her what has happened, but she will want to see Him, and I do not want her to do that alone."

When Joseph and I arrived at the praetorium, we found out that Pilate had already referred the charges against Jesus to Herod Antipas. Pilate decided that since Jesus was a Galilean and Herod was the governor over Galilee, he should determine Jesus's fate. But before we arrived at Herod's palace, we saw Jesus being taken back to stand before Pilate once again. Apparently, Herod had deferred the matter back to the Roman prefect since Jesus had been arrested in Judea.

Everything happened swiftly! Before we knew it, Pilate declared Jesus guilty despite his own protests to the contrary. He even went through a show of washing his hands of Jesus's blood. Had the entire world gone mad?

Now that the death order had been issued, we knew there was nothing anyone could do – short of a pardon from Caesar himself. Jesus was going to be crucified today. My mind couldn't comprehend it!

Joseph and I watched as members of the high council made their way to Golgotha to witness the crucifixion. I could not bring myself to follow them. I returned home where Tali and I wept for Jesus. We wept for His mother and His disciples. But we also wept for our people. God had sent His Son and we had rejected Him! His blood would forever be on our hands!

At noon, the sky turned black – day had become night. Surely it was a sign of the judgment awaiting us for what our people were doing to God's Son. Then a thought crossed my mind. The law precluded an honorable burial for one who was executed for violating the law. Jesus's body would be left hanging on the cross overnight in disgrace. There was no way I could permit that to happen to the body of my Lord.

I was certain His family and His disciples had not thought about this; they were overwhelmed by everything else happening. Whatever was to be done would need to happen quickly before sunset and the beginning of Sabbath.

I went to find Joseph to discuss what we could do. When I arrived at his home, I discovered he had already come to the same conclusion. We decided we first needed to go to Pilate and request Jesus's body. We were hoping Annas and Caiaphas had not done anything to block His body from being buried.

When we arrived at the praetorium, Pilate came outside to receive us. "I am told you want to bury the body of Jesus," he said with surprise. "Is that correct?"

"Yes, it is," we replied.

"How can that be when it was you religious leaders who demanded His death?" he asked.

"The two of us did not demand His death," I said. "He is an innocent Man. He has not done anything worthy of death!"

"I agree with you," Pilate replied. "But Caiaphas and Annas were adamant – and the crowd all shouted in agreement."

Pilate seemed to be seeking our forgiveness for his role in Jesus's death. He was looking to wash away the guilt he felt. We, however, stood in silence.

We would not help him justify his part in this travesty of justice. Eventually, he gave us a document granting us permission to receive Jesus's body once He was declared dead.

Joseph had recently acquired a tomb intended for his own burial, but he offered to let us bury Jesus's body in his tomb. We stopped at one of the shops in the city and purchased a linen shroud and the ointments we would need to prepare His body for burial.

We were horrified to see what had been done to Jesus when we arrived at the foot of His cross. The torture and pain they had inflicted to His body was obvious. Just then we heard Him say, *"It is finished!"*[1]

We both fell to our knees and wept. When we regained our composure, we approached the Roman centurion with the document Pilate had given us. There was also another man at the foot of the cross. We had seen him when we arrived. As we prepared to take Jesus's body to the tomb, he came to us and said, "I carried His cross to Golgotha, and now I will carry His body to the tomb."

As the three of us placed Jesus's body in the tomb and sealed it with a great stone, a group of Roman soldiers appeared. Evidently, Caiaphas and Annas had petitioned Pilate to post guards so no one could remove His body and declare that Jesus had risen from the grave.

∾

29

THE TOMB IS EMPTY!

∼

I was back home with Tali just as night began to fall. The two of us were reeling from the events of the past twenty-four hours. Jesus was dead! I had held His lifeless body in my arms as we laid Him in the tomb. How could it be?

I knew Jesus was the Son of the Living God. He was the Promised Messiah. He was the One whose coming was foretold by the prophets. He was the One who would set us free! But His own people had rejected Him. Most of our religious leaders had been complicit in His death!

I reflected on all the prophecies I had heard. Since I was a boy, I had antici-pated His arrival much like the generations before me. I thought everyone was looking forward to His coming. He was to establish His kingdom and rule over us. Had we somehow foiled God's plan by murdering His Son? That had never been part of the prophecies I remembered nor was it some-thing we talked about in synagogue or in the School of Hillel.

My mind was racing. Was there anything about the Messiah dying in the writings of any of the prophets? It was then God brought to mind these words from the prophet Isaiah:

He was despised and rejected — a man of sorrows, acquainted with deepest grief. We turned our backs on Him and looked the other way. He was despised, and we did not care. Yet it was our weaknesses He carried; it was our sorrows that weighed Him down.

And we thought His troubles were a punishment from God, a punishment for His own sins!

Or so Caiaphas and the others wanted us to believe. But Jesus was without sin, and Jehovah God had already set the record straight through the prophecy:

He was pierced for our rebellion, crushed for our sins. He was beaten so we could be whole. He was whipped so we could be healed.

I had seen the stripes on His flesh from being whipped. I had seen the opening in His side from being pierced by the spear. I had seen the bruises all over His body from being beaten by the Roman soldiers.

All of us, like sheep, have strayed away. We have left God's paths to follow our own. Yet the Lord laid on Him the sins of us all. He was oppressed and treated harshly,

yet He never said a word. He was led like a lamb to the slaughter. And as a sheep is silent before the shearers, He did not open His mouth. Unjustly condemned,

He was led away. No one cared that He died without descendants, that His life was cut short in midstream. But He was struck down for the rebellion of My people. He had done no wrong and had never deceived anyone ...

Today that prophecy had been fulfilled. He had been slaughtered for the sins of us all. He was unjustly condemned ... but willingly faced the punishment as our Passover Lamb. He was sent by the Father to be the spotless Passover Lamb whose blood had now been shed as a covering for our sins. How fitting that God had allowed this to occur on the very day that our people remember the Passover lamb.

And then I remembered the last words of that prophecy:

... but He was buried like a criminal; He was put in a rich man's grave.[1]

Unbeknownst to Joseph and me, we had fulfilled those words just moments ago. How many times had I read or heard those words? Today I had seen them come to pass. It was my own iniquity that led Jesus to the cross today. I couldn't blame Annas, or Caiaphas, or Pilate alone. It was the sinfulness of us all. As that reality flooded my mind and heart, I began to weep uncontrollably.

I wept throughout that night, the next day, and into the third day. That afternoon there was a knock on our door. To my surprise, it was my nephew, John. But instead of looking heartbroken, his face was radiant with joy!

"Uncle Nicodemus, Jesus is alive!" he exclaimed. "I have been to the tomb. His body is not there! He has risen from the grave! He had told us He would – but we had not understood. Now, He has appeared to many of our number this morning and this afternoon. Rejoice, Uncle ... Jesus is alive!"

I wanted to rejoice – but it was all so difficult to comprehend. For two days I had been consumed by grief, but now John was saying Jesus had conquered death and the grave. We all knew He had raised others from the dead, but now He Himself had walked out of the tomb!

I thought about the soldiers who had arrived at the tomb as Joseph and I were leaving. What must they have thought when they saw Jesus walk out of that grave!?!

"Uncle," John continued, "Jesus said we should all gather in the room over the home of Yitzhak the merchant. Get dressed and come with me."

"You go ahead!" I told him. "I will go and find Joseph and the man who carried Jesus's body to the tomb – the one named Simon. I will tell them what you have said, and we will all come to the upper room."

I did just that. When we arrived at the upper room, several men and women were excitedly telling us about seeing Jesus that day. All at once, Jesus appeared in our midst! I saw Him standing before us with my own eyes. Jesus is alive!

~

30

I NOW KNOW WHAT I HAVE TO DO!

~

*T*he next day, Joseph and I walked into the Hall of Hewn Stones together. The other members were already in their places discussing the news that Jesus had risen from the grave.

"We feared the disciples of Jesus would do something like this," Caiaphas said. "That's why we petitioned Pilate to post guards at the tomb. But by their own admission, the guards fell asleep. Yesterday they told us Jesus's disciples came while they were sleeping and stole His body.

"No resurrection has taken place – only an attempt at deception. The guards are searching the surrounding area to find out where His body has been placed. Brothers, I would admonish each of you to squelch this false rumor at every opportunity. Jesus is not alive! He has been crucified, and He is dead! God has punished Him for His sins."

I could no longer listen to these lies!

"My Sanhedrin brothers, I have come to tell you that Jesus is, in fact, alive!" I blurted out. "Joseph and I saw Him last evening and spoke with Him in this very city!"

An uproar immediately arose in the hall. Some were shouting to drown out my words while others shouted because they wanted to hear more. I waited for the noise to die down.

"Our leaders want us to believe the disciples of Jesus are attempting to deceive us," I continued. "In reality, it is our leaders who are attempting to deceive us. The same men who orchestrated the plot to have Him crucified now stand before you denying the truth of His resurrection.

"Each of you has witnessed the miracles He performed. Each of you has heard the words He taught. Many of you were involved in trying to discredit Him in some way – but all those attempts failed. And they failed because He is who He said He is. You may deny it with your words, but you cannot deny it with your hearts.

"When Jesus told us three years ago that if we destroyed the temple, He would raise it up in three days, He was talking about Himself. He knew the sin and wickedness and deceit in our hearts. He knew we would ultimately orchestrate the events of this past Friday – and He was telling us even then He would rise from the dead."

Some of the men began shouting again to keep me from speaking further, but this time it was quite a few members who quieted them down. "Let Nicodemus finish!" they shouted.

"Jesus was the slain Lamb Isaiah foretold," I continued. "But He is not one of many lambs who must be slain for our sin, He is the one and only

Lamb. And though His blood was shed, He alone has conquered death and the grave. He is a Living Sacrifice. He is the sacrifice God promised on this very hill to our Father Abraham many years ago when he was prepared to sacrifice his own son, Isaac. Jehovah God has sacrificed His own Son. But He who died for us is now alive. The prophecy is completed!"

As I looked around the room, I saw a handful of members carefully considering my words. But I could tell by their angry faces that the majority was refusing to accept the truth.

"That is a very interesting story, Nicodemus," Caiaphas began. "It is very creative. It is the kind of story you would make up to tell children. But we are not children. We are the religious leaders of our people, and we have done what needed to be done. No one has returned from the dead. Even the ones Jesus supposedly raised from the dead were merely tricks intended to deceive us."

"Be careful, Caiaphas," I said, "one of those you refer to is my grand-daughter. And I can assure you she was raised from the dead just as Jesus has been raised from the dead!"

"Nicodemus," Caiaphas continued in a condescending tone, "I have no doubt you believe that – but you have been deceived. I will no longer stand here and argue with you. I cannot permit a member of this Sanhedrin to embrace such heresy against God and such disrespect against our leadership. According to the laws of our land, I place the question before this body – should Nicodemus be discharged from his position on this Sanhedrin?"

Joseph interrupted, saying, "Caiaphas, I echo everything Nicodemus has said. I, too, have seen the risen Jesus. He is alive and He is my Lord and Savior. If you discharge Nicodemus, then you must discharge me as well!"

Caiaphas looked amazed. Then he shook his head and said, "Members, you have heard Joseph. What say you, should Nicodemus and Joseph both be discharged?"

By an overwhelming margin, Joseph and I were discharged from the Sanhedrin that day. Several men did not vote in agreement, which made them suspect among the others. One of them, my friend Gamaliel, would one day stand up for Jesus himself.

That day was the first of many in which God would lead me to take a stand for my Lord and Savior. I remained in Jerusalem for the next fifty days leading up to the Feast of Pentecost, experiencing snubs and ridicule from many of those with whom I had served. But in their stead, we found fellowship with those like us who had become followers of Jesus. Tali and I stood on the hill outside the city with many of them the day Jesus ascended into heaven to sit at the right hand of the Father.

And the two of us, together with Joseph, were back in the upper room over Yitzhak's home when the Holy Spirit came upon us all ten days after Jesus ascended. Soon afterward, Tali and I left Jerusalem. We returned home to Capernaum to bear witness throughout Galilee and Samaria to the words Jesus spoke to me that night long ago:

As Moses lifted up the bronze snake on a pole in the wilderness, so Jesus was lifted up on the cross, *so that everyone who believes in Him will have eternal life."*[1]

SCRIPTURE BIBLIOGRAPHY

～

Much of the story line of this book is taken from the Gospel according to John.
Certain fictional events or depictions of those events have been added.

Some of the dialogue in this story are direct quotations from Scripture.
Here are the specific references for those quotations:

Preface

[1] John 3:16

[2] John 7:51-52

[3] John 19:38-42

Chapter 2

[1] Psalm 100:1-5

Chapter 4

[1] Exodus 20: 2, 3, 6 (NASB)

Chapter 5

[1] Isaiah 61:1

Chapter 8

[1] Genesis 2:18 (HCSB)

[2] Job 1:21

[3] Psalm 23:4 (paraphrase)

Chapter 10

[1] Example of dispute taken from Deuteronomy 22:13-19

Chapter 14

[1] John 1:21

[2] John 1:22

[3] John 1:23

[4] Matthew 3:7-8, 11-12

Chapter 16

[1] John 2:16

Chapter 17

[1] John 2:18

[2] John 2:18

[3] John 2:19

(4) John 2:20

(5) Psalm 69:9

Chapter 18

(1) John 1:36

(2) Mark 1:11

Chapter 19

(1) John 3:2

(2) John 3:3

(3) John 3:4

(4) John 3:5-6

(5) John 3:9

(6) John 3:10-15

(7) John 3:16-17

(8) John 3:18-21

Chapter 20

(1) John 3:21

(2) Jeremiah 29:13

Chapter 21

(1) Luke 2:34-35 (CEV – paraphrase)

(2) Luke 2:29-30 (CEV)

Chapter 22

[1] John 4:50

[2] Mark 5:23

[3] Mark 5:35

[4] Mark 5:36

[5] Mark 5:39

[6] Mark 5:41

Chapter 23

[1] John 8:4

[2] John 8:7

[3] John 8:10

[4] John 8:11

[5] John 8:11

Chapter 24

[1] Zechariah 9:9

[2] Matthew 21:9

[3] Luke 19:39

[4] Luke 19:40

Chapter 25

[1] Luke 19:46 (ESV)

[2] Mark 11:28

[3] Mark 11:30

Chapter 27

(1) Luke 19:40

(2) Matthew 27:4

(3) Matthew 27:4

(4) Matthew 27:6

Chapter 28

(1) John 19:30

Chapter 29

(1) Isaiah 53:3-9

Chapter 30

(1) John 3:15

∿

LISTING OF CHARACTERS
(ALPHABETICAL ORDER)

~

Many of the characters in this book are real people pulled directly from the pages of Scripture. i have not changed any details about those individuals except in some instances their interactions with the fictional characters. They are noted below as "UN" (unchanged).

In other instances, fictional details have been added to real people to provide additional background about their lives where Scripture is silent. The intent is to provide further information for the story. They are noted as "FB" (fictional background).

In some instances, we are never told the names of certain individuals in the Bible. In those instances, where i have given them a name as well as a fictional background, they are noted as "FN" (fictional name).

Lastly, a few of the characters are purely fictional, added to convey the fictional elements of these stories . They are noted as "FC" (fictional character).

~

Adir – great-great-grandfather of Nicodemus (FC)

Andrew - brother of Simon Peter, friend of John, disciple of Jesus (UN)

Annas - high priest 6-15AD (FB)

Asher - grandfather of Nicodemus (FC)

Ashriel – great-grandson of Simeon, rabbi in Arimathea (FC)

Betzalel - a carpenter, father of Jairus (FC)

Caiaphas - high priest 18-36AD, son-in-law of Annas (FB)

Camydus – brother of Hillel & Shebna, grandfather of Annas (FC)

Devorah - wife of Adir (FC)

Eleazar ben Annas - son of Annas, High Priest 17-17AD, member of Sanhedrin (FB)

Gamaliel - member of Sanhedrin, grandson of Hillel (FB)

Herod, the Great - the tetrarch (UN)

Herod Antipas – sixth son of Herod the Great, ethnarch over Galilee and Perea (UN)

Hillel, the Elder - respected teacher, brother of Shebna & Camydus, grandfather of Gamaliel (FB)

Ilana - daughter of Jairus and Leah, granddaughter of Nicodemus, raised from the dead by Jesus (FN)

Ishmael - son of Shebna, business partner of Yaakov, father of Salome and Tali (FC)

Ishmael ben Phabi - High Priest 15-16AD, member of Sanhedrin (FB)

Jairus - rabbi in Capernaum, father of Ilana (FB)

James - son of Zebedee and Salome, disciple of Jesus (UN)

Jesus - Son of the Living God (UN)

John - son of Zebedee and Salome, disciple of Jesus (FB)

John the baptizer – a voice crying in the wilderness preparing the way (UN)

Jonah - father of Simon Peter and Andrew, fishing partner of Zebedee (UN)

Jonathan ben Annas - son of Annas, High Priest 36-37AD, member of Sanhedrin (FB)

Joseph of Arimathea - pharisee, member of Sanhedrin (FB)

Judas Maccabeus - led the revolt against the Seleucid Empire (FB)

Leah - daughter of Nicodemus and Tali, wife of Jairus, mother of Ilana (FC)

Marianne - wife (3rd) of Herod the Great, daughter of Simon ben Boethus (UN)

Mattathias Maccabeus – father of Judas Maccabeus (UN)

Matthew - tax collector in Capernaum, disciple of Jesus (UN)

Menahem - great-grandfather of Nicodemus, son of Adir (FC)

Nahum - GGG-grandfather of Nicodemus, fought with Judas Maccabeus in revolt, namesake of Capernaum (FC)

Nicodemus – rabbi, member of the Sanhedrin (FB)

Nissa - daughter of Shebna, younger sister of Ishmael, wife of Yaakov, mother of Nicodemus (FC)

Pontius Pilate – Roman prefect of Judea (UN)

Rebekah - daughter of Nicodemus and Tali (FC)

Reuben - son of Nicodemus (FC)

Salome - daughter of Ishmael, sister of Tali, wife of Zebedee, mother of James & John (FB)

Shebna - brother of Hillel & Camydus, business partner of Asher, father of Ishmael (FC)

Simeon - the ancient who God promised would see the Messiah (UN)

Simon ben Boethus - High Priest 23-5 B.C. (UN)

Simon ben Camithus - High Priest 17-18 A.D., member of Sanhedrin (FB)

Simon Peter - son of Jonah, disciple of Jesus (UN)

Simon the Cyrene - pulled from crowd to carry the cross of Jesus (FB)

Tali - wife of Nicodemus, daughter of Ishmael, sister of Salome (FC)

Theophilus ben Annas – son of Annas, High Priest 37-41AD, member of Sanhedrin (FB)

Unnamed father in case heard by local Sanhedrin (FC)

Unnamed husband in case heard by local Sanhedrin (FC)

Unnamed merchant in the temple (FC)

Unnamed priest who accused the adulterous woman (FB)

Unnamed wife in case heard by local Sanhedrin (FC)

Uriah – son of Yitzhak (FC)

Yaakov - father of Nicodemus, son of Asher, business partner of Ishmael (FC)

Yitzhak – merchant in Jerusalem, owner of the upper room used by Jesus (FC)

Zebedee - husband of Salome, father of James & John, fishing partner with Jonah and later Simon Peter (UN)

A MERCHANT CALLED LYDIA

KENNETH A. WINTER

DEDICATION

In memory of my mother,
Betty Winter,
a woman of grace and beauty,
who lived her life with the courage and strength of Lydia.

She loved her husband, her children, her grandchildren,
and her great-grandchildren well,
and
she desired for everyone she met to know the One she loved the most,
her Lord and Savior, Jesus Christ.

~

A woman who fears the LORD will be greatly praised.
(Proverbs 31:30)

~

PREFACE

～

This fictional novella is the fifth book in the series titled, *The Called*, which is about ordinary people whom God called to use in extraordinary ways. As i've said before, we tend to elevate the people we read about in Scripture and place them on a pedestal far beyond our reach. We then tend to think, "Of course God used them. They had extraordinary strength or extraordinary faith. But God could never use an ordinary person like me."

But nothing could be further from the truth. The reality is that throughout history God has used the ordinary to accomplish the extraordinary – and He has empowered them through His Holy Spirit.

Lydia was one of those people. She first appears in Scripture in Acts 16. Prior to our introduction to her, she had already achieved success in business. And though she was a Gentile, she was already seeking to know the God of the Jews. Through these pages, we'll explore how she could have achieved her success, and the possible circumstances in her life that led her to meet the apostle Paul.

Scripture does tell us that Lydia was from Thyatira, the same city referenced by the apostle John in Revelation 2. We read in Acts that Paul and Silas were prevented by the Spirit from entering Thyatira and the other cities of Asia on Paul's second missionary journey. It was that journey that subsequently led them to meet Lydia in Philippi.

i have often wondered if God didn't need them to stop in Thyatira because their role was to bring the Gospel to Lydia, and her role was then to bring the Gospel back to Thyatira. This story explores that possibility.

Also, you will see that the city of Rome plays an important role in this storyline. There is no indication in Scripture – or anywhere else, for that matter – that Lydia spent any time in Rome. It is a fictional device i have employed in the story to help describe how the cities of the empire were ruled by Rome, and how the city became the scene for significant events in the early history of the church.

Lastly, the story concludes just prior to the apostle John addressing the Thyatiran church in the Book of Revelation. It gives us a view of an important kingdom principle in the mission of God and the spread of the Gospel.

So, sit back and enjoy this walk through the life of Lydia and the others who surround her. Many of the characters in the story come directly from Scripture. You will recognize many of them from the pages of the Book of Acts, the Epistles written by Paul, and the Book of Revelation. In numerous instances, i have added background details about them that are not in Scripture so we might see them as people and not just names. i draw heavily on the historical writings of Josephus in doing so. But please always remember that i employ plausible fiction as well.

As in my other stories, i have added completely fictional characters to round out the narrative. They often represent people we know existed but are never given any details about, such as parents or children. Included in the back of this book is a character map you can use to clarify the historical vs. fictional elements of each character.

Whenever i directly quote Scripture during the story, it is italicized. The Scripture references are also included as an appendix in the book. Those remaining instances of dialogue related to individuals from Scripture, such as Paul, that are not italicized are a part of the fictional story that helps advance the narrative.

One of my greatest joys as a biblical teacher and author is when readers tell me they were prompted to go to the Bible and read the biblical account after reading one of my books; i hope you will do so. None of my books is intended to be a substitute for God's Word – rather, i hope they will lead you to spend time in His Word.

Finally, my prayer is, that as you read this story, you will see Lydia through fresh eyes – and be challenged to live out *your* walk with the Lord with the same boldness, humility, and courage she displayed. And most importantly, i pray you will be challenged to be an "ordinary" follower with the willingness and faith to be used by God in extraordinary ways . . . for His glory!

1

A ROMAN CITY

~

"*L*ydia, Macedonian blood flows through your veins. Be true to your heritage, and honor your Macedonian forefathers." My father began telling me that when I was just a toddler, though I didn't understand what he meant. Our city – the city of Thyatira – had very much become a Roman city.

Thyatira is surrounded by hills and lies in the mouth of a long valley that flows north from the Hermus River. We are fortunate that our fertile land remains fruitful without the hard work required in more parched regions of Asia. A continuous procession of camels transports Thyatira's produce to the bazaars of Pergamos, Sardis, and Smyrna.

Prior to its colonization by Macedonian King Seleucus Nicator, Thyatira was a small farming village, sparsely populated and clustered around a central pagan temple. But the Macedonians viewed Thyatira as a strategic military outpost. They believed it was key to protecting the great trade highway that wound through the valley.

Because of Thyatira's key location, they believed the protection of their rule and their provincial capital of Pergamos rested on the strength of our city. As a result, the fortunes of Pergamos and Thyatira were inextricably linked from that day forward.

The Macedonian soldiers brought little in the way of possessions with them, but they did bring their worship of the sun god Apollo to our city. The temple constructed in his honor is one of the few Macedonian structures that remain in the city today.

Though Thyatira was viewed as a gateway into Asia, it was never a fortified city. No one would ever mistake it as a powerful ruling city. Instead, our purpose was to protect whichever empire we happened to belong to at the time by preventing the enemy from penetrating deeper into imperial territory.

That all changed, however, when we became a part of the Roman Empire. Emperor Augustus instituted changes that enabled our city to blossom and prosper into the thriving city we are today. The Roman Empire, with its vast military might, did not view our location as a strategic military outpost; instead, they regarded us as a valuable city of industry and trade. Our city soon teemed with foundries for the production of brass and bronze instruments. Sweltering artisans toiled over white-hot flames fashioning Thyatiran wares that were coveted throughout the empire.

But those were not the only significant items produced in our city. We also became well-known for our linen and woolen cloth industry – especially our red and purple cloth. Purple is the more costly of the two and is used primarily by those who are wealthy or royal. Red cloth, on the other hand, is more widely used by the masses.

Purple cloth, generally sold throughout the empire, is produced using a dye derived from tiny Mediterranean mollusks found along the Phoenician and Spartan coasts. But the dye produced in Thyatira is refined from the roots of plants uniquely indigenous to our area. The combination of those roots and the waters of our region produce a dye that is a much richer hue and is resistant to fading – making it a more sought-after product.

The current Roman emperor, Vespasian, has done even more to foster the city's growth and prestige, including the addition of three new gymnasiums, an impressive colonnaded stoa of merchant shops and craftsmen stalls, and many more shrines to the Roman gods. We most definitely have come to reflect the best – and the worst – of Rome.

As the city grew in importance in industry, Thyatira became host to numerous guilds centered around the various trades. In fact, there are more trade guilds in our city than in any other city in Asia. The guilds are not solely the center of business life within the trades. If you belong to a guild, your life pretty much functions within the confines of the social, civic, and religious views of the guild, as well.

The three most powerful guilds in our city are the coppersmiths, the bronzesmiths, and the dyers. Those three greatly influence the thinking of our other guilds, which include the wool workers, the linen workers, the makers of outer garments, the leather workers, the tanners, the potters, the bakers, and the slave dealers. As you might expect, a person's position in the community is determined by which guild he belongs to and where he stands in the hierarchy of his respective guild.

Over the years, there has been a blending of races in our city. Our long-standing families are primarily of Macedonian descent. A considerable influx of families of pure Roman descent began to immigrate to the city once Rome took possession of our lands, as did peoples from other regions of the expanding empire. My family is a mixture of the two.

In more recent years, there has been an influx of people from Egypt, Judea, the Arabian Peninsula, Syria, and Cilicia. They have brought their diversity of religious beliefs, including the one perceived by most to be the most unique of them all – the Jews. Over time those beliefs have become syncretized into an amalgamation of beliefs. It has become acceptable to believe whatever you think is true – as long as you do not express the idea that one belief is more correct than another. Emperor Vespasian has even introduced the idea of the deification of Caesar himself.

As such, we have become a tolerant city as long as a person's beliefs do not violate the code of his guild. Yes, we are a city of contradictions, but many would also tell you that we have become a shining city within the empire – wealthy in riches and progressive in our beliefs. It is the city I became proud to call home.

∼

2

MY MACEDONIAN HERITAGE

~

or a brief time under the rule of Alexander the Great, the Macedonian Empire was the most powerful in the world. It was the epicenter from which Greek arts and literature flourished, and the enlightenment of philosophy, engineering, and science spread to the rest of the known world. The great philosopher and teacher, Aristotle, spent most of his adult life in Macedonia in the city of Pella after King Philip brought him there to tutor his son, Alexander the Great.

As my father often reminded me, our Macedonian ancestors were from Pella. He was confident that they too had acquired much of their knowledge from sitting at the feet of Aristotle. Perhaps the great philosopher had gained some of his knowledge from them as well!

After the death of Alexander the Great, the city soon lost its prestige and began to fade into the shadows as a small provincial town. My ancestors, like many others, began looking for opportunities in the new Asian colonies. As a result, when the Macedonian soldiers arrived in Thyatira, they were accompanied by a host of tradesmen and merchants seeking greater fortune. One of my ancestors was counted among their number.

By the time the Romans took control of our city and the surrounding region, four generations of my family had made their mark and prospered in their adopted city. They quickly learned that wealthy families – regardless of which empire they belonged to – always desired to clothe themselves and furnish their homes in the finest fabrics. My family's prosperity came through the discovery of our now infamous Tyrian purple dye.

The Romans had worked tirelessly to extend their empire and develop an expanded infrastructure of trade routes that fostered more opportunities for business. By the time my grandfather was in control of our family business, ours was one of the most prestigious in the city, and he had become one of its most powerful men.

As a matter of fact, my grandfather was instrumental in the establishment of the trade guilds for which Thyatira is famous. And he carefully mentored his son, Evander, preparing him to eventually take over the family business as well as maintain the family's influence in the city. He also wisely determined that our family's influence needed to extend beyond the boundaries of Thyatira into the ever-increasing regions that now made up the Roman Empire.

For that to happen, my grandfather sent his son to Rome – the seat of power for the empire – to further his education. But father and son both knew it would also afford him the opportunity to build solid relationships with powerful Roman families, which would be very beneficial in the days ahead. So, at the age of twelve, my father set sail on a merchant vessel bound for Rome.

The voyage was to take a little more than three weeks. It was quite a venture for a twelve-year-old boy to make without his family, but my father was not just any boy. By that age, he had already demonstrated a wisdom beyond his years and a capability to inspire and lead others – even those much older – to accomplish more than they had ever envisioned.

That ability was soon put to the test on his journey. Halfway through the voyage, about three days from their next port of call, Rhegium, a typhoon struck. The captain and crew bravely battled the storm; they enlisted the help of the eight passengers onboard, including my father, to throw the ship's cargo overboard and band the ship's hull.

On the third day of battling the destructive winds and waves, the captain was struck on the head by a damaged mast and swept overboard. He immediately disappeared in the violent waves; there was no time to rescue him.

Without the captain to give them direction, the crew began to panic as the day wore on. They believed the ship was doomed as it tossed to and fro in the waves. When they finally spotted land, they were afraid the ship would not make it through the shoals.

They quickly assessed their situation. The crew feared for their lives if they remained on the ship. They also knew they would not be paid since the captain and cargo were both lost at sea. There was one lifeboat aboard with room enough for the crew but no passengers. So, they decided to give the passengers a task to distract them while several crew members lowered the lifeboat to make their escape.

My father, however, noticed what the crew was doing and alerted the other passengers. He knew that without the crew the ship would be lost. Without any hesitation, he made his way to the stern, picked up a knife along the way, and cut the rope securing the lifeboat to the ship. When the crew realized what he had done and saw there was no way to reach the lifeboat, they ran toward him to throw him overboard.

3

MY ROMAN HERITAGE

~

*B*ut in the heat of the moment, my father called out, "I believe the only chance we have in surviving this storm is if we all stay together. You men have the experience and know-how to guide this ship to land, and the eight of us will add our strength to the effort. We passengers know that with the loss of the captain and cargo you will not be paid for this voyage. But we will all pay you a reward equal to three times what you would have received if you guide us to dry land!

"You know that your chances in that small lifeboat were not much better than on this ship. But if we all work together, we might just be able to tell the story to our children of how we survived this storm! And you men will be paid handsomely for the effort!"

As my father spoke, the crew members looked at one another. The men who had grabbed him relaxed their grip. Slowly, they all nodded their agreement and turned to look at their first mate.

The first mate asked, "How do we know the rest of these passengers will pay up the money needed to provide this bounty you have promised us?"

All the other passengers looked at him and nodded their heads in agreement. But then my father added, "Because if they don't, I will! You will receive your funds when we get to Rome – and if not, you can hold me captive until you do!"

"Well, young sir," the first mate exclaimed, "we accept your pledge and will hold you responsible to fulfill it. Otherwise, you will pay dearly for having cut that rope!"

Under the direction of the first mate and crew, the ship lurched in to shore the next day. We came aground about an hour's walk southeast of Rhegium, the most southern city on the coast of Italy. As the passengers made their way to the city, they discussed the bounty they had promised to pay the crew. Several men said they should report the crew to the authorities in Rhegium and have them arrested for extortion and abandonment at sea. But my father reminded them they had all given their pledge.

The crew set about locating a ship's captain who needed a crew for a voyage to Rome that also could accommodate eight passengers. It seemed like an impossible request, but unbeknownst to everyone involved, God was ordering their steps and just such an opportunity became available. My father and the other passengers had to pay an additional fare to their new captain to take them to Rome – but at that point, it was a small price to pay to get to their destination.

After docking in Rome, my father accessed the funds his father had already sent ahead to provide for his living expenses. Between those funds and those of the other passengers, they were able to settle their obligation to the sailors before they all parted ways. My father had to live frugally for his first three months. It took that long for word to reach my grandfather of his need for additional funds and for those funds to arrive in Rome.

But his depleted finances did not prevent my father from making inroads into Roman society from his very first day. His wit and charm quickly opened doors with his fellow students as well as their prestigious families. One of those students was a young man named Aurelius, who was the same age as my father. My father was always one step ahead of him – both in the classroom and on the athletic field. But the two students soon became inseparable, and my father became a frequent guest in his friend's home.

Aurelius was the son of Gaius, an influential member of the Roman senate and, as it turned out, a close friend of Emperor Augustus. Each visit to Aurelius's home gave my father the opportunity to meet another member of Rome's elite and solidify his place in that social circle.

But the one who truly captured my father's attention was Aurelius's younger sister, Caecilia. As the years passed, she transformed into the lovely young woman who captured my father's heart. However, unlike her brother, she was never one step behind my father in anything. As a matter of fact, my father often said he knew from the start he would always have to run just to keep up with her!

When Caecilia's father became aware that a relationship was blossoming between his daughter and my father, he made it clear he would not grant his permission for her to marry until she was twenty years of age. He told my father he would not allow her education to be interrupted.

By that time, my father had become firmly established as a member of Roman society and was a leading merchant in the city. Our family's Tyrian purple was now the only acceptable purple dye to be used in the clothing and household linens of the Roman elite, and it was only available through my father. So, neither my grandfather nor my father was in any rush for him to return home to Thyatira. The decision to send my father to Rome had become even more profitable than either of them had imagined.

When he and Caecilia were married, I am told it was one of the major events of that year's social calendar. Everyone who was anyone was in attendance. Even Emperor Augustus and the Empress Livia graced the event with their presence. But my father always told me that event paled in the eyes of both he and my mother in comparison to the occasion that took place just three years later. That was the day my mother gave birth to me.

4

GROWING UP IN THYATIRA

~

*D*uring my father's early years in Rome, he was introduced to a
man named Linus, a successful Roman trader in fabrics. He
specialized in exotic silks from the Far East and fine linens from the
Middle East. He and my father soon realized that between Linus's fabrics
and my father's exclusive dye, they could easily control the textile market
to the upper class of Rome. Their relationship began as a business partnership but soon the bond between them became even closer than brothers. I
even referred to him as my Uncle Linus.

He was the first one to receive the message from Thyatira that my grandfather had died. The merchant sailors who arrived with a shipment of dye
also carried the message to my father. Though I was too young to fully
understand, I knew my father was heartbroken when Uncle Linus delivered the news.

My father knew that he must return to Thyatira without delay. He needed
to comfort my grandmother and take over the affairs of the family business. His sorrow over his father's death was compounded by the sadness

both of my parents felt. My mother had never been separated from her family or her beloved Rome, and, after seventeen years, the city had become my father's adopted home. Though my father would always tell me that Macedonian blood flowed through our veins, he also knew that Rome would always hold a special place in his heart.

My parents quickly set about making arrangements for their departure. Uncle Linus would assume full responsibility for their joint business affairs in Rome. Passage was booked on a merchant ship scheduled to leave in three days. My Roman grandparents accompanied us to the ship and bade us a sad farewell. My mother often said they were sadder to see me go than they were to see her leave. At the time, I was their only grandchild!

Our three-week journey was uneventful, and my family soon settled into our new home with my grandmother Marijana. My father took over the family's business affairs without delay, while my mother was left to navigate the transition from the sophistication of Rome to the quaintness of Thyatira. Gratefully, she and my grandmother got along right from the beginning.

Even though I am a Roman citizen by birth, I have no memories of the city from when I was a baby. My earliest memories all begin in Thyatira. Even as a young child, I knew our family was one of the most important families in the city. From the day we arrived, my father was considered a city leader, and my mother set the social standard for what a proper household should be like. Our home was always filled with friends, neighbors, and guests seeking the opinion or the affirmation of my parents. Everyone wanted to be considered their friend, and my parents were gracious and hospitable to each one without regard to station in life.

When I was four years old, my brother Janus was born. Though I never questioned my father's love for me, I knew he was thankful to have a son he could raise to walk in his footsteps. But as the years passed, I was the one who began showing the greater interest in learning the family business.

Both my parents placed great value on education, and our mother taught Janus and me during our early years. I admired her for her understanding and proficiency in the studies of philosophy, mathematics, and history. She taught us to read and write in both Latin and Greek, and she passed on to us her great love for poetry.

When I reached the age of twelve, my father paid to have tutors further my education in the subjects of physical science, mechanics, and economics. But some of my greatest education in those areas came from my father. I would often listen as he carried on conversations about business, politics, and philosophy.

Although our family was not very religious, my father taught us that Greek and Roman gods were contrived to be answers to questions people were unwilling or unable to discover for themselves. He admonished Janus and me that we were above all of that. We had the ability to find our own answers and solve our own problems – we didn't need an imaginary god to do that for us.

As I entered my teens, I began to increasingly favor my mother in appearance. I was taller than most young women my age and had a slender frame. My father frequently told me I was becoming quite beautiful – just like my mother. Janus, on the other hand, closely resembled our father. He was very athletic and ruggedly handsome. But, in other ways, I was the one who truly favored our father. I had his skill in business. I was learning how to deal with people astutely but fairly. And I was learning how to lead others confidently – without being overbearing.

Eventually my father succumbed to my pleas to help him with the family business. He was reluctant at first, but ultimately he recognized my passion and skill for the work. My brother, on the other hand, was content to allow me to take a leading role. He was a hard worker, but he had no interest in being the leader.

"You are just like your mother," my father said to me one day. "I have always known she is smarter than I am. But she has always allowed me to think I am the one who is in charge. However, I know better.

"We need to find a husband for you who will not be intimidated by you. And one who will recognize not only your physical beauty but also the beauty of your mind, your will, and your spirit.

"Your mother and I believe it is time for you to return to Rome to further your education and spend some time with your grandparents there. It has been almost fifteen years since we arrived here in Thyatira. Your mother deserves the opportunity to go back and spend time with her family. The two of you will be setting sail for Rome next week!"

∾

5

MY ROMAN EDUCATION BEGINS

❀

*J*anus remained home with my father. Though I relished the opportunity of returning to Rome with my mother, a part of me wanted to stay in Thyatira. I knew my father was hoping Janus, in my absence, would begin to show interest in the affairs of our family business and aspire to lead it one day.

As my mother, two of our servants, and I made the journey across the seas, I couldn't help but wonder if my father secretly hoped I would become so enthralled with Rome – and perhaps even find a husband – that I would lose interest in our family business. Though he knew I had the ability to lead it, he favored leaving control of his business to his son rather than his daughter. I was resolved to win him over to my way of thinking, and I was busily making plans to do so.

Our ship docked at the harbor of Ostia, located on the mouth of the Tiber River, eleven miles downriver from Rome. Mother had sent word of our pending arrival to my grandparents, so they sent servants to meet us and accompany us on the riverboat journey to Rome. They greeted us as soon as we stepped off the ship. They fawned over my mother and reminded me I was only a baby when they had last seen me.

When the city came into view, I forgot everything else on my mind. It was magnificent! I had never seen anything so grand. I now know that the lustre of the city is paid for by the taxes of the working people throughout the rest of the empire. Citizens of Rome pay no taxes; the rest of the empire pays it for them. But that fact was nowhere in my mind as I took in the splendor of all that was before me.

Our family lives in one of the grandest homes in Thyatira, but as we approached my grandparents' palatial home, I suddenly felt very provincial. That was even before we walked inside and I witnessed the lavishly appointed mosaic floors and frescoes. But nothing took my breath away more than the sight of my grandmother, Cornelia. She looked like a queen – but her welcoming embrace of my mother and me immediately caused any apprehension to disappear. My surroundings suddenly felt familiar, and I felt at home!

My grandfather, Gaius, returned home from the senate later that after-noon. Although I was momentarily intimidated by the fact he was one of the most important men in the empire, his broad smile and outstretched arms immediately extinguished my fears.

My grandmother soon began making preparations for a grand celebration to announce my mother's and my return. She told me it would be a premier social event of the season. In the meantime, my mother wasted no time in arranging for three of her best tutors to begin my instruction.

Within the first week, I begged my grandfather to allow me to accompany him to the senate. I wanted to witness where and how our most powerful leaders conducted the business of ruling the empire. I hoped I might get a glimpse of the emperor himself. But my grandfather told me Emperor Tiberius had become a recluse and no longer resided in the city. He had delegated the administration of the empire to his Praetorian prefect, Sejanus. I could tell from my grandfather's description he did not think very highly of the man.

"The emperor and the senate are supposed to be two co-equal branches of government," my grandfather explained. "But in practice, the actual authority of the senate has become negligible as the emperor holds the true power. Since the rule of Augustus, our authority has slowly been diminished. As such, our position as senators is mainly one of prestige and social standing rather than actual authority. In recent days, Sejanus has orchestrated it so our independent legislative, judicial, and electoral authority is now completely nonexistent. We function solely as a vehicle through which the emperor exercises his autocratic powers."

As the session unfolded, my grandfather pointed out Sejanus as he was addressing the senate. But based upon the speech he was giving, I had already surmised who he was.

Late in the day, as we were leaving the senate chamber, a voice called out from behind us. "Gaius," he bellowed, "who is this young lady with you today?"

We stopped and turned toward the man as my grandfather answered. "Prefect Sejanus, please allow me to introduce my granddaughter, Lydia."

Sejanus bowed, taking my hand in his, and said, "Lydia, it is an honor to make your acquaintance. I had no idea Gaius had a granddaughter . . . and particularly one so beautiful."

"You are most kind, sir," I replied. "My mother and I have only recently arrived in Rome for a visit with my grandparents."

"Ah, yes, you are Caecilia's daughter," he replied with a smile. "I had heard she had returned for a visit, but my sources failed to tell me about you. I hope you will enjoy your stay. I find that most people who come to Rome love it so much they never leave. I hope that will be true of you, as well. Please call on me if I can be of service in any way."

With that, he walked away – after he and my grandfather clearly exchanged contemptuous glares at one another.

~

6

A GRAND WELCOME IN OUR HONOR

~

"*B*e wary of that man, Lydia," my grandfather warned. "Sejanus is the most powerful man in Rome, second only to the emperor. But he is a treacherous man who is not to be trusted. No matter how much he may ooze charm, his venom is poisonous, and his bite is deadly. Avoid him at all costs."

Since I didn't plan to return to the senate, I thought avoiding him would be no problem.

The next night was the welcome celebration my grandmother had planned for us. It was the second time since my arrival in Rome I felt very unsophisticated. I had never seen such a variety or quantity of exotic foods: pheasant, thrush, oysters, lobster, venison, wild boar, and peacock. In addition, I was told the cooks had prepared two special dishes in my honor: roasted pig stuffed with sausages and hare decorated with wings to resemble Pegasus.

I had also never seen such a large assembly of guests dressed in such finery. To her credit, mother remembered most of their names and greeted each one with her usual grace and charm before introducing me. I worked diligently to follow her lead and remember each name. I realized I was now seeing what her life had been like before she followed my father to Thyatira. It was a very different world!

As the evening progressed, she reintroduced me to Uncle Linus, whom I barely remembered since I was so young when we left Rome. I felt at ease in his company the moment I saw him. He instantly felt like family, and I could see how he and my father had become such good friends and partners.

"Uncle Linus," I asked, "may I come visit you at your place of business? I would like to see all that you are doing here. My father talks of you so fondly and so often."

"It would be my pleasure, my dear," he answered, after first giving my mother a questioning look to make sure it was all right with her. "Let me know what day works best for you, and I will arrange it."

"How about tomorrow?" I replied without hesitating.

My earnestness prompted a chuckle from him before he replied, "You are most definitely your father's daughter! Yes, by all means! Tomorrow it is!"

I was immediately excited about the appointment. My father always told me he credited much of his skill in business to the time he and Uncle Linus worked side by side. I knew I still had much to learn, and I knew my visit would be the beginning of that education. I soon found myself daydreaming about visiting the business as the guests and their chatter faded into the background.

However, I was startled back to reality when I heard someone call my name. "So Lydia, are you enjoying being the center of attention this evening?"

I turned to find myself face to face with Sejanus – and my grandfather was nowhere in sight to come to my rescue. "Prefect Sejanus, I didn't realize I would have the pleasure of seeing you again so soon! It is kind of you to take time out of your busy schedule to join us tonight. You honor my mother and me with your presence."

Suddenly, out of the corner of my eye, I saw my mother approaching. "Have you had the opportunity to meet my mother?" I asked, as I turned to introduce them.

"Yes, your mother and I knew one another before your father stole her heart," Sejanus said, with a sigh of regret. "Caecilia, it is a pleasure to see you again. I know your parents have missed you. I hope you are enjoying your days back here in the city."

"It is a delight to be back and to introduce Lydia to its charms and see the many changes that have occurred in my absence. Not the least of which is how you have risen to a position of such incredible responsibility and authority. I'm sure you must be very proud of your achievements."

My mother continued to flatter him for a few more minutes before she turned to me and said, "Lydia, please go join your grandmother and attend to our other guests while I continue to entertain the prefect. Though he is our most honored guest, we do not want to overlook the others."

Given how awkward I had felt both times around Sejanus, I was grateful to my mother for freeing me from his intimidating gaze. I hastily found my grandmother and shook off the sense of foreboding I felt around the prefect. But as I looked back at them, I noticed their conversation had become a bit animated. Mother looked stern and resolute, and Sejanus looked most displeased.

As I stood watching them, I wondered what they could possibly be discussing in hushed tones. Just then, Uncle Linus and a younger man approached me and captured my attention. "Lydia," Linus began, "my son, Lucius, has just arrived and I would like to introduce him to you."

I could tell Lucius was a few years older than I was, but he and I were most definitely the youngest people in the room. I was pleased to have someone closer in age with whom I could engage in conversation.

He told me he had actually seen me years ago when I was a baby. He was a boy of six when I was born, so his recollection of me was that I was tiny and slept a lot. "Obviously, you've changed quite a lot!" he said somewhat awkwardly.

As the night continued, I learned about his involvement in his father's business and his desire to take it over one day. Our conversation gradually became easier, and I knew we would become good friends.

∾

7

BUSY DAYS AND AN UNEXPECTED OVERTURE

~

*T*he next morning, I asked my mother what she and the prefect had been discussing. "Oh, that," she replied. "It was nothing really. Just a misunderstanding related to something that happened years ago. But I'm certain it is settled now, and we will hear nothing more about it!"

Then she deftly changed the subject. "I noticed that you and Lucius seemed to be enjoying getting to know one another. He has grown into such a handsome young man, and his father tells me he is very gifted in business. He reminds me of your father at that age," she concluded with a smile.

As the days and weeks passed, I found myself thinking less about Thyatira and becoming more preoccupied with Rome. I will confess that Lucius probably had something to do with that!

My days began to follow a consistent schedule. In the mornings I would attend to my studies with my tutors. They pushed me to open my mind as I studied the works of Aristotle. Though he lived almost 400 years before me, his writings on metaphysical philosophy captured my interest as did his theses on psychology and meteorology. And somewhat to my grandfather's chagrin, the tutors, at my mother's direction, pressed me to become even more skilled in debate and oratory.

"All the women in my family are already skilled at debating me on any subject they choose," he sighed. "You don't need any further training in that regard," he added, with a twinkle in his eye and a smile on his lips.

During the afternoons, I was most often with Uncle Linus as he negotiated with his suppliers or charmed his customers. After a time, he began allowing me to take part in the conversations, and we both realized I had a talent for it. I would disarm our suppliers with my youth and gender before I craftily led them to agree to terms that were far better than what my uncle had proposed. More than once they told my uncle that I drove a harder bargain than he did – and he knew they were right.

There was no denying I had the advantage when we were presenting our newest fine linens to our female clientele. They soon accepted that I was an authority on whatever was the most fashionable and durable. Uncle Linus confided to my mother that he was learning just as much from me as I was learning from him. Lucius often accompanied us on those visits, but he soon began to sit back and smile at me as I took control of the conversations.

However, he did take the lead on our evening schedule when he and I attended the galleries and theaters. He had a far greater appreciation for, and knowledge of, the arts than I would ever have. I marveled at his ability to see things in the arts that were much more obscure to me.

One day I asked my grandfather if I could again go with him to the senate, and he agreed to take me. "Grandfather, do you think we will encounter the prefect while we are there?" It was the first I had thought of him since the night of the celebration.

"We will likely see him from a distance," grandfather replied, "but I do not expect he will seek you out."

"I saw that he and mother were having a stern conversation the night he came to our home. Do you know what it was about?" I asked. "Mother would not tell me."

Grandfather hesitated before answering. "Yes, you have a right to know. Years ago, long before Sejanus was prefect and long before your mother and father were married, Sejanus sought my permission to court your mother. I have never trusted the man, even when he was young. But I also knew he would one day rise to a powerful position, so I did not want to offend him. I told him she had her eye on your father, and I had already given my permission to your father to court her, even though I had not yet officially given my blessing.

"He tried unsuccessfully to convince me to change my mind, but at the end of the day, he grudgingly accepted my answer. He and I have been at odds ever since.

"That night at the celebration, since your father is not here, he asked your mother for her permission to court you. There is no question he is the second most powerful man in the empire – at least for now. You would want for nothing, and you would immediately rise to the pinnacle of Roman society. But your mother also knows the man's heart. He is old enough to be your father, but he has absolutely none of your father's good character. Your mother would never agree to allow you to enter into what she knows would become a loveless relationship.

"But your mother also wisely knew to respond carefully. He is the prefect, after all. Many are the men who have been imprisoned – or worse – for having said 'no' to him. She first told him how flattered the family would be to learn the prefect had expressed interest in her daughter. She told him it was a great honor, beyond all imagination! But then she told him you are much too young to enter into such a commitment right now; and regardless, your age difference would prevent your father from ever agreeing to such a union. She again thanked him for honoring you and the family in such a way but told him her answer was 'no.' There could be no further discussion.

"I would venture to say the only person in Rome today who could get away with speaking to him like that is your mother. I believe he still has feelings for her. I believe his interest in courting you was because you are so much like her – in every way. But he uncharacteristically accepted her decision. He would never want the matter to be known publicly because it would damage his reputation if others knew he had been refused. So, he has not mentioned it again. He will now avoid talking to you or acknowledging you in any way. His pride will prevent him from doing so. He needs to treat you with indifference."

"I had no idea!" I told my grandfather. "I owe my mother a greater debt than I could ever imagine – in more ways than one."

8

THE YEARS PASS QUICKLY

~

*T*he first anniversary of our arrival in Rome came around quickly. The year had been a whirlwind of new experiences. Rome had become my home even though I longed to see my father and brother. My heart had been captured by its sophistication, its opportunities, and its openness to new ideas. I found myself with greater prospects than I had ever envisioned in Thyatira. Here I could be the woman I wanted to be – enlightened, cosmopolitan, and successful. Given my youthful outlook, I firmly believed there was no limit to what I could do.

My grandfather was my greatest champion. He encouraged me to stretch my wings and fly. Whenever my grandmother commented I was "stretching" beyond the bounds of propriety for a young woman my age, he would always retort, "The gods have given her wings to stretch those boundaries. She will set the standards by which others will one day aspire to achieve!"

I counted my time with all my family as precious, but I treasured my time with my grandfather the most; we had become very close. That's why the news I received from my mother one afternoon hit me hard. I was working alongside Uncle Linus when I received her message. It read: "Please come home at once. Something has happened!"

My mother was never overly dramatic, so I knew the matter must be urgent and I hurried home. As I entered the house, I saw my mother and grandmother consoling one another. Through her tears, my mother haltingly told me, "Your grandfather collapsed on the senate floor this afternoon. His heart appears to have just stopped. There was nothing anyone could do. Your grandfather is dead."

My legs buckled beneath me. I would have collapsed to the floor if my Uncle Aurelius had not reached out to steady me. He, his wife, Diana, and my younger cousin, Pudens, had also just learned the news and had immediately come to the house. To say we were all in shock would be an understatement. My grandfather had been the picture of health.

The days immediately following were a blur. Because of my grandfather's position in the senate, his funeral took on the magnitude of a public event over multiple days. He was laid out in his finest toga and wore a wreath that reflected his station. Even through my tears, I admired just how handsome he was. His body was placed on display in the main hall of our home for two days before being taken to the senate meeting chamber so the public could pay their respects.

My Uncle Aurelius was given the honor of bringing the public eulogy. I secretly wished I could have done it, but there was no doubt that would have not only been inappropriate but scandalous. My grandfather's cronies told my uncle the eulogy would be a good way for him to show the people he was ready to take his father's place in the senate.

All of Rome's ruling elite were in attendance. Even the prefect made a brief appearance. I watched as he spoke a few quiet words to my mother and grandmother. Though I knew he and my grandfather had never seen eye to eye, I was grateful he had come to pay his respects. I did notice, however, he never even glanced in my direction.

Following the eulogy, a public feast was held to honor my grandfather's memory. It continued for several hours until it was time for the procession to carry his body to the crematory pyre. The streets were lined with people paying their respects. Once his body was cremated, my grandfather's ashes were placed in an urn and interred in the cemetery reserved for the city's elite. My uncle and grandmother commissioned the creation of a suitable monument to mark my grandfather's final resting place.

Our lives gradually settled into a new normal. My father sent his heartfelt sympathies and condolences and asked my mother if he should come join us in Rome. She told him that wasn't necessary, but she would be delaying her return to Thyatira so she could stay and comfort her mother during her time of grief.

My uncle assumed my grandfather's seat in the senate. He and my aunt soon moved into my grandparents' home, taking occupancy as its new master and mistress. We had been in Rome for almost three years when my mother approached me about returning to Thyatira. Though my heart longed to see my father and brother, it longed even more to remain in Rome.

I knew my staying would help soften the absence of my mother for my grandmother. And truth be told, I didn't want to leave Lucius. Though we had not discussed marriage, it was becoming obvious to us, and all those around us, that day was approaching. I had decided I would not marry until I was twenty-one, and that was still two years away. In the meantime, I wanted to continue my education – both in my studies and in business. My mother agreed I should remain.

Lucius and I accompanied my mother to meet the ship that would carry her back to Thyatira. One of my grandmother's servants would be her companion on the voyage home.

Just before my mother boarded the ship, she turned to me and said, "Lydia, when we arrived in Rome, you were a wide-eyed girl. You have become an accomplished young woman with the poise and ability to accomplish anything you set your mind to do. Though I go with a sad heart knowing I am leaving you behind, I go with a heart that could not be prouder of who you are. I know you do not seek a husband *within* whom you will find purpose, but rather one *with* whom you will find purpose together. If you decide Lucius is that one, you have your father's and my blessing.

"Allow Rome to continue to teach you, but do not forget that Thyatira is in your heart. One day you will return to us. And you will know when that day has arrived."

~

9

THE DAY ARRIVES

~

a year later, when I was twenty, Lucius and I formally announced our engagement. We made plans to marry on my twenty-first birthday. Our engagement seemed to spark new life in my grandmother. She immediately began making all the plans. I was grateful for her help, and she was pleased to have the occasion to occupy her mind. Though I was no longer the unrefined sixteen-year-old who had arrived in the city, there were still parts of Roman society protocol that my grandmother understood far better than I ever would.

Our business trade continued to prosper. By this point, Uncle Linus considered me a full partner in our dye and linen business. Very few decisions were made without my being consulted. Linus said he was keeping my father apprised of my progress throughout my time in Rome.

A few weeks before Lucius and I were to be married, Linus confided in me, "I have told your father we would be foolish to exclude you from the management of the business. You understand it as well, if not better, than we do. Plus, you have a gift for negotiating the best price while leaving our customers and suppliers with a smile on their faces."

Then he added with a laugh, "I told your father if Lucius didn't ask you to marry him, I was going to – so we would be assured of your continued involvement in the business!"

Lucius knew how his father felt and told me he completely agreed. He was not threatened by my ability; rather, he felt our talents complemented one another – and I thought so too!

There was an uproar in Rome exactly one month before our wedding. Uncle Aurelius had been reporting for some time that the senate was receiving mixed messages from Emperor Tiberius about his confidence in Prefect Sejanus. Supporters were beginning to take sides and declare their allegiance. The senate was waiting to see how the emperor would respond.

On October 18, Sejanus was summoned to a senate meeting by a letter from the emperor, allegedly to grant him additional powers. However, Uncle Aurelius told us that afternoon, "Sejanus entered the senate hall at first light as a directive from the emperor was being read aloud. The letter addressed routine matters of business and Sejanus, as well as other members of the senate, anxiously awaited the announcement. But suddenly the letter took an unexpected turn. Tiberius denounced Sejanus and ordered he be arrested immediately and executed for treason against the emperor."

I couldn't help but feel sad for Sejanus. I would never know if he was really making treasonous plans, but I knew he had been the tragic victim of his own selfish ambition. I silently said a word of thanks to the gods for protecting me from being in the middle of that sadness and tragedy.

There was one element of personal sadness, however, that surrounded my wedding. Three weeks prior to the day of our celebration, I received a letter from my father which read:

MY DEAREST LYDIA,

EVER SINCE THE NEWS OF YOUR ENGAGEMENT, YOUR MOTHER AND I HAVE LOOKED FORWARD TO JOINING YOU IN ROME FOR THE OCCASION OF YOUR WEDDING. PLEASE KNOW HOW MUCH WE WOULD HAVE RELISHED BEING THERE WITH YOU AND LUCIUS TO CELEBRATE YOUR SPECIAL DAY. BUT, ALAS, CIRCUM-STANCES HAVE ARISEN THAT WILL PREVENT US FROM DOING SO.

DO NOT BE ALARMED, BUT MY PHYSICIANS HAVE DIAGNOSED ME WITH AN ILLNESS CALLED "PHTHISIS." IT IS CHARACTERIZED BY PROLONGED EPISODES OF FEVER AND FITFUL COUGHING. THEY HAVE ADVISED ME THAT A LONG JOURNEY WOULD NOT BE IN MY BEST INTEREST AT THIS TIME. THEY CONTINUE TO CONFINE ME TO MY BED AND TREAT ME WITH THEIR REMEDIES. THEY ASSURE ME THAT IF I FOLLOW THEIR ADVICE THE ILLNESS WILL PASS.

IT IS NOT SOMETHING THAT YOU NEED TO BE CONCERNED ABOUT. I WILL GET BETTER. BUT IT HAS COME AT A VERY INCONVENIENT TIME. I HAVE ENCOURAGED YOUR MOTHER TO COME TO ROME WITHOUT ME, BUT SHE IS REFUSING TO DO SO. SO, REGRETTABLY WE WILL NEED TO CELEBRATE WITH YOU FROM AFAR. PLEASE KNOW THAT OUR THOUGHTS AND HEARTS ARE WITH YOU, AND PLEASE DO NOT ALLOW OUR ABSENCE TO CAST A SHADOW ON YOUR SPECIAL DAY.

WITH ALL MY LOVE,

YOUR FATHER

In my father's absence, Uncle Linus did me the honor of giving me away to marry Lucius. Despite my parents' absence, it was a joyful day. The arrangements, all handled by my grandmother down to the smallest details, were perfect. She again remarked it was one of the social events of the year in Rome. But that honestly didn't make much difference to me. All I cared about was marrying the one with whom I wanted to spend the rest of my life!

That day I moved out of the palatial dwelling that had been my home for the past six years – now the home of Uncle Aurelius and Aunt Diana. I moved into the more modest home of a successful merchant and tradesman with my husband. In many ways, this house felt more like home, and I waved goodbye to the provincial girl of my past.

My father and mother continued to write that my father's health was improving, and they assured me there was no reason for me to return to Thyatira. However, tragedy soon struck right there in Rome. The year following my marriage, my grandmother was struck with a fever that passed through the city. Aunt Diana and I did all we could to nurse her and keep her comfortable. But nothing the physicians did was able to change the course of her fever. Ten days after falling ill, she died.

Her funeral was much less grand than my grandfather's. We buried the urn with her ashes beside those of my grandfather. I missed them both, and I would often walk to the cemetery and stand by their monument and talk to them. Somehow, I felt they were both still giving me good counsel – even from the grave.

Though I was grateful for the family around me – Lucius, Linus, Aurelius, Diana, and Pudens – I found myself missing my family in Thyatira. Rome no longer felt quite the same without my grandparents. For the first time in six years, I considered returning to Thyatira. I believed my time in Rome may soon be drawing to an end.

One morning I awakened to the news that the day of my return had arrived. My father had died. His condition had worsened – apparently at an alarming rate. My mother needed me … and truth be told, I needed her. Uncle Linus agreed that Lucius and I needed to go. We needed to comfort my family, but we also needed to tend to business affairs in Thyatira. He would keep everything running smoothly in Rome, but my brother would need our help in Thyatira.

Lucius made our travel arrangements, and we said goodbye to our family and friends in Rome not knowing when, or if, we would see them again. My voyage to Rome years ago had been exciting, but this trip was filled with sadness. I was despondent about leaving Rome, but I was absolutely heartbroken to return to a Thyatira that no longer included my father.

10

THE SURPRISE THAT AWAITED ME

~

*I*t took us two weeks to sail from Rome to Miletus, then another six days to make our way overland to Thyatira. As we stood on the hill overlooking the city, I was surprised that it looked much smaller than I remembered. I also missed seeing the grand buildings I had grown so accustomed to in Rome. But the hills surrounding the city were still as lush and beautiful as I remembered them.

We arrived at my parents' home just before nightfall. There was a part of me that hoped the message I had received was all a mistake – and my father would be there to greet me at the door. But that was not the case; my mother opened the door.

She looked worn and tired. I had never seen her like this. My father's illness and death had taken a great toll on her. She clung to me in a welcoming embrace, but it was more than just joy and relief to see us; she needed to draw from my strength.

Janus came into the room a few minutes later. My eighteen-year-old brother was now quite the man, looking ever so much like our father. But he too looked haggard, as if the weight of the world now rested on his shoulders.

The servants prepared a meal, and Lucius and I gratefully ate since we were hungry from our journey. But I noticed my mother and brother ate very little. I quickly realized the confident mother I had last seen in Rome was now completely overwrought with grief. Janus wasn't in much better shape. He was now the man of the house and the leader of our family business. However, the first was a position he wasn't ready for; the second was a role he never wanted.

I knew they both needed me to be strong right now – to help them walk through their grief and to navigate all the responsibilities they were facing. That night, Lucius and I listened as they expressed their pain, and we all cried together. We would talk about next steps later, but for now they needed to release the sorrow they had been holding in.

None of us got much sleep that night, but the glimmer of dawn reminded us that no matter how dark things may be, the sun will always rise to help us find the way. I suggested we all rest for a few hours. Then Janus and I would go to the family's place of business later in the morning. Lucius stayed with my mother and brightened her spirits with stories about Rome.

I had always known my father was an excellent salesman. Uncle Linus was always quick to remind me no one could outsell my father – but then he would add, "except you." But Linus had also confided that my father did not watch costs as closely as he should. That was one of the talents Linus contributed to their partnership. But their physical distance apart kept Linus from monitoring the business in Thyatira as closely as was needed.

Our business in Thyatira always appeared to be thriving because my father was very adept at borrowing money and enlisting new investors. Those funds offset the losses my father was actually incurring. Somehow, he had been able to juggle it all. But now that he was gone, the lenders and investors did not have that same confidence in my brother. They were demanding immediate payment, and as Janus told me, "There is no money with which to pay them!" My father had been deep in debt, and now the responsibility fell to us to pay off that debt.

Gratefully, I had not only acquired my father's sales ability, but I had also been an attentive student of my Uncle Linus. I knew we could make the business as profitable as the one in Rome; all it required was time. And it was up to me to convince the lenders and investors to give us that time.

Most of the men my father dealt with would remember me as the adorable little girl who followed in her father's shadow. So, I knew it would be hard for them to see me as a capable young businesswoman. I needed to assure them that the three of us – my brother, my husband, and I – were capable of providing them with the income they had expected to receive from my father. It would require every ounce of my sales ability.

I sent an invitation to the lenders and investors from Janus, Lucius, and me that read, "Please honor us with your presence at our place of business two weeks from today, at which time we will outline how you will be repaid the capital you entrusted to our father, together with the income your trust in him has yielded." Though I had no idea what the plan was going to be, I had at least given myself a two-week reprieve.

I dispatched Janus to work with the dye makers; he had always demonstrated an affinity for that part of the business. I was confident he would discover ways of reducing our costs without sacrificing quality – needed changes I knew my father had always resisted. Lucius had spent a lot of time in the linen shops in Rome. I tasked him with the responsibility of reducing our costs in that area. And I started meeting with our main patrons to convince them why our products were worth an increase in price.

By the end of the two-week period, we had increased our profit margins substantially and were able to present a plan to our investors and lenders that would repay them in two years' time with a handsome profit as well. They were so impressed with our work they unanimously agreed – and I don't think any of them saw me as that adorable little girl walking in her father's shadow any longer.

∿

11

A LIFE IS GIVEN, AND A LIFE IS TAKEN

~

*A*s the weeks passed, my mother's countenance began to brighten. She took strength from having all of us around her. And though we had never bothered her with business concerns, she could tell things had improved. She sensed Janus's relief and his confidence in me to provide the necessary leadership.

It surprised me that I was no longer homesick for Rome. I was gradually embracing Thyatira as the home I once held close to my heart, and I was thriving in the opportunity to lead our business. However, I was painfully aware that it was still a man's world. Representatives from the guild invited Janus and Lucius to take the seat vacated by my father; they never considered inviting me. But for now, I tried to be content with the progress we had made.

One week later, those concerns were set aside when I realized I was expecting my first child. The news of the baby breathed even more life into our home and family. Somehow the skies continued to brighten.

The favorite topic at every family gathering after that was whether Lucius's and my child would be a boy or a girl. Lucius and Janus were hoping for a boy. My mother vacillated –some days she wanted a boy, other days a girl. But I never wavered. I was trusting the gods for a daughter. I prided myself on having a strength of character I had inherited from my mother, and she had inherited from her mother. I wanted the opportunity to pass that strength on to my daughter.

The day of the baby's arrival came quickly for some, but I will confess it seemed much longer for me. As the months passed, I developed a greater appreciation for all my mother had gone through to bring me into the world. It doesn't matter how much your mother shares with you, you never really understand until you experience it for yourself!

I had just returned home from meeting with one of our patrons when I knew the time had come. I sent our servant, Sergius, to get the midwife as his wife, Oppia, and my mother helped me prepare. I knew Lucius would be of no help at this point, so I suggested he go for a long walk. My labor continued throughout the night and into the next morning. But finally, I was rewarded with the cries of . . . a baby girl.

"What will you name her?" my mother asked.

"We will name her Valeria," I answered. "Because she will grow up to be brave and strong."

"Just like her mother," my mother smiled through tears of joy. I knew she was wishing my father were here to witness the birth of his first grandchild.

Valeria lived up to her name from the time she was a little girl, demonstrating the same strength of character I had shown at her age. Lucius and I made sure she had a quality education. We hired some of the finest tutors, and when we discovered there were subjects for which experienced teachers were not available, Lucius, my mother, or I taught her. By the time she was ten, she had spent many afternoons with me at our place of business.

Our family business continued to thrive, and we had now expanded our trade into Macedonia. My father would have been proud! We were discussing the possibility of sending a representative to the city of Philippi, which would open up additional opportunities in Macedonia as well as in Thrace. Several of our former investors were pleading with me for the opportunity to invest in our expansion.

It was gratifying that the guild and investors finally acknowledged I was the one running the business. They no longer went to Lucius and Janus to discuss such matters. My husband and brother still held the seat in the guild, but I expected that too would soon change.

Lucius and I had been planning a trip to Rome to visit family. Linus had come to Thyatira for a visit a few years after Valeria was born. He said he came to discuss important business matters, but we all knew he had come to meet his granddaughter! Now another ten years had passed, and we longed for our daughter to spend more time with her grandfather and experience the great city.

A few days before we were to leave on the journey, a fever passed through our city. Lucius, Valeria, and Janus all came down with it. Gratefully, my mother and I escaped it, so we were able to care for the others. The midwife showed us how to prepare and apply the poultice being used to treat those with fever.

Valeria and Janus began to improve after several days and gradually regained their strength. But Lucius was showing no signs of improvement. I spoke to the midwife about trying a different treatment, but she told me there was nothing more she knew to do. I had never been a deeply religious woman, but I even called out to the gods to heal my husband. But those cries proved to be no more effective than the poultice.

On the ninth day of his fever, Lucius died. Though I had walked through the pain with my mother and grandmother when they lost their husbands, I realized you cannot truly understand how it feels to lose a spouse until you experience that grief yourself. Thankfully, my mother was there to help me through every step of my journey.

I've never told this to anyone, but I sometimes wonder if I would have made it through had my mother not been right beside me. Yes, I had my daughter to think about. She had just lost her father – much too soon. She needed me, and I needed to be strong for her. But truthfully, I had no strength left in me . . . and I had no gods to call upon.

I relied heavily on my mother's strength to make it out of that valley. And while I didn't realize it at the time, it was my husband's death that set me on a mission to find the true meaning of life. What was the purpose of life amid all this pain and death? I'd lost Lucius. I'd almost lost Valeria. The purpose had to be more than live well and die. And it most certainly wasn't the dye and cloth business!

∼

12

SEARCHING FOR THE UNKNOWN

∽

*W*ithout Lucius to help shoulder the responsibility, I had to assume his duties of managing the linen shops. I worked hard and in time increased the number of shops under our management. Having already been recognized as the manufacturer of the highest-quality dye, we were now also recognized as the largest supplier of dyed linen in Thyatira. Our business had never been better.

The guild could no longer ignore my accomplishments. They risked angering the patrons with their prejudicial disrespect. Reluctantly, they granted me a seat on the guild despite the reservations voiced by several longtime members. My only regret the day the seat was awarded to me was that my father and husband were not there to witness it. But I knew they both would have been proud of my accomplishment.

Looking back, I realize my increased workload was my way of masking the pain of losing Lucius. But in doing so, I robbed Valeria of the mother she needed. I am so thankful my mother was there to fill that void; but, nonetheless, I was wrong in what I did. The worst part is it cost me precious time with my daughter that I will never get back.

Around that time, I met a woman about my age named Rebecca. She also was an eldest daughter working for her father. He had established one of the successful linen shops we had recently acquired, but I quickly determined *she* was the primary reason for the shop's success. Her gender prevented her from receiving the recognition she deserved. But I planned to change that!

The more I got to know Rebecca, the more I admired her character. Since Lucius's death, I had become more interested in pursuing spiritual ideas. I quickly decided the Roman gods held no interest for me; they were simply imaginative stories. And the sun god, Apollo, who is so prominent in our city, held no place in my heart.

One day I asked Rebecca what she believed, and she began to tell me about the God of the Jews. Instead of a plethora of self-centered gods, she told me how her people, the Israelites, had been chosen by One called Jehovah God to be His people.

"The God of our patriarchs delivered us from slavery at the hands of our Egyptian taskmasters over 1,500 years ago and eventually led us to a land He promised to give us," she told me. "Our people prospered under His hand until we were taken captive by the Assyrians and Babylonians due to our disobedience to Him."

As she explained more about Him, I began to understand He was a just and compassionate God – not fickle – but true to His word. The more she spoke about Him, the more curious I became. I wasn't ready to join her in worship, but I could not get this God out of my mind.

As the months passed, I assigned additional responsibility to Rebecca. I was confident she could lead our other linen shops to become even more efficient. I was right! Within months, we were able to seek out additional patrons because of our increased production capability.

Janus and I decided we needed to make her a partner in our business. That action led to two important life changes for me. Though Valeria was with me most afternoons at the business, I still spent very little quality time with her. So, I decided to reduce my work hours and instead plan more mother-daughter activities with Valeria. She was approaching her sixteenth birthday, and I knew our remaining days would pass quickly.

I was mindful of the time my mother and I had spent together in Rome when I was Valeria's age. Those years had made an indelible impression on my life. That prompted me to consider doing the same with Valeria. It would give her time with her grandfather, Linus, and Uncle Aurelius, as well as an education that would be unmatched. But I could not find peace with the decision. Even my mother counseled me to consider an alternate plan.

That is when the idea for the second big change began to form. Our Roman heritage had always influenced our lives, but I also knew our Macedonian blood had helped shape us. I could hear my father's words playing over and over again in my head: "Lydia, Macedonian blood flows through your veins. Be true to your heritage and honor your Macedonian forefathers."

Our heritage was drawing me to take my daughter to Macedonia. But there was also a business opportunity there. Janus and Rebecca were quite capable of overseeing our business operations in Thyatira just as Linus was doing in Rome. This would be an opportunity to expand our business into Macedonia – and in many ways, to return to the place where it all started. And who better to do that than Valeria and me?

When I shared the idea with my mother, she agreed. "Your father would be so proud of you. You would be doing something he always wanted to do. In many ways, you and Valeria would be helping him achieve an unfulfilled dream. You should do it, Lydia! You will never know what could come from your time there if you don't."

"Should I return to the homeplace of our ancestors, the city of Pella?" I asked, not really expecting an answer.

"No," my mother replied. "Go to the city of Philippi. It is the new gateway to Macedonia."

I knew the moment she spoke those words I was to go there – but I had no idea why my heart had such certainty!

13

MY ARRIVAL IN PHILIPPI

~

$\mathcal{T}$wo months later, Valeria and I – together with our two servants, Sergius and Oppia – set out for Philippi. We traveled overland to Smyrna where we boarded a riverboat that navigated along the coast to Troas. After resting there overnight, we boarded the ferry and crossed the northern tip of the Aegean Sea landing at the island of Samothrace. The next day we continued on the rest of our journey and arrived at the harbor of Neapolis. It took us nine days to make the journey from Thyatira to the coast of Macedonia.

The minute we arrived in the harbor we knew we had stepped into a different world – it was a true mixture of diverse cultures. The port and surrounding towns were originally established by my Macedonian ancestors about 400 years earlier to mine gold. Soldiers had been assigned to several garrisons to protect the mining operations. One of those forts, situated sixteen kilometers inland from Neapolis, was the town of Philippi, named in honor of King Philip II, the father of Alexander the Great. For 200 years, it served as a strategic military outpost.

But that all changed when Macedonia came under Roman rule. One of Rome's massive accomplishments soon after conquering the region was the construction of the Via Egnatia, a highway built on the backs of slave labor that stretched almost 800 kilometers (nearly 500 miles) from the Adriatic Sea to the Aegean Sea. It created an efficient trade route on which to move soldiers and goods by land from Italy to Asia and back again.

Located at its eastern end, Philippi became a gateway center – politically, commercially, militarily, and culturally. The city was redeveloped using a pattern similar to that of Rome and was colonized by veteran soldiers, many of whom were from the elite Praetorian guard. Other Roman citizens seeking opportunity and good fortune also flocked to the city, and its borders eventually extended to Neapolis.

My first order of business was to introduce myself to the local Roman magistrate. I knew that a woman with a small entourage planning to take up residence and establish a business in the city – all without a man – would raise questions. I wanted to answer them before they even arose.

The ferry captain had explained to me the city magistrate was in fact two military officers who had been appointed to be the duumviri (the co-magistrates responsible for governing the city). Officers Camillus and Marcellus, the duumviri of Philippi, were easy to locate; they resided in a large home that overlooked the entire city. I found out they had been assigned to their positions by the Roman senate a little more than two years earlier.

When I first began speaking with the men, they showed little interest in me and even less courtesy. So I decided to get their attention. "Your honors," I began, "I am a merchant of purple cloth from the city of Thyatira seeking to expand our trade into this region. My father's ancestors are from this part of the world, whereas my mother is part of an important family in Rome. You may have heard of her deceased father and my grandfather, Senator Gaius, as well as my uncle, Senator Aurelius."

Both men immediately gave me their full attention. "Yes, we are very familiar with your grandfather and your uncle," Camillus, the older of the two, replied. "In fact, your uncle presented our credentials before the senate just two years ago so we might be appointed to this office. We are in his debt."

Marcellus nodded. "Yes, we wholeheartedly welcome you to our city. We are honored that someone of your station has chosen to come here. But we must ask, given the business you plan to establish here, will your husband be joining you?"

"No, I'm afraid not," I replied. "Sadly, he passed away almost three years ago. Today I run our business. My grandfather always taught me to apply myself. I work in partnership with my brother, who manages our operations in Thyatira, and a good family friend who manages the business in Rome on the Vicus Sobrius, which as you know houses only the finest businesses of the city." The two men were now practically standing at attention.

"I would appreciate your assistance in finding accommodations that are commensurate with my station for both my daughter and me, as well as my servants," I continued. "And I will need to find a suitable place to conduct my trade in the better part of your business district. In the meantime, where might you recommend we lodge for the evening?"

After that, I wanted for nothing. The duumviri were most attentive to my every need. That evening we stayed in their guest quarters, and the following day we moved into our new home situated on the hill overlooking the city. Once settled, I began to explore the three locations the duumviri suggested might be suitable for my business.

When I entered the second location – and what proved to be the last in my search – I was greeted by a young woman named Naomi. It was a linen shop that appeared to be successfully catering to an elite clientele in the city. From the first moment, I was impressed with Naomi's demeanor. Her father owned the business, but it only took moments to realize she was running it. I could not get over how much she reminded me of Rebecca – her manner, her competence, and her character.

After we talked about business for a while, I changed the subject. "Are you a follower of Jehovah God? Are you a Jew?"

"Yes, I am," she replied. "I am surprised you would ask if I am a Jew. Very few people in our city know about the Jews; there are only a handful of us here. Why do you ask?"

"Because a good friend of mine in Thyatira is Jewish," I answered, "and she has begun to teach me about your beliefs. She told me to find the synagogue when I arrived here in Philippi."

"We don't yet have a synagogue in this city since there aren't enough of us," Naomi explained. "In our religion there must be ten men in order to establish a synagogue, and of our few number most are women. We gather by the river each Sabbath to pray. You are welcome to join us."

"I may do just that," I told her. "Besides, you and I will be spending a lot of time together. I intend to buy your business – so very soon you will be working for me."

∾

14

GATHERING FOR PRAYER

~

There is no question that the city of Philippi has prospered under the influence of Rome. Though the city is surrounded by Macedonian-era walls, vestiges of Roman life have slowly been added to its interior. A forum, or public marketplace, is situated on either side of the main road. It is the center of daily life and houses some of the most prestigious enterprises of the city, including mine. A large theater has also been built for the city's chief entertainment – the Roman games.

On the next Sabbath day, I joined Naomi and four other women along the river as they gathered to pray. I learned that one of the women was also not Jewish. She had been seeking the one true God and had been drawn to the God of the Jews. With the arrival of Valeria, my two servants, and me, we nearly doubled the size of the gathering.

Naomi and the other women took turns reading aloud from their holy book, the Torah. That day they were reading words written by a prophet named Isaiah. After a while, they invited me to read these words:

"The Spirit of the Sovereign Lord is upon Me,
for the Lord has anointed Me
to bring good news to the poor.
He has sent Me to comfort the brokenhearted
and to proclaim that captives will be released
and prisoners will be freed.
He has sent Me to tell those who mourn
that the time of the Lord's favor has come,
and with it, the day of God's anger against their enemies.
To all who mourn in Israel,
He will give a crown of beauty for ashes,
a joyous blessing instead of mourning,
festive praise instead of despair.
In their righteousness, they will be like great oaks
that the Lord has planted for His own glory."[1]

No god I had ever heard of promised to exchange beauty for ashes, blessing for mourning, or praise for despair. Every other god I knew about had always wanted something from me. My desire to know this God of the Jews increased.

The other women began to praise their God, speaking these words in unison:

"I prayed to the Lord, and He answered me.
He freed me from all my fears.
Those who look to Him for help will be radiant with joy;
no shadow of shame will darken their faces.
In my desperation I prayed, and the Lord listened;
He saved me from all my troubles.
For the angel of the Lord is a guard;
He surrounds and defends all who fear Him.[2]

I looked at Valeria, Sergius, and Oppia; tears were streaming down their faces. None of us could describe what was happening, but I sensed a presence I had never felt before. We continued to read and pray throughout the morning – and I didn't want our time to end.

But when it was over, I knew I would return to that place and join those women every week; Valeria and my servants felt the same. The next words in that psalm spoke to me as well:

> *Taste and see that the Lord is good.*
> *Oh, the joys of those who take refuge in Him!*[3]

That's exactly what I wanted to do. I had tasted of His goodness and I wanted to know Him more – His peace, His love, His mercy. The rest of that day and in the days that followed, I continued to hear those words in my mind.

My business in Philippi was flourishing. The purple dye was now arriving regularly from Thyatira on the merchant ships, and we had three linen shops producing our cloth for dyeing. With Naomi overseeing our production in Philippi, I was able to travel to other cities along the Via Egnatia, including Berea and Thessalonica.

Demand for our product increased everywhere I visited once buyers heard that these were the fabrics being worn by the elite of Rome. Ours were becoming the most sought-after fabrics of Macedonia, just as they were throughout Asia and Italy.

Though Valeria was not receiving the Roman education I had hoped for her, she was blossoming as she traveled to different places and experienced a diversity of cultures. Her father would have said she was becoming just like me – and he would have been right! I knew Lucius would be so proud if he could see the young lady she was now.

One day as we were returning to Philippi, Valeria asked, "Mother, we have lived in Macedonia for almost a year. Do you believe we will remain here, or do you think we will move elsewhere?"

"Why do you ask?" I inquired.

"Because I do not want to live anywhere else! I like the sights, the sounds, the sea, and the people. I particularly like Naomi, and our other friends, and our weekly gatherings at the riverbank on the Sabbath. I like the way it makes me feel. It has helped me work through the pain of Daddy's death. I'm not sure if it's the gathering or Jehovah God who has made me feel better. Maybe it's both. All I know is I don't want to leave. I want to stay here and bask in the way it makes me feel."

"So do I, Valeria," I said, as I pondered her words. I couldn't have said it better myself! I had tasted and seen that the Lord is good, and I didn't want to risk losing that feeling.

～

15

AN UNEXPECTED VISITOR AT THE RIVER

❧

One Sabbath day, as everyone in my household was walking to the riverbank, we were approached by a girl at least four or five years younger than Valeria.

"Matron, may I tell you your fortune?" she asked, as she stared at me with a curious expression. "I am able to tell you what will happen in your life – love that will be gained, love that will be lost, fortune that will be gained, and the like. All you have to do is ask me and give me a few coins. I have much I can tell you about yourself."

"I fear there is little you can tell me that I don't already know, my girl," I answered. I saw two men leaning against a tree nearby who were listening to our every word and watching our every move. "But I also fear these men may be taking advantage of you," I said as I looked at the two men. "What is your name, girl?"

"They call me Rumena, matron," the girl replied, "and no, these men do not take advantage of me; they take good care of me and treat me well. I couldn't ask for better, and I know it to be so because I've looked into my future. How about you? Can I tell you what I see in your future?"

"No, Rumena," I responded. "I am not in the habit of giving my coins to line the pockets of men who take advantage of young girls. But if you ever need someone to help you when you are free of their bondage, you come see me."

Then I called out to the men, "And you see that you take good care of her and bring her no harm. Or I will see that you feel the full sting of Roman justice across your backs!"

Both men waved me off and turned their heads, but I knew they had heard me – and knew I was true to my word. After all, the whole city now knew me as the wealthy woman who lives on the hill next to the duumviri.

As we continued to the river, I turned back to Rumena and said, "We are going to the bank of the river to sing and pray to Jehovah God. Would you like to join us?"

She looked at the men and then back to me as she answered, "No, matron, I cannot worship Jehovah God. But thank you for your kindness. And if I ever need a hand, I will come see you."

As we set off, she whispered to me, "You will meet a man there today who will answer all your questions."

I do not believe in fortunetelling so I did not take her words to heart, but I could not get the girl out of mind. She was being used by those men – and though I knew legally she was their property – I couldn't help but ponder how I might rescue her from her life of bondage.

When we arrived at the riverbank, Naomi and the other women were already there. But we were surprised to see four men whom I did not recognize speaking with them. One of the men – slightly older than I am and small of stature – was doing most of the talking. He was introduced to us as Paul from the town of Tarsus.

The other three were his traveling companions. The oldest was a physician named Luke who told us he was from Antioch in Syria. He was the quietest of the four and seemed intent on listening to everything being said. The third man, Silas, was about my age and originally from Alexandria. He told me he had been traveling with Paul for about two years.

Timothy was the youngest of the four and about the age of my cousin, Pudens, but he looked even younger. He was from Lystra and was apparently being mentored by Paul.

The men had just arrived in Macedonia. Paul and Silas had begun their journey in Antioch and the other two had joined them along the way. It soon became obvious that Paul was a learned teacher and preacher.

As we read from the Torah together, Paul opened it to the same writing in Isaiah that I had read on my first Sabbath with the women. The words warmed my heart just as they had before. I had seen how Jehovah God could bring joy where there was mourning and praise where there had been despair.

Paul went on to tell us that the One sent by Jehovah God to set the captives free was named Jesus – the Promised One. He came to earth to be born of a virgin and live a righteous life without sin. His blood was shed on a cross as the covering for our sin. God had come to earth in the person of Jesus to set us free.

Because of His sacrifice on the cross, our mourning and despair could be wiped away – our sins forgiven. But Paul told us Jesus had not remained in the grave after His crucifixion. If He had, we would have had no hope! Rather, He arose from the grave on the third day. He is not a dead sacrifice . . . He is a living Savior!

The more Paul spoke, the more my heart leapt. I knew this was the truth. My spirit within me bore witness. So I asked Paul, "What must I do to be saved?"

He replied, "*Repent of your sins and turn to God, and be baptized in the name of Jesus Christ for the forgiveness of your sins. And you will receive the gift of the Holy Spirit. This promise is to you, to your children, and to those far away – all who have been called by the Lord our God.*"[1]

As I listened, the Lord opened my heart and made it clear what I should do next.

∾

16

COME AND STAY AT MY HOME

~

I knew I must be baptized. We were already on the bank of the river; there would never be a better time. I called out to Paul, "I do repent, and I believe in the name of Jesus. Will you baptize me?"

The next voice I heard, though, was not Paul's – it was Valeria's. "I also repent and believe. And I, too, want to be baptized in the name of Jesus!" I turned to my daughter and we embraced. Within moments, Sergius and Oppia spoke the same confession. All four of us stood there with our arms wrapped around one another, tears of joy streaming down our faces.

With the other men and women as witnesses, Paul baptized the four of us. The other women weren't quite sure what they should do. They did not take their step of belief that day – though each would do so in the days to come.

Once we were standing back on dry land, I asked Paul, "Do you and your companions have a place to stay here in Philippi?"

"God has provided us with a room for the past several nights," he replied.

I felt prompted to invite them to stay in my home. *"If you agree that I am faithful to the Lord,"* I said, *"come and stay at my home."*[1]

I knew it was highly unusual for an unmarried woman to extend such an invitation to four men, but I felt compelled to do so. I believed the Lord had plans for my home that extended beyond simple lodging. Apparently, so did Paul, because after a few moments he accepted my invitation.

Later that day as we ate a meal together, he recounted the journey that had brought them to Philippi.

"After staying with Timothy and his parents for a while, I received their permission to bring him along on a journey I thought would take us only as far as those cities of Asia immediately surrounding Lystra. I had given them assurances we would travel no farther," Paul said. "But those plans had not included the redirection we subsequently received from the Holy Spirit!

"As we approached the cities on the western border of Phrygia, Silas and I were restrained from entering them by the Spirit of the Lord. Rather, He directed us to turn northward and go toward the provinces of Bithynia and Pontus. Though I had not visited those regions, Timothy told us some believers from Iconium had been there to share the Good News. This path would allow us to preach and encourage the believers in those cities – or so I thought.

"But, as we approached that border, the Spirit again redirected us and turned us back toward the west. He again restrained us from entering the cities along the way – including your home of Thyatira. Instead, we found ourselves in the seaport town of Troas on the eastern shore of the Aegean Sea. When we had set out from Antioch, I never envisioned God would lead us there. But obviously He had other plans.

"Our next surprise was when we encountered Luke on the streets of Troas not long after we arrived. 'Shortly after the two of you left Antioch,' he told us, 'the Spirit of the Lord came to me in a dream and told me to come to Troas.' Luke had asked Him, 'For what purpose?' And the Spirit of the Lord had responded, 'I will show you once you get there.'

"Luke questioned whether or not it was really the Lord. But when the Lord directed him a second time, he knew he must act quickly. He arrived in Troas the very morning that Silas, Timothy, and I arrived."

Paul continued, "That night, I had a vision. I saw a man from Macedonia pleading with me, saying, '*Come over here and help us.*'[2] The next morning, I shared my dream with the other men. We all agreed there was no question what God was directing us to do next!

"We boarded a ferry that day and set sail to the harbor of Neapolis. That was four days ago. Today the Spirit of the Lord allowed me to see that the man standing on the shore in my vision was really a group of women praying by the riverbank. The Spirit of the Lord was at work in this place long before we ever set foot on this shore – and what He begins, He will complete!" Paul concluded.

As a new follower of Jesus, I had much to learn and absorb. But it didn't take long before I was taught a painful lesson – the devil does not like his territory invaded.

The day after Paul baptized me, I traveled to Amphipolis on business and took Valeria with me. I told Paul and his companions to make themselves comfortable in my home, and I charged my servants with attending to their needs.

Paul decided to return each morning to the riverbank to teach about Jesus to those who gathered. The crowds grew larger day after day. On the second day, Paul and Silas noticed a young girl following them on the path. They didn't know her, but it was Rumena. As she walked behind them, she began to shout, "*These men are servants of the Most High God, and they have come to tell you how to be saved.*"(3)

This continued for several days until Paul became so exasperated by the distraction he finally spoke up. He had known from the first day it was not Rumena talking but the demon who had control over her. He addressed the demon directly: "*I command you in the name of Jesus Christ to come out of her!*"(4) Instantly it left her – and immediately her shouting stopped.

Paul and Silas continued on their way to the riverbank and began to teach. But it didn't take long for her masters to discover that Rumena's ability to tell fortunes left with the demon – and their hopes of wealth with it. When the two men realized what had happened, they cast her aside and set out to find Paul and Silas.

～

17

WRONGFULLY PUNISHED

~

*M*ost of the townspeople in Philippi were wary of the Jews. They knew Jewish people believed in only one God – which was contrary to their own beliefs. A large number of the residents did not want the Jews living in their city.

But since there were so few Jews, the duumviri had decided they were not a threat. A majority of the people accepted that decision, but there remained a few who would never be trusting or accepting. Rumena's masters knew this smaller group could easily be swayed to attack the Jews and stir the greater population into turmoil.

Within an hour, the two men had worked a small mob into a frenzy, which they then led to the riverbank where Paul and Silas were teaching. The mob grabbed Paul and Silas and dragged them to the center of the forum shouting, *"The whole city is in an uproar because of these Jews. They are teaching customs that are illegal for us Romans to practice."*[1]

If I had been there, I could have spoken on their behalf and calmed the crowd. But God in His sovereignty chose for me to be away from the city. The gathering began to grow even larger. Camillus and Marcellus were summoned to address the matter and rule on what needed to be done to Paul and Silas.

In light of their own religious and racial prejudices, the duumviri did not listen to any defense from Paul or Silas. Instead, they assessed the overwhelming accusations of the crowd and decided to follow their lead. They ordered Paul and Silas to be stripped and beaten. The fact the two men were Roman citizens should have prevented that action, but the duumviri never bothered to ask the question – and they never allowed Paul or Silas to speak. Instead, they ordered the city jailer to severely beat them with wooden rods and lock them in prison. The jailer, on his part, took no chances. He locked them in the inner dungeon and clamped their feet in stocks.

Paul and Silas were wrongfully accused, wrongfully judged, and wrongfully punished. Despite that, Paul later told me, "As we sat in the dungeon, an overwhelming peace came over us – a peace that could only be explained by the presence of the Holy Spirit. Our heads told us we should shout at the top of our lungs with pleas of innocence and injustice, but our spirits told us to lift our voices to God with praises and hymns.

"Around midnight, as the other prisoners were listening to us praying and singing, a great earthquake shook the very foundation of the prison. All the doors flew open, and the chains of every prisoner fell off. Although the prisoners could have fled to freedom, they remained right where they were. They sat there in awe of God, which overshadowed any fear they had of our Roman captors. I don't know with complete certainty, but I believe a number of our fellow prisoners came to faith in Jesus that night.

"My attention was fixed on the jailer. Roman law demands that if a jailer loses a prisoner, he will receive the same punishment as the prisoner. Several of the men imprisoned were facing severe punishments. When the jailer saw the doors were open and feared the prisoners had escaped, he knew the penalty he would face. I watched as he drew his sword to kill himself.

"It would have been easy to justify taking vengeance on our persecutor by allowing him to take his own life. But I knew the jailer was really the prisoner – imprisoned by his own sin. Silas and I were truly freed men – set free from the bondage of sin. I knew I was no more worthy of the grace extended to me through the compassion of Christ than this cruel jailer. So, I shouted out, *'Don't kill yourself! We are all here!'*[2]

"The power of God is what had seized the jailer's attention, but it was the grace and compassion of God that made him understand his need for a Savior. It wasn't the supernatural power of the earthquake that God used to draw this man to Himself; it was a spirit of humility, grace, and kindness that drew him to the Gospel.

"Trembling with fear, the jailer, whose name we learned is Aeropos, asked us, *'Sirs, what must I do to be saved?'*[3] That night, he and all the members of his household heard the Good News, believed, and were baptized. An evening that started with Aeropos subjecting us to severe beatings ended with him washing our wounds and extending us hospitality," Paul concluded.

Valeria and I arrived back in Philippi late that night. Early the next morning, Timothy and Luke reported to me what had happened. They told me Paul and Silas were wrongfully imprisoned; I feared for what had happened to them.

I immediately sought out Camillus and Marcellus. "Do you men know what you have done?" I asked as soon as I entered their hall.

"About what?" they asked, startled by my tone.

"You have ordered that two of the guests living in my home be beaten and imprisoned! Not only have you greatly offended me, but you also have violated the law of the empire by subjecting Roman citizens to illegal treatment! By law, you are required to have given them a fair trial – not punish them at the whim of an angry mob. Believe me when I say, the senate will hear of your offenses!"

The two men looked at one another in fear. Camillus stuttered, "But the witnesses accused them of inciting a riot, and the crowd bore further witness."

"So you took the word of the men who have oppressed that young girl as their slave over the word of two men who are guests in my home?" I demanded. "And you have allowed the very people you told to set aside their prejudices against the Jews to now sway your opinion?

"I can assure you my uncle would never condone the action you have taken. Apparently, his trust has been greatly misplaced in you! I will be sending word to him immediately!"

Camillus and Marcellus looked at one another in fear. "Our honorable patrician, that will not be necessary," Marcellus insisted. "Obviously, a grave error has occurred. Thank you for bringing it to our attention. We relied upon testimony that we now know to be false. We will immediately set it right by sending word for the prisoners to be released."

~

18

A CHURCH IS BORN

~

*T*he soldiers dispatched by the duumviri soon arrived at the jail with this message, *"Let those men go!"*[1]

Aeropos later told me that he was overjoyed to receive the news. He had been considering a way to release Paul and Silas without endangering his family or himself. So he happily entered the jail to announce to Paul, *"The city officials have said you and Silas are free to leave. Go in peace."*[2]

But he was shocked when Paul replied, *"They have publicly beaten us without a trial and put us in prison – and we are Roman citizens. So now they want us to leave secretly? Certainly not! Let them come themselves to release us!"*[3]

When the soldiers reported back to the duumviri that Paul and Silas were refusing to leave, Camillus and Marcellus again became frightened about what would happen to them if news about this made its way to Rome. Would I tell my uncle? Would Paul and Silas report them to the officials in Rome?

They came to me hoping I would come to their defense as an ally. "The men are refusing to leave the jail," Marcellus exclaimed in disbelief. "They want us to go in person to release them! Would you go on our behalf and tell them the matter has been settled, and they don't need to press this any further?"

I hesitated a moment for effect before replying, "No. They apparently want to hear it directly from you. If you want to avoid any repercussions, I suggest you go to them."

Reluctantly, they went to the jail and apologized to Paul and Silas. In all my years, I have never seen a Roman official apologize for anything!

After they asked forgiveness and personally escorted Paul and Silas out of jail, the duumviri begged them to leave the city. They were afraid the mob would erupt again if Paul and Silas remained. Camillus and Marcellus knew if that occurred, they would be caught in the middle.

Paul assured them they would leave after attending to some matters in the city. Camillus and Marcellus nervously watched as Paul and Silas walked to my home. When they arrived, Paul told me, "The Spirit of the Lord has shown me my work here is done. You and your household, together with Aeropos and his household, are the ones the Spirit will use to make the Gospel known to the rest of the city. You will be His witnesses now!"

"But there is so much we have to learn," I said. "How can we learn if there is no one here to teach us?"

"The Spirit of God will guide you in all truth through the Torah you have and the witness about Jesus you have received," Paul replied. "Also, I have come to believe the Lord led Luke here to train up leaders in Philippi. He will remain and assist in that work until he has completed his task."

Paul sent word for Aeropos to come join us as he shared more words of encouragement. Then just before Silas, Timothy, and he left town, Paul said to us, *"Remain faithful to the things you have been taught. You know they are true, for you know you can trust those who taught you."*[4]

Later that day, after the men had departed, Rumena arrived at my home. "Matron, is the one they call Paul here?" she asked.

"No, he and his companions have left the city," I replied. "Why do you seek him?"

"Because he has set me free," Rumena answered. "For as long as I can remember, I have been enslaved by a spirit within me and masters who owned me. I have never been able to go where I wanted to go or do what I wanted to do. But ever since Paul told the spirit to come out of me, I have been set free. The spirit is no longer within me, and my masters have told me to leave them because I can no longer make them wealthy.

"At first, I was in despair, not knowing what I should do. I have always had someone to tell me what to do, but now I am free. I came to ask Paul's advice since he was the one who freed me."

"Rumena, Paul did not set you free. He may have been the one you heard speak the words, but the name of the One who set you free is Jesus. He is the Son of the living God, and He came to earth to set us all free from our sins. Twenty-two years ago, He was crucified on a cross as a sacrifice for our sins. But three days later He rose from the grave just as God promised He would do. He is not dead in a grave. He is alive!

"Think about it! We have always been told that we are to sacrifice ourselves for our gods, but He is a God who sacrificed Himself for us. He came so that you, and I, and Paul could be set free – as well as anyone else who repents of their sins and believes in Him. I was set free just a few days before Paul spoke those words to you.

"Yes, you have been set free," I continued. "But you still have one thing to do. If Paul were here, he would tell you to do the same thing he told me: 'repent of your sins, turn to God, and be baptized in the name of Jesus Christ.'"

"Then that is what I will do," Rumena said, smiling through her tears. "I repent and believe, and I want to be baptized!"

We all walked down to the riverbank that afternoon and Luke baptized Rumena. She became my sister in Christ that day and she moved into my home as one of the members of my household. Her masters couldn't possibly have been more mistaken about her – for she is now a treasure of immeasurable worth!

～

19

THE CHURCH GROWS

~

*I*n the weeks following Paul's departure, we continued to see more men and women declare their belief in Jesus and follow Him in baptism. One of the first to do so was Naomi. I rejoiced in the knowledge that my trusted business partner was now also my sister in Christ.

There were about fifty people, both men and women, gathered at the riverbank that Sabbath morning. Many had come out of curiosity; word had spread about Paul's arrest and release the week before. Others had heard about Rumena's transformation. They had encountered her many times when she offered to tell their fortune. Now she told them what Jesus had done for her.

We read aloud from the Torah the account of God's promise to Abraham:

The Lord took Abram outside and said to him, "Look up into the sky and count the stars if you can. That's how many descendants you will have!" And Abram believed the Lord, and the Lord counted him as righteous because of his faith.[1]

Then Luke told us, "Just as Abraham believed God, and God counted him as righteous because of his faith, the real children of Abraham are those who put their faith in God. What's more, the Scriptures looked forward to this time when God would make us Gentiles right in His sight because of our faith. God proclaimed this good news to Abraham long ago when He said, 'All nations will be blessed through you.' So all who put their faith in Christ share the same blessing Abraham received because of his faith."

In addition to Naomi, two other women – Euodia and Syntyche – and a man named Epaphroditus repented of their sins, placed their faith in Christ, and were baptized that day. All of us were excited to share our newfound faith with everyone we could. We began gathering each night in my home to read God's Word and learn more about Jesus. Our numbers continued to increase until we eventually had to move outside.

The large gathering began to draw the attention of my neighbors – the duumviri. Anytime large crowds gathered, the duumviri were always watchful to ensure the gathering was not fostering rebellion against Rome. I expected a visit from them soon – and I was not disappointed.

Camillus and Marcellus arrived at my home under the pretense of paying a social visit, but the conversation soon took a turn. "Lydia," Camillus began, "we have been watching the nightly gatherings outside your home with growing interest. We know some of the people are Jews, but many like yourself and our city jailer are not. As you know, we have been watching the Jews to make sure they do not disrupt our city with their beliefs. However, as we understand it, you are now hosting this gathering to worship and teach about the God of the Jews. Is that true?"

"Many of us who are gathered believe the God of the Jews is the one true God – the Creator of us all," I replied. "Like you, I have heard the many stories over the years about the Greek gods, the Roman gods, and the Macedonian gods. But I have always found those stories to be myths and fables with no basis in fact. But a few years ago, I was introduced to Jehovah God – the God of the Jews. And there is too much historical and scientific fact to dispute His existence.

"But I didn't come to believe in Him until I learned He had sent His Son, Jesus, to suffer death on a Roman cross as the sacrifice for our sin. He died as a sacrifice for us all. But He didn't remain in the grave, He rose again. I know of no other god who was willing to lay down his life for me. I know of no other god who has died and come back from the dead. And yes, I worship Him . . . because He is worthy of my worship."

"We have heard about this Jesus," Marcellus responded. "We have been told that He declared Himself to be the King of the Jews and died a humiliating death on the cross. But He sounds as if He was a pathetic creature."

"He made the blind to see, the lame to walk, and the dead to come alive. He stilled the winds and the waves, cast out demons, and overcame death itself," I responded. "There isn't anything pathetic about Him, Marcellus!

"The men you arrested – Paul and Silas – simply spoke in His name and a demon was cast out of Rumena. Just ask her former masters if they believe what happened to her was true. But then again, you don't need to, do you? They already told you it was true.

"So, what would you two have me do – deny the truth? Ignore the irrefutable reality I know to be true? My Roman education tells me to embrace truth. My grandfather Gaius taught me to stand for what is true! Would you now wish me to deny it because there are some who are close-minded to truth? No, I think not. I don't believe the men my uncle sponsored to be the duumviri of this city would show such little intellect and conviction.

"Rather, I invite you to no longer stand at a distance but come join our gathering tonight so you might better understand the truth. After all, as it is said, the truth will set you free!"

I truly hoped the duumviri would be open to seeking the truth of the Gospel, but they responded as I feared they would. "Thank you for your kind invitation, Lydia," Camillus replied, "but we will remain neutral on this matter. We will, however, guarantee you that no one will be permitted to disrupt your gathering. You, and your uncle, have our assurance of that."

The duumviri never questioned me again or threatened to disrupt our gathering. But sadly, they remained steadfast in their unbelief.

As the weeks passed, more men and women continued coming to faith. The Spirit of the Lord raised up those with spiritual gifts to be elders, deacons, and teachers. Among them were Aeropos, Epaphroditus, and Clement. I was grateful Paul had left Luke to shepherd us.

∾

20

MY RETURN TO THYATIRA

∾

*T*wo years later, I began to sense it was time for me to return to Thyatira. The church was growing in number and maturity under the pastoral leadership of Luke. Though we both knew he would one day soon move on, our elders believed God was raising up Clement to become the next pastor of the church. Luke was working closely with him to prepare him for the role. We all sensed God was raising up the needed leadership from within.

My business in Philippi was also prospering under the guiding hand of Naomi. I was confident the business would continue to thrive without my presence, despite Naomi's protests to the contrary. Also, she, Valeria, and I had all had a part in mentoring Rumena over the past two years and we were all equally confident in her ability to assist Naomi.

Valeria had recently turned nineteen, and I longed for her to spend some time in Rome with her grandfather Linus. But before she did, I wanted us to reunite with my mother in Thyatira. Janus had sent me word her health was declining, so I did not want to delay much longer.

The Spirit of the Lord was giving me confidence that my work here was done, so I arranged passage for Valeria, Sergius, Oppia, and me to return home. Before I departed, though, I knew there was one last thing I needed to do.

The duumviri were somewhat surprised to see me. Though we had by no means hidden from one another, our interactions had been limited over the past couple of years. But I knew my presence had been a deterrent against them doing anything that might harm the church.

"Camillus and Marcellus," I began, "I have come to thank you for all the assistance you have provided me since my arrival in Philippi. I plan to travel to Rome in the near future, and I will be certain to pass along my compliments to my uncle regarding you."

"You are most kind," Camillus replied humbly. "It has been our great privilege to assist you in whatever small way we have been able to do so. We do, however, regret you will be leaving our fair city." Then he added respectfully, "You have become one of our most prestigious residents, and we know your presence will be greatly missed by the entire city."

"Please be assured, Camillus, that I will continue to stay in close communication with my business associates here, no matter where I am. If I have any concerns, I will not hesitate to call upon you – or my uncle. And I am confident you will respond to my requests with the same level of courtesy you have always shown." The expressions on the two men's faces made it clear my point had not been lost on them. I could now leave knowing they would not create any problems for the church.

Three days later we boarded the ferry to Troas, and a week after that we arrived back in Thyatira. It was good to be home. Though God had done much in our lives through our time in Philippi, it had never felt like home.

Valeria and I spent the next several days catching up on all the news with mother and Janus.

Janus had married while we were away. He and his wife, Clelia, now had a baby son. I was enjoying getting to know my little nephew, and Valeria, her little cousin. But Janus's reports about our mother had been understated. I wasn't prepared for how frail she had become. The strength and confidence she always exuded were gone.

Though I had written my family about my newfound faith in Jesus, I was grateful for this opportunity to tell them in person. I shared with them the truth I had learned from the Scriptures and the good news of Jesus. Valeria and I explained how Jesus had transformed our lives and the lives of so many in Philippi. I was grateful that mother, Janus, and Clelia all continued to ask me questions. They obviously had a desire to know and understand.

By our third day together, all three of them confessed their faith in Jesus. I baptized my brother in the river, and he and I together baptized our mother because of her frailty. Janus then baptized his wife. It was a great night of rejoicing as the rest of our household also placed their faith in Jesus and were baptized.

Two weeks later, I knew God had orchestrated the timing of our return to Thyatira. It was on that day we said goodbye to my mother as she passed from this life into the next. Because of her decision to follow Jesus, I knew I would see her again. We would be parted for a time, but we would spend all of eternity together in the presence of Jesus.

"Thank You, Lord," I prayed as I knelt beside her bed. "Thank You for allowing me to tell her about You and for granting me the opportunity to see her surrender her life to You. Thank You for saving her. And thank You for loving her – and all of us – so much that You sent Jesus."

To the best of our knowledge, there were no other believers in the city outside of our household, so there was no church. We made preparations to bury her body in a grave next to my father's. We knew our many friends would want to pay their respects. So we invited everyone to come to her graveside as Janus and I spoke.

As the oldest child, I did most of the speaking. It was the first time the Gospel was shared publicly in our city. Though I was grieving my mother's death, the Spirit of God gave me the strength and the words to share. I told them how I had placed my faith and trust in Jesus, as had my mother and the rest of our family. "We know right where our mother is. She's with Jesus! We will see her again . . . and so can you!"

21

RESISTANCE FROM THE GUILDS

~

*A*fter my mother's body had been committed to the ground, many friends returned home with us for a meal. I was overwhelmed by the number who told me they wanted to hear more about Jesus. After we ate, I invited those who wanted to learn more to stay.

Well into the evening I told them, "Since we were children, we have been told to seek the gods. Well, I am here to tell you about the *God who made the world and everything in it. Since He is Lord of heaven and earth, He doesn't live in man-made temples like Apollo, or the other gods of the Romans and the Greeks. Human hands can't serve His needs – for He has no needs. He himself gives life and breath to everything, and He satisfies every need.*

"From one man He created all the nations throughout the whole earth. He decided beforehand when they should rise and fall, and He determined their boundaries. His purpose was for the nations to seek after Him and perhaps feel their way toward Him and find Him – though He is not far from any one of us.

"For in Him we live and move and exist. As some of our own poets have said, 'We are His offspring.' And since this is true, we shouldn't think of God as an idol designed by craftsmen from gold or silver or stone.

"God overlooked people's ignorance about these things in earlier times, but now He commands everyone everywhere to repent of their sins and turn to Him. For He has set a day for judging the world with justice by the Man He has appointed, and He proved to everyone who this is by raising Him from the dead.[1]

"And that Man's name is Jesus. But He is not any man. He is God Himself who took on flesh as the Son of God and came to live among His creation. He lived and ate and breathed just as we do – with one important difference: He never sinned. Then when the time was right, Jehovah God permitted His Son to be crucified on a cross and His blood shed as the sacrifice for our sins.

"But though He was dead, three days later He rose from the grave. He lived, and died, and rose again so we might be redeemed from our sin. He paid the price, and all we must do to receive His redemption is to believe in Him, repent of our sins, and receive His forgiveness. As a man once told me, 'Repent, believe on His name, and be baptized!'"

Before the evening was over, twenty of our friends and neighbors had believed in Jesus and were baptized in the river! Every night afterward, those friends and others they brought gathered to hear more about Jesus. Each night a different person would share their testimony and the Gospel, and each night we saw more people believe and be baptized.

As I looked out over the growing crowd each evening I prayed, "Lord, to whom should we turn to shepherd these people? Luke is not here, neither is Paul, nor Silas, nor Timothy. What would You have us do?"

And I believe I heard the Spirit of the Lord reply, "I am not raising up followers of Paul, or Luke, or Silas, or Timothy. Neither am I raising up followers of Lydia or Janus. I am raising up followers of Jesus. Trust me to shepherd My people."

By faith, we took it a day at a time and saw God raise up teachers and leaders from within our midst. By His Spirit, He gave each one gifts according to the needs of the church – which He grew and nurtured.

But that growth was not without opposition. Every month the guild sponsored feasts for its members that involved worship of the emperor together with Apollo and other local pagan deities. The worship of those gods involved sexual immorality. Before I had become a follower of Jesus, those practices had not bothered me. But now Janus and I realized we could no longer continue to maintain our seats on the guild.

The guild did not take kindly to our position. Neither did they take kindly to what they saw as a threat against guild-led life in Thyatira. Not to participate in their pagan practices placed us at significant economic risk, some threatened, particularly if we wanted to continue to be successful in business and society.

But ours was the most successful dye and cloth business in Thyatira. We alone had a presence in Asia, Italy, and Macedonia. We were the recognized leaders of our trade – and by extension, the leaders of our guild – the same guild we were now rejecting. The other members knew they would be hard-pressed to compete against our business. We had the best dyes, the finest linens, and the most established and elite client base. We could survive without the guild – but the guild would suffer without us.

So, the guild leaders decided to attack us in the one place they felt we were vulnerable – the church. First, they pressured seekers or recent followers of Jesus by telling them it was fine for Janus and me to profess Jesus because we were successful and did not depend on the guild's support for our livelihood. But that was not the case for everyone else. The guild threatened to ruin them financially if they continued to pursue this Jesus.

Second, they began to stir up the rest of the city against the church saying, *"Brothers, you know that much of your wealth comes from the manufacture of shrines and goods used in the worship of the sun god Apollo. These followers of the One they call Jesus are attempting to persuade our citizens that Apollo is not a god at all. We're not just talking about the loss of respect for our businesses. We're also concerned that our magnificent god Apollo will be robbed of his prestige.*[2] We must convince our neighbors who have turned to this Jesus to put an end to their practice. Go to your neighbors who have been deceived and make them see the truth!"

22

RETURNING TO ROME

~

*D*espite those attempts by the guild and the persecution by their neighbors, the church remained strong and banded together. We all sold many of our possessions and shared the proceeds with those in need. As our neighbors witnessed how we cared for one another, the persecution died down. As a matter of fact, many of them came seeking to know more about Jesus.

Eventually the guild abandoned its pagan practices as more members became followers of Jesus. Many in our city still worshiped their false gods, but the church was growing, and the city was changing – for the better.

I began to sense the Spirit of the Lord telling me now was the time to take Valeria to Rome. I had no idea what the journey would bring, but I knew it would be a good opportunity for Valeria. Plus, I longed to see my uncle and his family, as well as Linus. Three weeks later, Valeria and I, together with Sergius and Oppia, set out for Rome.

After three weeks of travel, we found ourselves on the boat headed upriver toward Rome. I delighted in how Valeria reacted to the sights of the city as they came into view. I remembered my first view of the city nearly thirty years earlier. I understood the wonderment and amazement she was experiencing.

Even I was surprised by how much the city had changed during my twenty-four year absence. The Circus Maximus had been extended and was even more magnificent. More palatial homes were scattered throughout the city, and construction had just been completed on Emperor Nero's new grand palace. More of the streets had been paved with rocks, and everything appeared to be more pristine than I recalled.

I hoped my letter regarding our visit had reached Aurelius and Linus so they would be expecting us. When we arrived at Linus's home, he was eagerly awaiting us. Valeria was only three years old when he had last seen his granddaughter in Thyatira, and now she was a grown woman of twenty-two. We all had much to catch up on. I sent word to my Uncle Aurelius that we would call on him and his family the next day.

In the meantime, Valeria and I told Linus about our experiences in Philippi, which quickly turned to telling him how we had come to believe in Jesus. Linus listened intently, but he showed no interest in pursuing the subject further. We knew we needed to allow the Spirit of the Lord time to do His work in Linus, so we said nothing more.

Linus already knew about Naomi and the way she was leading our business in Philippi. He had become impressed with her ability through the messages we exchanged over the years. "And I have someone I want you to meet," Linus added. He sent word for someone in the house to join us.

When the man entered, Linus continued, "Lydia and Valeria, allow me to introduce my assistant, Eubulus. He has been assisting me for several years and in many ways has become like a son to me."

I could see from Valeria's reaction she was quite taken by this handsome young man who was a few years her senior – and he appeared to be equally taken with her. "Eubulus, it is a pleasure to meet you," I said. "We look forward to becoming better acquainted."

Our conversation continued well past dinner and into the evening. It was apparent that Valeria and Eubulus were not ready for the evening to end when I announced we needed to retire for the night. As I prepared for bed, I couldn't help but reflect on the many similarities between Eubulus and my Lucius.

The next day, we went to visit my Uncle Aurelius. He had aged greatly since I last saw him, particularly since the death of his wife, my Aunt Diana, one year earlier. He confided that he was considering stepping down from the senate and turning his seat over to his son, Pudens. As if on cue, my cousin and his wife, Priscilla, walked into the room to join us. I was happy to see that Pudens and his wife were quite capable of assuming the roles of master and mistress of this home.

During our time together, Valeria and I both shared about our decision to place our faith in Jesus. I was pleased and surprised when Pudens spoke up. "Well, if you are followers of Jesus of Nazareth then I must introduce you to my friend, Pontius Aquila. He was in Jerusalem when Jesus was crucified. In fact, his father was the prefect who condemned Him to death."

I could not believe my ears. Though Paul had told me he had seen Jesus in different ways over the years, I had yet to meet anyone who had actually seen Him in Jerusalem. "I look forward to meeting him," I replied.

"Then we will arrange for him and his mother to join us for dinner very soon," Pudens replied, sensing my excitement.

Two weeks later, Valeria and I were invited to join my uncle and cousin for dinner with Pontius Aquila and his mother, Claudia. As the night progressed, I asked them to tell us everything they knew of Jesus.

"I spent my youth in the palace in Caesarea Maritima," Pontius Aquila began. "My mother and I were both in Jerusalem when the religious leaders brought Jesus of Nazareth before my father, Pontius Pilate. I watched from the roof as my father condemned Jesus to die on the cross. My father knew He was innocent, and so did my mother and I.

"Tears flowed down our cheeks as we watched my father come before that crowd and refuse to stand up for what he knew was right. I watched in shame as he ceremoniously washed his hands. It was a turning point in my life. Until that moment, I would have followed my father anywhere.

"When the soldiers led Jesus to the cross, I covered myself with a cloak and followed from a distance. I watched as He was crucified under my father's order. I knew He was not only an innocent man, falsely accused – I knew He was a righteous man and so did my mother. I later heard He had risen from the grave, though my father denied the reports. He contended that Jesus's disciples had moved His body. But I never believed that.

"Lydia, Pudens tells me you are a follower of Jesus. Please tell us how that came to be."

◠

23

ARRESTED!

～

*I*t was about a week later Valeria and I joined my uncle for dinner at his home again. I was delighted to find Pudens and Priscilla were also there, as well as Pontius Aquila. All three were animatedly discussing something that had occurred earlier that day.

"Cousin Lydia," Pudens greeted me, "we have the most exciting news to share with you! Today, Priscilla and I became followers of Jesus! We repented of our sins, placed our faith in Him, and were baptized!"

I was overjoyed. "How did you come to your decision?" I asked. "I know you have been considering all we have spoken about these past few weeks. But how did the Spirit of the Lord lead you to make that decision today?"

"We were talking with Aquila, and he told us he and his mother had just been baptized two days ago," Pudens answered. "As he spoke, Priscilla and I looked at each other and asked, 'What is keeping us from being baptized?' We knew at that moment we believed, and if we delayed any longer we would be disobeying what God was telling us to do. So earlier today we went to the river and Aquila's new friend, Luke, baptized us."

I wondered if it could be the same Luke I knew. "Who is this Luke and how do you know him, Aquila?"

"He is a friend of the apostle Paul who led my mother and me to faith in Jesus three nights ago," Aquila answered. "He told us the same good news you had shared with us a few weeks ago, and as he did, we knew we believed. The truth is, we believed in Jerusalem all those years ago; we just failed to act on what we believed."

"Where did you see Paul?" I asked excitedly. "Is he here in Rome? And Luke is with him?"

I went on to tell them how it had been Paul who preached the Gospel to Valeria and me and baptized us in Philippi. "Then Luke stayed in my home for two years until I returned to Thyatira," I explained. "Where are these men? Can we go get them and have them come join us for dinner?"

I could not contain my excitement over this news. My cousins were now my brother and sister in Christ, and my dear friends, Paul and Luke, were here in the city!

"Paul can't come join us, Lydia," Aquila replied slowly. "He is under house arrest, awaiting a hearing before Caesar."

"He's what?" I asked in disbelief. "How is it he was arrested and how is it he is here? Can I see him? Will you take me to him?"

"Yes, you can see him. I will take you tomorrow," Aquila answered. "I will let him explain why he is here. But I will tell you he is here because God led him here. His three-year journey to get here is a testimony of God's ability to order our steps to accomplish His purpose – no matter how unlikely it may appear. And because of God's faithfulness, Priscilla, Pudens, and I stand before you tonight as trophies of God's grace – just like you and Valeria.

Suddenly Uncle Aurelius spoke up. He had obviously been listening to our conversation. "I, too, have now repented and believed. What must I do to be baptized?"

Little had I known when I set out to come for dinner that the evening would become such a great night of celebration! Every living member of my family had now come to faith in Jesus!

The next day, Aquila and Pudens took me to visit Paul. I discovered he was staying in rooms directly below those of Eubulus. Ironically, the house he was staying in was owned by Eubulus's family. Apparently, everyone in my circle of influence knew Paul was in Rome except me! And what's more, Eubulus had just placed his faith in Jesus that morning!

Paul explained how he had been falsely accused and arrested by the religious leaders in Jerusalem. I was aware of Paul's history of being falsely accused and wrongfully imprisoned, but I was amazed as I listened to his account of the two long years he had awaited trial in Caesarea Maritima, his appeal to Caesar, and his treacherous voyage to Rome.[1]

As I told him about the church the Spirit had birthed in Thyatira, it was his turn to rejoice. He said he was sending letters of encouragement to the churches in Asia and Macedonia, and he would also send one to Thyatira. It was obvious Paul's eyesight was continuing to fail, so I asked how he was writing those letters. He quickly introduced me to Aristarchus, his companion and secretary.

Paul remained chained between two soldiers the entire time we spoke. But I knew they were brothers in Christ by their reactions to what was being said. I joined Paul in prayer that God would soon open the door for him to share the Gospel with Emperor Nero. With what I had witnessed over the past twenty-four hours, I was certain a mighty movement of God was about to take place across Rome!

And God was not done working in my family. Aquila and Eubulus accompanied me back to Linus's home for the night. As we told him about our day, he too surrendered his life to Jesus. Arrangements were made for Eubulus and him to be baptized the next morning.

Everyone I partnered with in business was now also a brother or sister in Christ. Regardless of whether our business continued to be a financial success, I was jubilant to realize we were now all united in Christ's purpose and mission!

~

24

NEWS FROM PHILIPPI

~

few months later, Valeria and I were pleased when Epaphroditus arrived in Rome to see Paul. He stayed with Paul in his rooms, together with Luke and Aristarchus, so they could all serve Paul and assist him with errands. Frequently during our visits with Paul, we would catch up on news about the church in Philippi. Though I received periodic reports from Naomi, it was entirely different to hear Epaphroditus's detailed accounts firsthand of how God was growing the church – numerically and in maturity.

"Clement is continuing to serve as pastor of the church," he told us. Luke had informed me about the ease of transition when he left Philippi five years earlier to rejoin Paul.

"Clement has grown in knowledge and maturity," Epaphroditus continued, "and has been, without any doubt, the man God chose and equipped to pastor the church. Under his leadership, the saints continue to grow in knowledge and understanding of the Word.

"The carpenter, Syzygus, has become an elder in the church. You may recall he came to faith while Paul was still with us and has become a steadfast witness who is undeniably filled with the Holy Spirit. The church relies on him greatly for his godly wisdom."

Other good news was that Aeropos had been elevated from his role as jailer to one of the magistrates of the city, assisting the duumviri. That happened as a result of the night Paul and Silas had been entrusted to his care. When word reached the duumviri that all the prison doors had opened that night and all the chains had fallen off every prisoner, Aeropos was recognized for his valiant effort in keeping every prisoner from escaping.

"Aeropos knew it was solely the work of the Spirit of the Lord," Epaphroditus recounted, "and he tried to communicate that to the duumviri. But they had ignored what they considered his humility and promoted him for his bravery and quick thinking. Though we all knew they were failing to acknowledge who was truly responsible, we also knew God was using it to place one of His servants in a position of authority for the furtherance of His purpose."

Epaphroditus went on to say that because of Aeropos's new position, he had unlimited access to the duumviri – which gave him opportunities to tell Camillus what had truly taken place. Though my own access to the duumviri had been limited by Marcellus during my last two years in the city, apparently the Spirit of God had silently been at work in the heart of Camillus.

On multiple occasions, when just the two of them were together, Camillus had questioned Aeropos about that night. Aeropos had the opportunity to share the Gospel with him, and one evening Camillus surrendered his life to Jesus. When I heard the news, I was thrilled and began to praise the Lord for His saving work!

"Over the years," Epaphroditus added, "Camillus has grown bold in his witness and has become one of the leaders in the church. Marcellus has yet to become a follower of Jesus, but the church has been able to prosper in a season of newfound freedoms without any concern of reprisal from the magistrates."

When the church heard about Paul's arrest and imprisonment, they immediately dispatched Epaphroditus as one of the elders to Rome. Since the officials in Caesarea Maritima would have released Paul if he had not appealed to Caesar, he was burdened with the cost for his own transportation to Rome, the salaries of those who accompanied him, the cost of his housing, and the wages of the guards who were chained to him.

The Philippian church took up an offering to assist Paul with those living expenses, just as many of us did. Epaphroditus brought the church's offering along with a cloak Rumena had sewn for him.

I was distressed to hear my good friends Euodia and Syntyche were at odds with each other. Apparently, their fighting was dividing the church and placing the unity of the body in jeopardy. Paul was troubled by this news, as well.

"I will need to send you back to Philippi with instructions for Syzygus to help them settle their dispute," Paul told Epaphroditus. "Since he is an elder, and their senior by a few years, he is in the best position to give them counsel. I'm afraid they may not listen to Clement because of his young age."

Several days later, Epaphroditus fell ill with fever. We feared he had contracted the illness from Uncle Aurelius, who was now also confined to his bed. We knew Epaphroditus could no longer stay with Paul for fear he and the others might contract it. Pudens suggested Epaphroditus stay at his father's home so the same physicians could attend to them both.

The two men's conditions deteriorated and became critical. Neither was showing any sign of improvement despite the care of the city's finest physicians. Luke, at great personal risk, quarantined himself in my uncle's home so he could provide additional care for them.

Despite those best efforts, my uncle died. Though Pudens, Priscilla, Valeria, and I grieved his death, we had peace knowing he and my mother had now been reunited, and we would all see him again. Because of his position in the senate, there typically would have been an elaborate funeral proceeding. Instead, due to a growing fear across the city about the contagion of the fever, we quietly buried him.

We were afraid Epaphroditus would soon follow my uncle in death. But, in God's mercy, he miraculously recovered. And by God's grace, none of the rest of us contracted the fever. It reminded us that God knows – and controls – the number of our days. He obviously had more for all of us to accomplish for His glory. Because as Paul often said, *"He who began a good work in you will complete it!"*[1]

～

25

MY RETURN TO PHILIPPI

❧

*H*aving received reports about many of the churches, Paul proceeded to write each of them a letter. One of those letters was addressed to the church in Philippi, and Paul wanted Epaphroditus to deliver it. Several of us felt he had not yet recovered enough to make the journey by himself.

As we discussed it, I sensed the Spirit leading Sergius, Oppia, and me to make the journey with him. Valeria, on the other hand, told me she wanted to remain in Rome. I knew her grandfather and her older cousin Pudens, who had now taken his father's seat in the senate, would keep a watchful eye on her. Valeria had begun to find her place in Roman society, and she was becoming one of the leaders of the new church here.

My heart ached to be separated from her, but I knew it was time. She was a twenty-seven-year-old woman, and a relationship was budding between her and Eubulus. When I looked at her, I saw myself: an independent young woman with plans to change the world – for the sake of the Kingdom. It was time for me to grant her that independence.

She and Eubulus accompanied us to the docks where Epaphroditus, Sergius, Oppia, and I boarded a Macedonian merchant ship. It was a three-week journey with stops along the way in Messana, Athens, Miletus, and Troas. When we landed in Miletus, I realized I was only a short distance over land from Thyatira, but that was not my destination.

When we finally arrived in Philippi, the church – made up of old friends and new – greeted us warmly. I had been away for eight years, but in some ways, it was if I never left as we picked right back up on conversations. The church had grown to the point the body was now gathering in multiple locations around the city.

None greeted us more warmly than Camillus. He was without question a changed man, and I rejoiced with him in the work God had done in his life. When we told him we were delivering a letter from Paul to the church, Camillus said he would arrange for us to use the city's amphitheater that night so everyone could meet together to hear what Paul had written.

When it was time for Epaphroditus to address the gathering, he began by saying, "The church in Philippi is probably closer to Paul's heart than any other. Our love for him and his for us has been deeply rooted from the start. He writes to thank us for our constant help throughout his times of need, but he also wants to encourage us to remain true to the Lord."

He then began to read Paul's letter:

"I am writing to all of God's holy people in Philippi who belong to Christ Jesus, including the church leaders and deacons. May God our Father and the Lord Jesus Christ give you grace and peace.

"Every time I think of you, I give thanks to my God. Whenever I pray, I make my requests for all of you with joy, for you have been my partners in spreading the Good News about Christ from the time you first heard it until now. And I am

certain that God, who began the good work within you, will continue His work until it is finally finished on the day when Christ Jesus returns."[1]

He continued reading the letter of exhortation and then came to this specific message:

"Therefore, my dear brothers and sisters, stay true to the Lord. I love you and long to see you, dear friends, for you are my joy and the crown I receive for my work.

"Now I appeal to Euodia and Syntyche. Please, because you belong to the Lord, settle your disagreement. And I ask you, loyal Syzygus, to help these two women, for they worked hard with me in telling others the Good News. They worked along with Clement and the rest of my co-workers, whose names are written in the Book of Life."[2]

I looked over at Euodia and Syntyche, whom I loved as sisters. These two women and I had been together at that very first prayer gathering at the riverbank. They had been closer than sisters. But now they were estranged, and it was affecting the church. The two women looked embarrassed as Epaphroditus read Paul's words. But more than that, their expressions registered a deep sense of remorse. I prayed that the Spirit would bring reconciliation and restoration to my friends – and I was confident He would.

Epaphroditus continued:

"Fix your thoughts on what is true and honorable and right. Think about things that are pure and lovely and admirable. Think about things that are excellent and worthy of praise. Keep putting into practice all you learned from me and heard from me and saw me doing, and the God of peace will be with you."[3]

When Epaphroditus finished, the church members embraced one another, cried with each other, and praised the Lord together for His goodness. Yes, the One who had begun the work would complete it, and they were ready to follow Him to that end – even Euodia and Syntyche.

Several months later, I learned that Paul had been released from his house arrest in Rome. His accusers from Jerusalem never made an appearance in Rome, so he could make no appeal if there was no one to make a charge. Accordingly, Pontius Aquila and Pudens appealed for his release, and it was granted. He hadn't been given the opportunity to proclaim the Good News to Emperor Nero, but the Spirit had given him the opportunity to preach to many others.

Paul traveled for five years after that, including a three-month stay in Philippi. During that time, we received news that Emperor Nero had ordered the apostle Peter be crucified on a cross in Rome. The winds of persecution were beginning to blow throughout the empire, fanned by the flames in Rome. These had become uncertain times, but we clung to the certainty of our Savior.

By the time Paul arrived in Philippi, I had already returned to Thyatira. He sent me a message that he would soon come and spend time with the church there. But he only made it as far as Troas. I soon received another message that Paul had again been arrested and was being taken to Rome – not to appeal to the emperor but to be executed by him.

I feared for Paul . . . but with all of the unrest in the city, I also feared for Valeria. I immediately set out for Rome.

∿

26

A CITY IN FLAMES

～

*T*his time as Sergius, Oppia, and I traveled to Rome from the new harbor of Portus, the city looked very different. It had been over two-and-one-half years since the fire had destroyed a good deal of the city. Though much rebuilding had already occurred, there still were many physical reminders of the devastation that had taken place.

But much more visible was the deathly pallor that had now befallen the city. Even from the river, I could see crosses scattered along the horizon, casting their shadows of death in every corner of the city. I wept as I saw my brothers and sisters hanging on crosses. I asked the Lord to comfort them and give them strength to endure their final moments of agony before they entered His presence.

The sight made me even more afraid for Valeria and my family and friends who were followers of Jesus. When we arrived in the city, we immediately made our way to Valeria's home. She and Eubulus had now been married for five years and she had recently given birth to my granddaughter, Olivia. My heart slowed to a normal rhythm as soon as I saw Valeria and her infant daughter. It was a moment of overwhelming joy in the midst of the oppressive horror that surrounded us.

After Valeria placed my granddaughter in my arms, she began to update me on all that was happening. "All our family members are safe and have not received any threats. Most of our brothers and sisters in Christ who are being crucified have been brought to Rome from other places, just like Paul. Emperor Nero apparently does not want to risk inciting a revolt of Roman citizens."

"How did this all start?" I asked.

"The fire in the city broke out in one of the cook shops situated near the Circus Maximus," Valeria replied. "It was a windy day, and the fire spread quickly. It took nine days before it could be contained. As you have already seen, the fire destroyed a substantial part of the city, leaving many dead and many others homeless. It was only by God's grace that our home was spared, as well as the homes of Grandfather Linus and cousin Pudens.

"The surviving citizens of Rome became incensed against Emperor Nero. Many were shouting in the streets, 'Why did the emperor not lead the city to react more quickly to extinguish the fire?' There were some who accused him of setting the fire himself.

"He quickly took action to divert the blame from himself to the Christians. He announced we were a threat to the empire. He accused us of being troublemakers who followed a leader who had been crucified in Jerusalem because of His acts of rebellion. He told the entire empire they needed to be purged of Christians or risk being destroyed. He sent out troops to arrest believers. Our Christian brothers in the senate, like Pudens and Aquila, together with officers of the military, attempted to reason with him – but he would not listen.

"He began gathering up Christians from around the empire and having them crucified on the streets of Rome. He learned that the apostle Peter was one of the leaders of the movement and was here in Rome. He sent out soldiers to apprehend him at once. There was no trial; Nero had him crucified immediately.

"We only recently learned Paul was here. He was held in the dungeon for several weeks before we received the news when Luke and Aristarchus arrived. As soon as we heard, Pudens and Aquila began making pleas on his behalf with fellow members of the senate. But their influence has greatly diminished because they are Christians. Though their efforts were unsuccessful, they were able to arrange for Luke and Aristarchus to stay with Paul in his cell so he would not be alone.

"One of our Christian brothers is an officer in the Praetorian guard, and he is able to deliver food and clothing to Paul and the others on occasion. He has become our only lifeline of communication with Paul. Short of miraculous intervention by God, Paul will soon be executed. Apparently, the only detail in question is the form of execution to be used.

"Paul has declared he is unworthy to be executed in the same way as our Lord. He pled before the judge that since he is a Roman citizen that he be beheaded according to the law. There has been a delay in his execution awaiting that decision. Apparently, Emperor Nero has been called upon to decide his fate. Word could come at any moment.

"The church is gathering in secret small groups each night to pray for Paul and all of those who are being apprehended and sentenced to death. Tonight, we will gather in grandfather's home, and you will join us."

When Eubulus, Valeria, Olivia, my servants, and I arrived, I was again overcome with conflicting emotions. I wanted to spend some time with Linus before the others arrived. Though he was now eighty-two years of age, he had continued to remain remarkably active. Eubulus was now attending to most of the details of our business, but Linus still maintained a visible presence. He also had been actively serving as an elder of the Roman church almost since its inception.

I fondly remembered the first time I had met him at my grandparents' home almost forty-two years earlier. I thought back to those carefree days. With the passing of so many loved ones in my life, Linus had been my one constant over the years. But as I looked at him that night, I realized the events surrounding us were taking a heavy toll on him. I knew one day soon he would be passing on to his reward in heaven.

Pudens and Priscilla, Aquila and his mother, Claudia, who was also looking frail, and a few others I did not know assembled at Linus's home and we began to pray.

We continued to meet together nightly for prayer for several months – until the night Luke and Aristarchus joined us. Paul had been beheaded that day. He had entered into the eternal presence of his Lord. He had finished his race.

Luke showed us Paul's last words, written in his own hand:

> "HERE IS MY FINAL GREETING IN MY OWN HAND – PAUL.
> REMEMBER MY CHAINS.
> MAY THE GRACE OF GOD BE WITH YOU."[1]

~

27

FINISHING MY RACE

~

I decided I would stay in Rome. I was approaching sixty years of age, and I wanted to live out the rest of my life close to my daughter and granddaughter. I wanted to be an encouragement and support to them, just like my mother had been to me.

The political landscape soon changed dramatically when Emperor Nero was declared a public enemy by the senate, largely due to the efforts of Pudens and Aquila. Within a few months of Paul's death, Nero committed suicide, resulting in an end to the persecution of Christians. We praised God for His mercy and deliverance.

But Rome continued in political turmoil. During the eighteen months following Nero's death, we were ruled by four different emperors, the fourth of which – Emperor Vespasian – assumed his rule by executing his predecessor through a military takeover. The city remained under a cloud of oppression. Though Christians were no longer being persecuted, no one outside the church knew whom they could trust. The group in power today could be tomorrow's enemy. Everyday interactions between people on the streets became cautious and stilted; relationships became strained.

As a result of the tensions, our trade in the city was impacted. Gratefully, many of our patrons had been working with us for a long time, so we weren't as affected as other businesses. In the midst of that time, Linus passed away peacefully in his sleep. The physicians told us his heart had simply stopped beating. I was grateful he had not suffered.

Most of our community came together to remember his life and the impact he had on so many. He finished his race well, and I rejoiced in the knowledge of how many lives he touched as each one took a moment to tell me. Though he would have been the first to tell you he wasn't a preacher or a teacher like Paul, many had come to believe in Jesus because of the testimony of his life. I would miss him – but I knew it would only be for a season.

As I looked ahead at what was in store for our business, I was thankful the partnership he and my father had forged so many years earlier remained strong. They had laid a solid foundation on which I was able to build. And by all indications, it would continue to prosper. Valeria was assuming more of my role as Eubulus managed our trade in Rome, Naomi continued to do so in Philippi, and Janus was grooming his son to manage the work in Thyatira. And I knew each one would add his or her unique stamp to it as well. It was a business God had prospered for His Kingdom purpose as we sought to further His mission and honor Him through all our dealings.

One year after Linus died, Emperor Vespasian dispatched his army to besiege the city of Jerusalem. During the previous four years, Jewish leaders had led their people in anti-tax protests and attacks on Roman citizens who were in positions of authority. The attacks had now escalated into full-scale rebellion. After only a few short months, Jerusalem fell, and the Temple was destroyed.

The church in Rome gathered to pray for our brothers and sisters in Jerusalem. We knew the seeds of the Gospel had first been planted there forty years earlier through the crucifixion and resurrection of our Lord. The church had soon scattered, and in so doing the Gospel had been spread throughout Asia, Macedonia, and Europe by Paul and others. We were the product of their faithfulness. We were fruit the Spirit of the Lord had produced from their vineyard.

Several months later, we received word the church had again scattered from Jerusalem as a result of the siege. The apostle John – the only original apostle still living in Jerusalem at the time – traveled to Asia, stopping to spend time with each of the churches along the way, including Thyatira. Janus wrote me of how God had used John to encourage the Thyatiran church. Even though Paul never made it to Thyatira, God had another plan – and that plan included John. Along the way, John also stopped at Laodicea, Philadelphia, Sardis, Pergamum, and Smyrna before settling in Ephesus to pastor the church there.

It caused me to remember something I had heard Paul say on multiple occasions:

"I planted the seed in your hearts, and another watered it, but it was God who made it grow. It's not important who does the planting, or who does the watering. What's important is that God makes the seed grow. The one who plants and the one who waters work together with the same purpose. And both will be rewarded for their own hard work. For we are both God's workers. And you are God's field. You are God's building."[1]

Another twenty years has now passed. My granddaughter Olivia is preparing to marry a godly young man who has been assisting Valeria and Eubulus in the business here in Rome. God has greatly blessed our business and our family. I have so much for which I am thankful.

As the end of my life on this earth approaches, I am blessed that God has permitted me to be part of three churches – in Philippi, Thyatira, and Rome. I have seen the principle of sowing, planting, and harvesting lived out in each one of those churches. And I've seen that the life cycle continues. I have seen the church when it pursues Jesus wholeheartedly, when it becomes distracted by worldly desires, and when it is led away from truth by an instrument of Satan.

I understand from Janus there is one now who has planted herself within the body of Thyatira and is sowing seeds of destruction and division. The task of correction will now fall to someone else. I trust the Lord to redeem her or cast her out. I trust Him to protect His church and bring to perfection that which He has begun.

As Paul wrote:

"I am certain that God, who began the good work within you, will continue His work until it is finally finished on the day when Christ Jesus returns."[2]

Until that day, may the grace of our Lord Jesus Christ be with you.

SCRIPTURE BIBLIOGRAPHY

༄

Much of the story line of this book is taken from the Acts of the Apostles, the Epistle of Paul the Apostle to the Philippians, and The Revelation of Jesus Christ as recorded in Scripture. Certain fictional events or depictions of those events have been added.

Some of the dialogue in this story are direct quotations from Scripture. Here are the specific references for those quotations:

Chapter 14

[1] Isaiah 61:1-3

[2] Psalm 34:4-7

[3] Psalm 34:8

Chapter 15

[1] Acts 2:38

Chapter 16

(1) Acts 16:15

(2) Acts 16:9

(3) Acts 16:17

(4) Acts 16:18

Chapter 17

(1) Acts 16:20-21

(2) Acts 16:28

(3) Acts 16:30

Chapter 18

(1) Acts 16:35

(2) Acts 16:36

(3) Acts 16:37

(4) 2 Timothy 3:14

Chapter 19

(1) Genesis 15:5-6

Chapter 21

(1) Adapted from Acts 17:24-31

(2) Adapted from Acts 19:25-27

Chapter 23

(1) For the complete account of Paul's journey read Acts chapters 21 through 28

Chapter 24

(1) Philippians 1:6 (NKJ)

Chapter 25

(1) Philippians 1:1-6

(2) Philippians 4:1-3

(3) Philippians 4:8-9

Chapter 26

(1) Colossians 4:18

Chapter 27

(1) 1 Corinthians 3:6-9

(2) Philippians 1:6

∼

LISTING OF CHARACTERS
(ALPHABETICAL ORDER)

~

Many of the characters in this book are real people pulled directly from the pages of Scripture. i have not changed any details about a number of those individuals, except the addition of their interactions with fictional characters. They are noted below as "UN" (unchanged).

In other instances, fictional details have been added to real people to provide backgrounds about their lives where Scripture is silent. The intent is that you understand these were real people, whose lives were full of all of the many details that fill our own lives. They are noted as "FB" (fictional background).

In some instances, we are not told the names of certain individuals in the Bible. In those instances, where i have given them a name, as well as a fictional background, they are noted as "FN" (fictional name).

Lastly, some of the characters are purely fictional, added to convey the fictional elements of these stories. They are noted as "FC" (fictional character).

~

Aeropos – jailer in Philippi (FN)
Aristarchus – early believer in Thessalonica with noble background, companion of Paul (FB)
Aurelius – son of Gaius, husband of Diana, father of Pudens, member of senate (FC)
Caecilia – daughter of Gaius, wife of Evander, mother of Lydia & Janus (FC)
Camillus – one of the duumviri of Philippi (FN)
Claudia – wife of Pontius Pilate, mother of Pontius Aquila II, friend of Paul (FB)
Clelia – wife of Janus, mother of unnamed son (FC)
Clement – pastor of Philippian church (FB)
Cornelia – wife of Gaius, mother of Aurelius & Caecilia, grandmother of Lydia (FC)
Diana – wife of Aurelius, mother of Pudens (FC)
Emperor Augustus – 1st Roman emperor (UN)
Emperor Caligula – 3rd Roman emperor (UN)
Emperor Claudius – 4th Roman emperor (UN)
Emperor Galba – 6th Roman emperor (UN)
Emperor Nero – 5th Roman emperor (UN)
Emperor Otho – 7th Roman emperor (UN)
Emperor Tiberius – 2nd Roman emperor (UN)
Emperor Vespasian – 9th Roman emperor (UN)
Emperor Vitellius – 8th Roman emperor (UN)
Empress Livia – wife of Emperor Augustus (UN)
Epaphroditus – leader in Philippian church, friend of Paul (FB)
Eubulus – associate of Linus, husband of Valeria, father of Olivia, friend of Paul (FB)
Euodia – part of prayer group at riverbank, leader of Philippian church (FB)
Evander – husband of Caecilia, father of Lydia & Janus, merchant of purple cloth (FC)

Gaius – husband of Cornelia, father of Aurelius & Caecilia, grandfather of Lydia, member of senate (FC)

Janus – son of Evander & Caecilia, brother of Lydia, husband of Clelia, father of unnamed son, merchant of purple cloth (FC)

John – apostle of Jesus, elder of Jerusalem church, pastor of Ephesian church (UN)

Linus – father of Lucius, father-in-law of Lydia, grandfather of Valeria, elder of church in Rome, merchant of purple cloth (FB)

Lucius – son of Linus, husband of Lydia, father of Valeria (FC)

Luke – physician, travel companion of Paul, pastor of Philippian church, writer of *The Gospel according to Luke* and *The Acts of the Apostles* (FB)

Lydia – daughter of Evander & Caecilia, wife of Lucius, mother of Valeria, grandmother of Olivia, merchant of purple cloth (FB)

Marcellus – one of the duumviri of Philippi (FN)

Marijana – mother of Evander, grandmother of Lydia & Janus (FC)

Naomi – Jewish business partner of Lydia in Philippi (FC)

Olivia – daughter of Eubulus & Valeria, granddaughter of Lydia (FC)

Oppia – servant & companion of Lydia, wife of Sergius (FC)

Paul – apostle to the Gentiles, follower of Jesus (FB)

Pontius Aquila II (aka Aquila) – son of Pontius Pilate & Claudia, witness of Jesus's crucifixion, member of senate, friend of Paul (FC)

Pontius Pilate – 5th prefect of Judea, husband of Claudia, father of Aquila (FB)

Priscilla – wife of Pudens, friend of Paul (FB)

Pudens – son of Aurelius & Diana, husband of Priscilla, cousin of Lydia, member of senate, friend of Paul (FB)

Rebecca – Jewish business partner of Lydia in Thyatira (FC)

Rumena – fortuneteller until demon was cast out of her by Paul (FN)

Sejanus – Praetorian prefect, administrator of Roman Empire under Emperor Tiberius (FB)

Sergius – servant & companion of Lydia, husband of Oppia (FC)

Silas – traveling companion of Paul (FB)

Syntyche – part of prayer group at riverbank, leader of Philippian church (FB)

Syzygus – elder of Philippian church (FB)

Timothy – traveling companion of Paul, pastor of Ephesian church (FB)

Unnamed father of Evander – grandfather of Lydia & Janus, merchant of purple cloth (FC)

PLEASE HELP ME BY LEAVING A REVIEW!

i would be very grateful if you would leave a review of this book. Your feedback will be helpful to me in my future writing endeavors and will also assist others as they consider picking up a copy of the book.

To leave a review:

Go to: amazon.com/dp/B0CJL3VP45

Or scan this QR code using your camera on your smartphone:

Thanks for your help!

∾

THE COMPLETE SERIES OF "THE CALLED"

Stories of these ordinary men and women called by God to be used in extraordinary ways.

A Carpenter Called Joseph (Book 1)

A Prophet Called Isaiah (Book 2)

A Teacher Called Nicodemus (Book 3)

A Judge Called Deborah (Book 4)

A Merchant Called Lydia (Book 5)

A Friend Called Enoch (Book 6)

A Fisherman Called Simon (Book 7)

A Heroine Called Rahab (Book 8)

A Witness Called Mary (Book 9)

A Cupbearer Called Nehemiah (Book 10)

AVAILABLE IN PAPERBACK, LARGE PRINT, AUDIO, AND FOR KINDLE ON AMAZON.

Scan this QR code using your camera on your smartphone to see the entire series.

∾

"THE PARABLES" SERIES

An Elusive Pursuit (Book 1)

Twenty-three year old R. Eugene Fearsithe boarded a train on the first day of April 1912 in pursuit of his elusive dream. Little did he know where the journey would take him, or what . . . and who . . . he would discover along the way.

A Belated Discovery (Book 2)

(releasing Spring 2024)

Nineteen year old Robert E. Fearsithe, Jr. enlisted in the army on the fifteenth day of December 1941 to fight for his family, his friends, and his neighbors. Along the way, he discovered just who his neighbor truly was.

ALSO BY KENNETH A. WINTER

THROUGH THE EYES
(a series of biblical fiction novels)

Through the Eyes of a Shepherd
Through the Eyes of a Spy
Through the Eyes of a Prisoner

THE EYEWITNESSES
(a series of biblical fiction short story collections)

For Christmas/Advent
Little Did We Know – the advent of Jesus — for adults
Not Too Little To Know – the advent – ages 8 thru adult

For Easter/Lent
The One Who Stood Before Us – the ministry and passion of Jesus — for adults
The Little Ones Who Came – the ministry and passion – ages 8 thru adult

LESSONS LEARNED IN THE WILDERNESS SERIES
(a non-fiction series of biblical devotional studies)

The Journey Begins (Exodus) – Book 1
The Wandering Years (Numbers and Deuteronomy) – Book 2
Possessing The Promise (Joshua and Judges) – Book 3
Walking With The Master (The Gospels leading up to Palm Sunday) – Book 4
Taking Up The Cross (The Gospels – the passion through ascension) – Book 5
Until He Returns (The Book of Acts) – Book 6

ALSO AVAILABLE AS AUDIOBOOKS

THE CALLED

(the complete series)

A Carpenter Called Joseph

A Prophet Called Isaiah

A Teacher Called Nicodemus

A Judge Called Deborah

A Merchant Called Lydia

A Friend Called Enoch

A Fisherman Called Simon

A Heroine Called Rahab

A Witness Called Mary

A Cupbearer Called Nehemiah

❧

Through the Eyes of a Shepherd

❧

Little Did We Know

Not Too Little to Know

❧

ACKNOWLEDGMENTS

I do not cease to give thanks for you ....
Ephesians 1:16 (ESV)

… my partner in all things, LaVonne,
for choosing to trust God as we follow Him in this faith adventure
together;

… my family,
for your love, support and encouragement;

… Sheryl,
for always helping me tell the story in a better way;

… Scott,
for the way you use your creative abilities to bring glory to God;

… a great group of friends who have read advance copies of these books,
for all of your help, feedback and encouragement;

… and most importantly,
the One who is truly the Author and Finisher of it all
– our Lord and Savior Jesus Christ!

〜

FROM THE AUTHOR

A word of explanation for those of you who are new to my writing.

You will notice that whenever i use the pronoun "I" referring to myself, i have chosen to use a lowercase "i." This only applies to me personally (in the Preface). i do not impose my personal conviction on any of the characters in this book. It is not a typographical error. i know this is contrary to proper English grammar and accepted editorial style guides. i drive editors (and "spell check") crazy by doing this. But years ago, the Lord convicted me – personally – that in all things i must decrease and He must increase.

And as a way of continuing personal reminder, from that day forward, i have chosen to use a lowercase "i" whenever referring to myself. Because of the same conviction, i use a capital letter for any pronoun referring to God throughout the entire book. The style guide for most of the Bible translations do not share that conviction. However, you will see that i have intentionally made that slight revision and capitalized any pronoun referring to God in my quotations of Scripture. If i have violated any style guides as a result, please accept my apology, but i must honor this conviction.

Lastly, regarding this matter – this is a <u>personal</u> conviction – and i share it only so you will understand why i have chosen to deviate from normal editorial practice. i am in no way suggesting or endeavoring to have anyone else subscribe to my conviction. Thanks for your understanding.

ABOUT THE AUTHOR

Ken Winter is a follower of Jesus, an extremely blessed husband, and a proud father and grandfather – all by the grace of God. His journey with Jesus has led him to serve on the pastoral staffs of two local churches – one in West Palm Beach, Florida and the other in Richmond, Virginia – and as the vice president of mobilization of an international missions organization.

Today, Ken continues in that journey as a full-time author, teacher and speaker. You can read his weekly blog posts at kenwinter.blog and listen to his weekly podcast at kenwinter.org/podcast.

And we proclaim Him, admonishing every man and teaching every man with all wisdom, that we may present every man complete in Christ. And for this purpose also I labor, striving according to His power, which mightily works within me.
(Colossians 1:28-29 NASB)

PLEASE JOIN MY READERS' GROUP

Please join my Readers' Group in order to receive updates and information about future releases, etc.

Also, i will send you a free copy of *The Journey Begins* e-book — the first book in the *Lessons Learned In The Wilderness* series. It is yours to keep or share with a friend or family member that you think might benefit from it.

It's completely free to sign up. i value your privacy and will not spam you. Also, you can unsubscribe at any time.

Go to kenwinter.org to subscribe.

Or scan this QR code using your camera on your smartphone:

~

www.ingramcontent.com/pod-product-compliance
Lightning Source LLC
Chambersburg PA
CBHW060410030726
47495CB00003B/511